A YEAR

IN THE
life of a

PLAYGROUND
MOTHER

CW00420896

Also By Christie Barlow:
The Misadventures of a Playground Mother

A YEAR
IN THE
life of a
PLAYGROUND
MOTHER

CHRISTIE BARLOW

bookouture

Published by Bookouture

An imprint of StoryFire Ltd.
23 Sussex Road, Ickenham, UB10 8PN
United Kingdom

www.bookouture.com

ISBN: 978-1-910751-27-5

For my husband Christian, my children, Emily, Jack, Ruby and Tilly, Mum and Dad and my loyal companion Woody.

ACKNOWLEDGEMENTS

In respect to this particular book, I owe a debt of gratitude to many people for their belief, encouragement and continuous support. My agent Madeleine Milburn who believed in me, my husband and children who have always supported me and my lovely friends who have put up with me.

A special mention to the wonderful Christian Barlow, Mum and Dad, Anita Redfern, Haley Hill, Lucy Davey, Chantal Chatfield, Kim Nash, Catherine Snook, Sue Stevens, Suzanne Toner, Nicola Rickus, Sarah Lees, Bev Smith. Alison Smithies, Andrew Nutley, Ilona Hampson and Sarah Yeats who have always been on hand in person or at the end of a telephone listening to plot dilemmas and their everyday support has not gone unnoticed. Thank you.

Dreams can come true.

Warmest wishes
Christie x

INTRODUCTION

So this was it, today had finally arrived. The day we had been looking forward to for so long. I was making a big move, from a reasonably well-to-do part of the north to the rolling hills and valleys of the countryside. Well, to put this into some kind of perspective, I was moving from a half-decent detached house in the north of England to a dilapidated shack that had land and lots of potential in a southern country village. A glamorous lifestyle is definitely one I do not lead but, my Lord, an eventful one it was about to become.

My name is Rachel Young and this was an incredibly courageous step for me. I'm married to Matt and we have four children, Eva, Samuel, Matilda and Daisy. We had thought long and hard about the merits of such a move for a long time but once the decision had been made, I was eager for it to happen. The move was intended to improve the quality of our family life and allow us to spend more time together, away from the routine of the rat-race and the monotony of the one-upmanship that plagued our lives on our modern, executive-home estate. The removal truck was bursting at the seams with all our belongings, the side-effect of years and years engaged in the real-life struggle to keep up with the Jones'. The car was packed with four children and numerous animals, including our standard poodle that was the spitting image of my grandmother. Just for the record my grandmother wasn't covered in black curly hair but she did resemble one of the blokes from the *Two Ronnies* and so did the dog but I can't actually explain why!

Matt was due to follow in a day or two, once our house sale had completed and he had wrapped up some loose ends at work. At least that's what he had convinced me; he was probably banking on escaping from the unpacking and shelf-erecting and having a few final nights in the pub with his mates, without the threat of earache from me. And what work did he have to wrap up anyway? He was a business consultant who spent most of his time on clients' sites or working from home, he was hardly ever in the office. That's why the move would have little effect on him, he could do his job from anywhere, as long as there was access to the Internet, taxis and trains.

As we pulled off I thought I would feel sad, I thought I would be fighting back the tears. I got married here, all my kids were born here and my friends lived here – but no.

I revved the engine and steered the car round the corner and there they were as usual, the group that gathered here every morning for their daily dose of gossip. My friends – well that was what they liked you to think. These people were no more than my acquaintances; the women I had the unfortunate pleasure of crossing skipping ropes with on a daily basis. The worst breed of humans that one could meet – primary school mothers – better known to the likes of you and me as the Playground Mafia.

For the last twelve months I felt that my life had been catapulted onto another planet – Planet School. I thought it would be lovely to meet new people with children of the same age as mine. I thought coffee mornings would be a great way to escape from household daily chores, to sit and converse with people who had similar interests. But these people were a different breed. The fifteen minutes that they spent in the playground dropping off their sprogs had taken over their lives. These mothers were the kind who drove their Range Rovers two hundred yards to school trying to give the impression that they were something special. These mothers constantly tried to outdo each other with their fake Gucci handbags, blonde hair extensions and their torrid bright pink nail varnish. It was a competitive world out there and even more so in the playground. These mothers chose names such as Gabriella and Troy for their children, after the main characters in *High School Musical.* These mothers should not – I repeat not – be allowed in the real world and should certainly not be trusted with a Range Rover.

It was apparent these mothers changed their outfits numerous times during the day; their afternoon pick-up apparel was always different to the morning drop-off attire. I, on the other hand, had no qualms about turning up with unwashed hair and baby sick over my shoulder whilst wearing my worn-out trainers.

Unbelievably, the highlight of their day is 3.15pm, when Troy skips out of the classroom into the playground clutching his new reading book. His mother's smugness is duly noticed by all the other mothers standing in the playground, her shrieks of delight echoing all around.

With his maths skills more advanced than Carol Vorderman and his seat on *Mastermind* already scheduled in, the mother stands there as proud as punch.

You can hear the shuffling of feet and the resentful whispering increasing in volume of the disgruntled mothers of those without a reading book and their faces slowly start to turn crimson. At this point you can imagine the word and timetables charts immediately being Blu-Tacked to the back of the kitchen door as soon as they return home from school. Their extra-curricular activities completely abandoned until they have secured first position on the reading scheme.

It's times like this when you wish children would turn around and say, 'Mum, it's not about you; I'm five years old, why can't I just play?'

It crossed my mind to pull the car over for one last goodbye. Actually it crossed my mind to run the bloody lot of them over but I did neither. I delivered a quick hand wave and put my foot down. It is times like this I would love to be driving a Range Rover too instead of my clapped out Citroën Picasso that had lost its va-va-voom some time ago.

I knew I would be the talk of the town for at least the next fifteen minutes. They would engineer some implausible story about why I was relocating to the country. I had actually just returned from a six-month stay in hospital after being injected twice a day just to stay alive. I had given birth to my fourth child, Daisy, and the whole pregnancy had taken its toll in many areas and changed my viewpoint on life. You only get one life, so live it. I had no intentions of spending the rest of my days in this place.

Don't get me wrong, the house I was leaving behind was fabulous. I had some lovely memories there but it hadn't felt like home for the last couple of years, well since the creepy bloke next door moved in. I spent most of my days dodging him, I'm always up for seeing the good in people but I couldn't find any in him. This bloke thought he was an International Sex God and would take every opportunity to take hold of my hand and give it a quick squeeze whilst peering down my top.

Every time he held a conversation with me his innuendos made me want to projectile vomit all over his open-buttoned shirt onto his tanned waxed chest.

This bloke was called Charles. He looked like a Charles if you close your eyes and picture a Charles in your mind, that's exactly what he looked like. I have three subjects that spring to mind when I think of this bloke – trees, water beds and New Year's Eve.

Charles was married to Lois but he had absolutely no re-semblance to Superman whatsoever. She was a lot younger than him, give or take twenty years or so. Her character was that of a timid mouse, never making eye contact and constantly scuttling in and out of her house as quickly as she could. If Lois didn't have to speak she wouldn't, unlike Charles. It surely wasn't a coincidence that every time I pulled my car onto the drive he was always there, loitering. You can't help but laugh that I had begun to wear polo neck jumpers, even in the middle of sum-mer, just so he didn't have the opportunity to peek at my chest. Matt thought it was highly amusing at first and suggested that I should be flattered other men found me attractive. Other men might have been a compliment but Charles really wasn't much of a man – or a compliment – and certainly no Gary Barlow or David Tennant. Charles was surely well into his sixties, not an appealing prospect for a thirty-four year old; clearly like most men, he had an eye for the younger woman.

Matt's opinion of Charles was soon about to change.

Charles had a thing about the trees in our back garden. These trees became the bane of my life. Charles would loiter outside the house day after day, month after month to discuss the trees. These trees were situated in the corner of our garden, just out-side the patio doors. According to Charles, their branches hung down over his side of the fence and were blocking the light to his fish pond. To the average person the solution would have been simple. He just needed to trim the branches back, but Charles, being a little unreasonable, wanted them completely removed.

Understandably my patience was running a little low. With a new baby, not much sleep, three other children and Matt who still demanded his weekly attention, trees were simply not my priority. I'd even started to dream about trees, chainsaws and timber!

One day after an afternoon trip to the supermarket, I arrived home to find my garden stripped of trees. The lunatic of a man had chopped them back so bloody far I could see his pond, which meant only one thing – he could see into my living room.

I was furious.

My mother has brought me up to be polite and always respect my elders but this was one of those times I was thankful she lived miles away, so she couldn't hear the abuse I hurled over the fence. Usually Charles wouldn't have heard me for the trees but on this occasion he heard everything, because the bloody trees had gone!

My head was splitting and quite frankly I'd had the day from hell. My body lacked sleep, the tumble dryer was bust – a story I will come back to – and the Playground Mafia had neglected to invite me to their latest quasi posh luncheon.

Obviously I didn't drive the right car, have children on the right reading books or own a fake Gucci handbag. I wasn't in the 'In Crowd' but who decides they are the 'In Crowd' anyway?

That night, I took myself off to bed hoping for a couple of hours' sleep before Daisy was due her feed. I didn't really ask for much in life, just sleep. Unfortunately there was no sleep on the cards for me tonight. No sooner had I fallen asleep when I was woken by the sound of distinct pan-piped music. I ventured downstairs to find Matt had done his usual trick of falling asleep on the couch watching *Match of the Day*. It's funny how nothing wakes him; even the baby screaming and the dog howling along to her cries does little to disturb his slumber.

After flicking Matt's ear and placing an After Eight mint wrapper in his open mouth, he gave a choking sound and finally opened his eyes.

I think he thought his luck was in, until I mouthed the words, 'Not a bloody chance, feed the baby.'

I followed the sound of the strange music and discovered it was filtering through the patio doors. After locking the howling dog in the utility room I made my way towards the back of the house. The music was definitely coming from the garden so I sneaked a peep from behind the dining room curtains – and shut them again instantly! Was this for real? Had I actually just seen what I thought I had seen? I beckoned to Matt to turn off the big light and move his backside quick, reminding him that his luck still wasn't in, just so there was no misunderstanding.

As we glimpsed through the curtains again my stomach lurched. We were greeted by a sight that no woman should be subjected to: Charles and Lois, dancing to music around their garden, completely naked.

Taking a deep breath I looked at Matt. There was no mistaking my firm, matter of fact tone. 'Tomorrow get your backside to the garden centre and buy the largest, tallest trees you can find. Oh, and on your way back, call into the estate agents, make an appointment, we are putting the house up for sale.'

Our cul-de-sac wasn't all bad. Our other neighbour was a lovely lady called May. She was the kindest, most genuine person I have ever had the pleasure of meeting. Matt was away a lot on business trips and May would always look after me, making sure I was all right with my brood of kids. Every time we booked a holiday, May was the first one to offer to look after my mini zoo, which consisted of two cats, one mad standard poodle, guinea pigs and rabbits. One of my cats I named Suggs after my obsession for the lead singer of Madness. He was certainly not blessed with the good-looking gene. In fact if the truth be known he was the ugliest cat anyone had ever set eyes on. Unfortunately, he had taken a dislike to babies and the

crying sound they made. When Daisy was brought home from
the hospital he wasn't impressed at all; with a look of contempt
and a meow of disgust he dived straight through the cat flap and
took up permanent residence at Aunty May's. I couldn't blame
him, it was a no brainer. She fed him the best fish, hopefully
straight from Charles' pond.

Fergus by contrast was the most beautiful of cats but her life
unfortunately ended in a complete spin – in the tumble dryer.
What a stupid place to take a nap – why did she think it was a
good idea to sleep on the wet washing? Tumble dryers no longer
have a place in my life.

It was official. The house was up for sale. I knew the minute
the 'For Sale' board went up that the Playground Mafia would
be buzzing around like blood-sucking mosquitoes. They would
try to extract the information from anyone to discover the reason we were moving.

They didn't disappoint me. Unfortunately, one of the Playground Mafia sent me a text accidentally. It probably should have
gone to Mrs High School Musical. According to the text my
house was up for sale because I was getting divorced – Matt had
left me for the woman in the local kebab shop. Other rumours
circulating were that I was divorcing him because I had changed
my sexual preference – and was sleeping with the woman in the
kebab shop. To put you all straight, neither of us like kebabs! It
was simple – nothing sinister, and sorry to disappoint – we just
wanted a new life in the country away from hair extensions, fake
pink nails and anyone whose kids were called Gabriella or Troy.

This one morning I had trudged to the primary school with
my feet stuffed in my Wellington boots, wearing my dishev-
elled, moth eaten duffle coat which was thrown over the top
of my PJs. I had begun to arrive at the dreaded school gates as
late as possible. Every morning I met my normal friend Emma

on the corner of the road. She was in the same boat as me. Her husband was also apparently having an affair with the woman in the kebab shop. Without a doubt the Playground Mafia lacked creativity with their rumours.

Emma had been my friend for six months, my ally at the school gates. She was a copper on maternity leave, a lovely, down to earth person who kept herself to herself, the exact antithesis of the Playground Mafia. Emma and I braved the school run together, metaphorically crossing off each day until the next school holiday. It felt like we were under constant scrutiny when we dropped our children at the school gates and usually with good reason too; on an almost daily basis we were subjected to the looks of disgust and muffled whispering of the Playground Mafia as they analysed our dress sense.

I couldn't begin to imagine the time they woke up in the morning to re-apply their torrid pink nail varnish or untangle their hair extensions. There would be no time to go to bed, which was unfortunate because it was apparent some of them really did need their beauty sleep. Who are these people actually trying to impress? It's not as though there are any famous fathers at the school. It was rumoured that one child's uncle was Bez from the Happy Mondays but believe me no Monday at this school was happy – or any other day for that matter.

I was completely knackered with the arrival of the new baby and it had only just crossed my mind to let Emma know my house was going up for sale. As we approached the corner of the close, Emma and I witnessed the estate agent hammering the 'For Sale' sign into the ground of my front garden. It was official. I would soon be asked questions – why, where and when we would be moving.

It was just at that moment Emma had the unfortunate pleasure of witnessing Charles, the International Sex God, in action. There he was leaning out of his bedroom window scooping out buckets of water – and I mean buckets – while semi-naked. Well, due to the brickwork we could only hope he was semi-naked. Charles was yelling down at us for help. I wasn't feeling in a heroic mood and certainly wasn't in the frame of mind to venture into his house to find out what all the commotion was about.

Emma took control of the situation and telephoned her colleagues at the local station on the grounds that Charles was disturbing the peace and organised for a newly qualified constable to make a visit as soon as possible to the house.

Fifteen minutes later the officer arrived on the scene and the mystery was soon solved. It was at that unfortunate moment we all discovered that the International Sex God was the proud owner of a deflated water bed. It transpired he had been partaking in some sort of solitary sex act whilst viewing a dodgy adult movie. After hearing the unfamiliar noise of the estate agent erecting the 'For Sale' sign, he was panicked into thinking Lois had returned home. The only way to prevent her from entering the bedroom and discovering his early morning extra-curricular activities was to burst the water bed. This was an image I immediately tried to block from my mind. At least now Emma fully understood why I wanted to move away from these people.

Now I've covered trees and the water bed, it just leaves the story of New Year's Eve last year.

Christmas was just around the corner, a time of year that I truly love. The shops are transformed into enchanting places, full of sparkle with tinsel draped from every possible appendage and the festive tunes that belt out over the supermarket speakers fill the aisles with festive cheer. I was really looking forward to this Christmas as the previous one had been no fun at all. I had been on the verge of being read my last rites carrying Daisy and I was determined this one was going to be different. Not only would I enjoy myself but this year I could participate in the demon drink.

This was a must in the weeks running up to Christmas especially the last few weeks of the school term. A cheeky glass of pinot grigio always helped to numb the pain of sitting through the school nativity plays.

The hard work of the teaching staff and children always seemed to be overshadowed by the Playground Mafia. They perch themselves on the front row to obtain the best views of their offspring. They have had the seats adorned with handwritten 'Reserved' notices that they have been able to sneak into the hall because of their PTA 'special access' rights. The rest of us mere mortals would need a current CRB check and a letter from the Prime Minister to get access to the hall during the school day.

They take great pride in scanning the programme and smiling smugly to themselves when they see their child's name printed in the cast list next to the main parts of Mary and Joseph.

For the duration of the play, they sit there with their noses in the air pretending they are at the Royal Ballet, constantly muttering.

'Did you know my Arabella has the main part?'

'Look at my Tristram, I'm certain he will be a Hollywood actor when he grows up.'

The closest their child will probably get to Hollywood is the town in County Down, Northern Ireland, that bears a similar name.

The parts of Mary and Joseph are so over rated: all they do is stand there, by a manger in a barn.

One piece of information that I never volunteered to any member of the Playground Mafia was the fact we had a second home. This type of information would have been like winning the golden ticket to Willy Wonka's Chocolate Factory and no doubt would secure my immediate place in the 'In Crowd' in a flash. The property was located in southern Spain. So why didn't I tell them? Probably because I knew the first thing they would do – after checking their child's bag for a new reading book – would be to search the Internet to pinpoint the property. No doubt the result of their find would ensure I became their new best friend as they inevitably try to blag a free holiday from us. At this moment I didn't need any new best friends and I certainly didn't need to holiday with any of the Playground Mafia. I decided sometimes it was better to keep this type of information to myself.

We shared the Spanish house with a couple of great people. These two weren't acquaintances; Alex and Susan were *real* friends. Alex was Matt's old business partner, Susan was his wife and they were great fun. There was a small amount of cash left over after Matt and Alex sold their business, so during one drunken evening we decided to send the boys off to Spain for a weekend in search of a villa for us to purchase. I'm not quite sure how much actual viewing took place but on their return we were the proud owners of a patch of land and some architects' plans which incorporated the largest swimming pool on the complex. A little over a year later, the house was finished and we were soaking up the Spanish sun, sipping champagne in our Jacuzzi.

Alex and Susan were joining us this New Year's Eve for our celebrations. It was always great fun when we got together and between us we have six kids. We were past the party animal stage and had progressed from drinking senseless amounts of alcohol in the local nightclub to drinking senseless amounts of alcohol at home, while in charge of the little people.

The boys planned to collect the curry early evening from the local curry house, leaving Susan and I attempting to entice the children into bed. The only problem with this plan was that Eva, my eldest, was a knowledgeable child and didn't miss a trick. She knew it was New Year's Eve and that this was the one night of the year where everyone stayed up until midnight – including children! It was proving a little difficult to lure her into bed so plan B kicked into action. Susan and I hurried around the house changing all of the clocks to 11.50pm. We quickly downloaded 'Auld Lang Syne' on to the iPod and counted down the time to midnight. Eva was completely oblivious to our cunning trickery and it worked an absolute treat. By 7.30pm she was in bed, sound asleep.

Susan and I were always up for the comfy life. We imagined Mrs High School Musical dressed up to the nines, playing hostess to the other members of the Playground Mafia at her over-the-top dinner and champagne party. Not us, we dressed up in our fluffy PJs and slippers and cracked open a beer. It was also my birthday in less than five hours but in all honesty New Year's Day is the worst day in the year for a birthday. Usually everyone is suffering from the hangover from hell after consuming vast amounts of alcohol the night before, so finding people to celebrate it with you was always a challenge. On the flip-side, the night before my birthday is traditionally the biggest party night on the social calendar for excessive drinking so I simply adopt that night instead for my birthday celebrations. The highlight of my birthday is the telephone call I dutifully receive from my mother – usually with a hangover – when she reminds me that I utterly ruined her New Year's Eve plans all those years ago when I decided to arrive two weeks early.

I was really looking forward to the night ahead. All the children were now in bed, a chicken balti was on its way, a bottle of Lanson Black Label was chilling for midnight and a game of poker and a right good chin-wag with our friends was on the cards. Unexpectedly the doorbell rang so I made some comment about the boys forgetting their keys and bounded to the door in my bright pink fluffy pyjamas and monster feet slippers. Opening the front door I found the International Sex God standing there in front of me. This was something I hadn't anticipated. Staring at him I asked him politely what I could do for him. As soon as the words left my mouth, I knew I had phrased that wrongly.

I thought I'd been rescued by the men's impeccable timing. After parking the car on the drive they hurried straight past him into the house with the curry in hand. Whilst the International Sex God answered my question.

'Are you staying in tonight?' he enquired.

I couldn't make up my mind whether this was a serious question only because I was standing there, in front of him dressed in my PJs and slippers. I didn't usually go out dressed in this attire. I continued staring at him as the next sentence escaped from his thin, creepy lips.

'We aren't doing anything tonight, is it OK if Lois and I pop in and join you?'

I grimaced.

I wanted to scream 'No!'

I wanted to give him Mrs High School Musical's address and catapult him anywhere in the world except my living room. I thought I was thinking fast when I replied.

'I'm sorry, we are about to sit down with our friends for a curry.'

I thought this was a polite way of saying 'No.'

His response was not one I was expecting.

'OK,' he said. 'You enjoy your meal and we will see you in a hour,' he continued.

Ugh.

I clearly didn't have a handle on this.

How on earth did that just happen?

What was I supposed to do now?

Most people usually organise their party arrangements for New Year's Eve well in advance.

Shutting the door in a dazed state the buoyant mood of the evening had completely evaporated. Taking a massive swig from my beer can I gazed at Matt. The look of astonishment on his face said it all as I shared the unfortunate news we were also about to spend New Year's Eve with the International Sex God and Lois – his timid mouse of a wife. Could our night get any worse? Immediately witnessing the look of disbelief on Susan's face we rapidly drank the next two cans of beer and decided to move on to the harder stuff. There was only one solution in times like this – sherry!

Feeling anxious, I had suddenly lost my appetite. We all sat around the table breaking up bits of poppadum while trying to come up with a plan to lose the neighbours. Unless we gate-crashed Mrs High School Musical's party and did the conga with the Playground Mafia, we were stuck with them. Thinking about it seriously, a night with the International Sex God was probably the better option but only just.

An hour later we were alerted to a tap, tap, tap on the window pane; pulling back the curtains we were faced with the neighbours staring straight back at us. At this point the sherry had rapidly begun to travel through my body and their faces were somewhat blurry. The thought crossed my mind to swiftly drink the rest of the bottle with the hope I'd put myself in a coma. Drastic measures I know.

Staggering towards the front door, I was more than a little tipsy and was finding it difficult to manoeuvre down the hallway wearing my monster slippers. Opening the front door, I did a double-take. That sherry must have been strong stuff because I could swear that Lois was standing in front of me in wearing a ball gown and Mr International Sex God was wearing a tuxedo. No, on second thoughts, it wasn't the sherry. Lois was actually standing in front of me wearing a ball gown and Mr International Sex God was actually sporting a tuxedo. Was it possible I had got the dress code wrong at my own party?

It was also quite quickly apparent that they had come without booze. The cheeky, tight-fisted neighbours had not only gate-crashed my house on New Year's Eve wearing some ridiculous attire they expected to drink all our drink and eat all our food. I had a feeling this was definitely going to be a night to remember. The only way to completely block this night out of my mind forever was to drink more sherry.

Feeling like I was a bridesmaid at her wedding I ended up easing Lois onto the sofa in her ball gown leaving not much room for anyone else to sit down. In no uncertain terms, I repeat, there was no way I was going to assist Lois to the toilet. I was beginning to feel a little ridiculous and underdressed in my pink fluffy pyjamas and monster feet slippers.

'Would you like a drink,' I asked. 'We have beer, wine, vodka, Bacardi and maybe a little Advocaat that has been festering in the drinks cupboard for years. I could make you a Snowball if you like.'

I had no intention of offering her any sherry, the sherry bottle was mine and mine only! I had hidden the bottle safely behind the dog's bed. Lois' reply was unexpected, causing Susan and I to raise our eyebrows in disbelief.

'I'm teetotal, have you got any fruit juice?'

Fruit juice? Bloody fruit juice! It was New Year's Eve and I was already three sheets to the wind, did I look like I was the kind of girl that had fruit juice? Mischievously I did think about offering her some of the baby's milk that I had expressed earlier in the day – probably the only soft-drink in the house.

Charles helped himself to a beer and before he perched on the edge of the couch next to Lois he tossed his car keys into the empty bowl on the coffee table. His smirk twitched slightly followed by a wink in my direction. Why the hell did he need his car keys, he only lived next door?

No sooner had Charles sat down than Susan leapt up and I followed her into the kitchen. She stuffed her pyjama sleeves completely into her mouth to muffle the sound of her uncontrollable fit of giggles. Yesterday's mascara was now smeared under her eyes leaving her resembling an ancient pop star.

Pushing Susan out of the kitchen and up the stairs before our fits of giggles were busted by the unwanted neighbours, we fell through the bedroom door and landed on the floor like a pair of teenagers who had just taken a sip of alcohol for the very first time. Attempting to control her laughter Susan wiped her panda black eyes clean.

'Why on earth would they need to gate-crash our fun, where are their friends and what's with the dress?' Susan chuckled, 'They look like the entertainment act for the evening.'

'I thought their dress sense was very current,' I guffawed.

'It's a tragedy,' Susan howled.

Instantly we both stood up and immediately began to belt out the tune 'Tragedy' by Steps whilst breaking into synchronised dance moves.

The tears were free-flowing down Susan's face, her arms flailing whilst stomping her feet on the ground, I thought it was possible any minute now she may die from laughing.

'And him, wearing a tuxedo, for God's sake, they are in a modest detached house on an estate not the ballroom at Blackpool.' Susan hooted some more.

'You are all heart, you are,' I chuckled.

'If I was married to the International Sex God I would need to be constantly inebriated to keep my sanity, teetotal would not be an option.'

Finally managing to pull ourselves together we headed downstairs straight towards the dog's bed for a quick top-up, before returning to the living room.

Entering the living room it fell completely silent and all eyes were on us, especially Matt's. His behaviour resembled that of a demented octopus, waving his arms around and pointing, first at the neighbours and then at his ears. He was obviously trying to tell me something but I was way too drunk for an impromptu game of charades. Suddenly, in the corner of the room a red flashing light caught my eye and I realised that the baby monitor was switched on and everyone in the room had heard our laughing and derogatory remarks.

Alex was finding it difficult to hide the fact he found the situation hilarious, he was biting down hard on his bottom lip to stop his laughter from escaping.

There was only one thing for it – more sherry!

At this point you would have hoped they would make their excuses to leave and go home, as much for our sakes as well as theirs. Instead, Lois looked in my direction and made eye contact for the first time ever.

'I think I will have a drink, if it's OK with you,' she said. 'Whatever you pair are drinking will do for me.'

To be honest I was very reluctant to share my sherry but thought it was only fair as we had given her and her husband a right good slating and everyone had heard us. Susan retrieved the sherry bottle and poured her a very large tumbler full and I picked a spot to sit down in the living room as far away from the International Sex God as I could manage.

Quick-thinking Alex decided to play some tunes on the iPod to drown out the awkward silence in the room. Susan raised her eyebrows in my direction; we both noticed Lois had sneaked a cheeky refill and was now on her second tumbler of sherry and as a consequence was starting to relax. Her lips were becoming very loose indeed and her words were beginning to slur. I, on the other hand, had begun to sober up. I think that was down to the game of musical chairs that Alex had instigated in a further attempt to lighten the mood. Unfortunately for me every time I sat down the International Sex God would move and sit next to me so I purposely forfeited the game by ensuring I was the last to find a chair. When the game had ended I decided to throw a few questions at them both, mainly to remind Charles that he was married and his wife was in the room sitting beside him.

'How did you two meet?' I enquired.

I was thirty-four years old and quite naïve to be fair, living a normal low-key existence in a regular house with my four children, my hard-working husband and a standard poodle. My eyes were about to be opened wide.

Lois started to rattle on about school. I was astounded because I'd hardly heard her speak before but now she was like a verbal machine gun. She told us that she had met Charles at school. I thought this was a bit strange because she certainly looked around twenty years younger than him but I was useless at guessing ages. Maybe he was younger than he looked? Maybe he had just had a hard life?

Lois giggled that it was love at first sight when their eyes met across the Bunsen burner in a chemistry lesson. She chuckled that at that very moment they both knew they were going to be together forever.

They started dating secretly – her family were very strict – and she would regularly catch the bus to Charles' house. It all sounded so very innocent – a young girl taking the bus to her boyfriend's parents' house was normal, wasn't it?

Then the curiosity got the better of me.

'How old are you both?'

'I am forty-five years old,' Lois replied. 'And Charles is sixty-seven next month.'

I could see the look of confusion on Alex and Susan's faces but Matt and I were obviously joining the dots faster than they were. Lois was making her own chemistry with the chemistry teacher! Charles was having it away with his pupil and Lois wasn't catching the bus to Charles' parents' house – Lois was catching the bus to his house!

Charles hijacked the conversation and we all listened intently. Actually I couldn't move, I needed the toilet so badly but didn't dare go in case I missed anything. Charles had our full attention as he continued to tell us about their first holiday together. As he reminisced, I tuned in to the words 'nudist beach', 'swingers' and 'car keys' as though I was playing a game of Voyeurs Bingo. I was just about to shout 'House' when it hit me like a bolt of lightning – they thought their luck was in. They had put their car keys in OUR bowl on OUR table.

I gasped.

Jeez.

Matt looked at me quizzically.

'They are swingers, you dope,' I mouthed at Matt.

The look of horror spread across Matt's face; instantly he coughed and cleared his throat.

Matt looked at Charles squarely in his eyes. 'I think it may easier all round if you leave now please,' he insisted firmly, handing him back his car keys from the bowl on the table. 'This is not our thing.'

Awkward silence.

Immediately scooping up her gown Lois scurried through the front door. Charles followed but not before muttering, 'You don't know what you are missing.'

That was a chance I was willing to take.

Once the front door was safely closed and locked behind them we all fell about laughing. With only a minute to go until midnight we carried on with our festivities and pulled the party poppers.

Hearing the chimes of Big Ben ringing out from the television we popped the cork from the bottle of champagne.

'Happy New Year,' we all cheered.

'Happy Birthday to me too.'

From that moment on we were lucky to avoid our neighbours from here on in, always making sure the coast was clear whenever we left the house.

Now, on moving day, as I drove away, I glanced into my rear view mirror. The Playground Mafia – still standing on the corner of the road – were about to become a distant memory, wiped out of my life forever as they got smaller and smaller. I knew once we arrived in the new village and the Internet was connected up to the Shack, I would have six fewer friends on Facebook. I had decided on a new motto – 'don't pretend, just un-friend'. That delete button was going to be very active.

Joining the busy motorway I put my foot down and glanced over and smiled at my grandma sat next to me – sorry, my mistake – I mean the dog. My four children were all strapped in, squashed amongst blankets, pillows and a picnic. I knew I had finally out-grown that place.

Apart from Aunty May there were a few people I was going to miss, including Margaret and Henry, who were both professional people in the finance world. It was safe to say Margaret was more successful than Henry but he liked to think it was the other way round. As the years went on, Henry had begun to get under Margaret's feet – so she did what any kind wife would do – she encouraged him to play golf, which gave her hours and hours to herself. I thought this was a genius plan and it is a lead I will follow I'm sure in years to come when the kids can look after themselves.

At one point we used to live next door to them but I kept producing offspring and we could no longer fit them all into that house. Margaret and Henry were sensible and had stuck to two kids. In my eyes any friendship that exceeds the seven year mark is more than likely to last an entire lifetime. Margaret and Henry definitely passed my seven-year rule of friendship and were classed as true friends.

Margaret was genuinely upset to see us leave. Her parting words I will never forget.

'Just remember, the first person who invites your kids for tea – AVOID!'

Margaret was convinced the Playground Mafia were all the same no matter what school you attended and these people would have an axe to grind. They will have caused animosity all around them, fallen out with everyone and usually want to influence your opinion of others.

There was one good thing about this move, I was moving closer to my best mate in the world ever. We were about to be joined up in the same county of Hampshire even though there would still be an hour's distance between us – but what's a few miles between friends?

Fay has known me since I was nineteen years old, she knows everything about me and keeps me on the straight and narrow. Over the years she has more than established herself as my best friend and there is no way she could ever be replaced. She knows way too much about me.

I first met Fay when I was employed to work as a civil servant in the local Job Centre. To the likes of you and me, that's someone who gets paid to be spat at, shouted at and have computers chucked at their heads from time to time. Fay already worked there. After a few weeks I had been promoted from the girl who answered the telephone and got abuse to the girl who sat behind the front counter and got abuse. My whole day would sound like a cassette tape being played out, over and over again.

'Have you done any work in the last fortnight?'

If the claimant had failed to seek employment they were immediately at risk of being interrogated by us, the end result possibly leading to the suspension of their benefits. The criteria for this process was pure and simple, we measured them on our make-believe shagometer – I think this scale is self-explanatory. If they were lucky and scored above a seven they had been successful and would receive their benefit as normal.

Fay and I hit it off good style. I think the partnership worked well. Her sevens on the shagometer were my mingers and my sevens were her mingers, so we knew we would never end up falling out over a bloke.

This job wasn't all bad. There were a few hardcore 'doleys' who had signed on for years but we knew the score. If we didn't give them hassle and paid their benefit on a fortnightly basis, they would look after us every Friday night in the local pub.

Often we would end up in a slanging match with the mingers whose benefits we had stopped but the hardcore crew took care of them and made sure we came to no harm. Usually, they would keep them talking in the pub while Fay and I sneaked out of the toilet window to avoid being spotted. Such classy birds! If you have ever seen two women wearing pink hot pants, shinning down a drainpipe and ending up face down in a pile of geraniums under a pub window let me apologise to you now, as that would have been us. We were not hammered, it was usually too early in the evenings – we were just on minger-escape. At the start of the evening I convinced myself I was more Kylie Minogue in my pink sequinned hot pants but by the end of the evening I most definitely resembled Boy George. These times were great times; the best times.

Fay and I spent most of our time clubbing at Maxine's night-club, a classy joint on the outskirts of the local town. These nights were fun.

We would start out on a Thursday night usually booking the Friday off work and on more than one occasion arriving straight back at our desks on a Monday morning, often just in time to log on to the computer and start the repertoire.

'Next.'

'Have you done any work in the last fortnight?'

Breakfast usually consisted of pinching a pint of milk from the milkman's float on our way past. Regularly I crossed paths with my father on the doorstep in the early hours of the morning when he was on his way out to play golf. Obviously Margaret had taken advice from my mother on the golf thing. We were the Thelma and Louise of the dole office. It's such a shame you can't keep these times forever but responsibilities get the better of you at some point.

Twenty odd years later Fay and I are still the best of friends and always will be. She's definitely passed my seven-year rule of friendship numerous times over.

My other best mate, Andy, I have known since I was five years old. We attended the same local primary school together where his father was a teacher. Andy used to make fun of me because by the time we went to high school my long curly permed hair resembled that of a standard poodle. I was also the spitting image of my grandma. Maybe I wanted to re-live my youth years later when the first pet I owned was a poodle.

Andy has a theory about life: he thinks the world is full of muppets – and we are not talking about the puppet kind. He has an imaginary bus and every month he allocates the vacant seats to particular people – usually celebrities – and once all the seats are occupied the bus will be driven over the side of a cliff. Those on board will never cross his path again – or the general public's for that matter – although of course it is all hypothetical!

Andy's current passengers include Robbie Williams. I do not agree with this seat. I think he is a born entertainer and he definitely earns the title of International Sex God, unlike Charles aka International Sex Pest.

Next to Robbie is Katie Price. Enough said, I'm afraid; I am Team Peter Andre all the way. The next two seats are occupied by the Gallagher brothers. To be perfectly honest I agree that one of these brothers is a legitimate candidate for a seat on the bus but the other brother is my guilty pleasure and an extremely talented musician in my opinion. I love Noel.

Other spaces on Andy's bus are occupied by Gervais, Barrowman, Walliams, Cowell and Savile. I twice wrote to *Jim'll Fix It* as a kid – the first time I hoped to meet Roland Rat and the second time I wanted to dance with a pop group called Five Star. It was actually thanks to my mother that I didn't end up on the show – she never posted the letters as she didn't want the family name disgraced.

Andy and I have often argued about Simon Cowell's seat on the bus. I think he should be saved because with four young children I need brain numbing TV to get me through a Saturday night. Sometimes two bottles of wine is just not enough and secretly if I could spend a night with Simon Cowell and Noel Gallagher – with Gary Barlow thrown in for good measure – my life would be complete. Andy has only one place left on his bus, to be filled at a later date.

I didn't need to give much thought as to who would fill the seats on *my* bus. That was simple, they were going to be filled by the Playground Mafia.

These were the good memories that helped me during the long drive to my new life in the country. I was going to be on my own in a new house for a couple of days, settling the kids into a new school before Matt could join me. I was actually excited because it was a fresh start. What would the country life have in store for us? Little did I know…

CHAPTER 1

January

The High School Musical gang thought we had left the north under a cloud – the only cloud we left under was a bloody snow cloud. To be precise, five inches of snow covered the ground when we entered our new village Tattersfield.

I continued to drive, fighting through the snow that was falling heavily. I imagined the snowflakes as little flies; the faces of the flies were identical to those of the mothers I had left behind. Hitting the windscreen with force they were squashed and disintegrated into nothing.

This was a move to village life. I wanted the good life. I wanted my children to grow up running and skipping through fields – coughing and spluttering with their hay fever. I wanted chickens and ponies and maybe – if it wasn't asking too much – a normal person to be my friend who wasn't in competition with me over the kids' reading books. I spared a thought for little Troy and wondered what reading level he was up to now?

This village was sold to me as the perfect rural idyll; a great little place with its quaint village hall, blooming hanging baskets, friendly residents, good pub and local shops.

Feeling thankful our long journey was nearly over, I drove through the heart of the village. The weather conditions were still appalling and the snow was falling thick and fast from the murky grey skies above. I was exhausted.

Mixed emotions surged through my body, I was exhausted from the drive but excited too. I spotted the new house in front of us – finally we had arrived. Parking the car on our new driveway I glanced behind me and saw that all of the children were snuggled up, fast asleep, including the dog who was snoring lightly. Ahead of me stood our brand new home, our 'dream'. A Shack complete with aluminium windows and the ugliest garage you have ever seen, stuck on the front of the house like an afterthought. Why did we buy this house? I'll tell you why – this house had potential. Although it was small and needed serious attention, it had a massive plot of land and that plot of land was our motivation. The house dated back to the 1950s and in all likelihood hadn't been decorated since then. It still had orange and brown swirly carpets, avocado kitchen units with a free-standing cooker and an original avocado green bathroom suite. In fact the previous owners had fully bought into the avocado theme. On top of the avocado bathroom suite were avocado tiles, an avocado shower curtain and, to complete the look, an avocado carpet. I knew immediately all the carpets had to go. The swirly ones certainly wouldn't bode well with a hangover.

By far the funniest feature of the house – which is really difficult to explain – was the internal corridor. When you walked out of the back door, you stepped into a passageway of exposed brickwork and quarry floor tiles. Across the passageway was a toilet, utility room and coal scuttle. At one end of the corridor was the ugly garage and at the other was a conservatory. It was as though there was a collection of outbuildings that had been connected to the main house as an add-on. It turned out that the previous owner of the house had been the headmaster of the local school. He and his wife were highly respected in this village. I could imagine the headmaster pacing up and down this corridor just like the corridors in his school. He must have loved his job so much that he decided to create his own personal corridor in his home. When we first viewed the house I fell in love but this love affair had nothing to do with the colour avocado I can assure you. To the front of the house the views were spectacular, countryside that spanned for miles and miles. There was a certain calm and tranquillity about the place.

The children had moved from a newly decorated five bedroom house to a tin-pot Shack, but we kept reminding ourselves that it had potential. The children would need to share bedrooms and sit on an avocado toilet – at least until we could complete the renovations – but on the plus side, had a garden they could get lost in. I knew this move was the right thing. There were no Disney shops, McDonald's, pretentious boutiques, or celebrity bistros. Apart from the pub and local shops, there was nothing – just open fields and the promise of healthy country living.

Once inside, the house felt icy, the radiators were stone cold, the heating wasn't working, it was possible the boiler had been installed at approximately the same time as the avocado suite and we had no beds until the removal men finally turned up. Setting up makeshift beds on the living room floor, the children snuggled deep down into the warmth of their sleeping bags. Daisy was the only one with a proper bed; luckily for her I'd remembered to place her Moses basket in the boot of the car along with numerous blankets and, wrapped up tightly, she was a snug as a bug in a rug and murmuring quite happily.

By the time we appointed an architect, a builder and not forgetting we needed plans approved from the local council, it would be approximately a year before any reconstruction of the property could begin. We were under no illusion it was going to be anything but hard work with four kids. We would have to demolish parts of the house and rebuild it in stages but the land suited us fine.

When the first knock on the door came, the children and I just stared at each other. The dog tipped his head to one side in the funny way dogs do, trying to decide whether he should bark or not. I went to the front door and opened it. There was no-one there. Had I been hearing things? Then I heard footsteps and couldn't quite work out where they were coming from. Suddenly the back door – that wasn't really a back door at all because it was halfway down the ridiculous corridor – burst open revealing a rather round, portly man whose cheeks glowed like Alex Ferguson's after dishing out a particularly ferocious hairdryer tirade. He looked like a posh version of Compo from *Last of the Summer Wine*. A kind of 'smart-scruffy' appearance, as though he spent four nights sleeping under a crisp, duck-down duvet but the other three rooting in bins and sleeping rough behind the skip at the local restaurant. Smart in the sense that he was wearing a suit but scruffy because the suit looked like it was probably bought from Montague & Burton in 1931 and his trousers were literally secured round his over-sized waist with a piece of tatty string. He was clutching a bottle of red wine and a card.

'Welcome to the village,' he bellowed.

So this was a villager, a true villager, a real villager in the flesh. The words of Margaret popped into my mind.

'The first person who invites your kids for tea – AVOID!'

I felt the relief rush over me. It was OK, surely he hardly seemed likely to invite the kids for tea. He introduced himself as Mr Fletcher-Parker. Placing the wine and the card on top of the kitchen worktop he held out a short, stubby hand and took mine, placing his other equally stubby hand over the top in a tight vice grip. I struggled to retrieve my hand but after a bit of wriggling and a final wrench it was free. This was all very well and neighbourly but Mr Fletcher-Parker had shuffled up my corridor and burst through my locked back door uninvited.

I was still trying to decide whether I was pleased to meet him or not.

'How did you get in, the door was locked?' I involuntarily blurted out.

He could have been a magician or maybe a ghost, but my money was on neither.

'I've been a key-holder for over twenty years,' he announced.

'Over twenty years,' I repeated.

'Yes twenty years,' he replied grandly with a beaming smile.

Oh goodness, I wanted that key back.

I didn't want to appear dramatic but if the truth be known I didn't feel comfortable with a stranger having a key to my Shack.

'How lovely, you must certainly be the world's most trusting neighbour holding a key for over twenty years.' I smiled.

I didn't want to upset my new neighbour.

I took a deep breath and opened my mouth. 'Well it will be no use to you any more. All the locks will be changed when the building work starts, which hopefully will be very soon,' I said, knowing full well it wouldn't be that soon.

I held out my hand and reluctantly, unhooking the key from his caravan club key ring, he placed the key back into my hand.

'Thank you,' I said earnestly.

With a nod of his head he turned and shuffled back down the corridor, one key worse off than he had been when he arrived.

The snow had continued to fall thick and fast and the older two children were starting their new school the following day. Understandably they were a little unsettled and nervous. I laid their new red uniforms out on the floor ready for the morning and set the alarm clock for an early morning call. Hopefully some sort of normality would be restored by the time they returned home from school tomorrow, the removal men would have delivered the rest of the furniture and Matt would be here.

The next morning I woke up to the shrill sound of the alarm and for a moment couldn't quite remember where I was. Surprisingly I had slept like a log. Opening the curtains I admired the blanket of snow covering the never-ending fields in front of the Shack. The sheep were difficult to spot as they blended in but their dark eyes stared balefully back at me.

So this was it, the first day at their new schools for the two older children. Eva and Samuel were very nervous whilst getting dressed into their uniforms and by the time they were standing in their class line for the first time they looked incredibly anxious. Understandably everyone was staring at them, pointing and whispering, wondering who the new kids were. The school bell rang and the lines of children began to filter into the building. I gave them a kiss, ruffled their hair and headed for the gate. I looked back and caught a final glimpse of their faces as they disappeared inside – they looked at me as though I had abandoned them in the lion's den.

I was in need of a few supplies and headed up the high street to check out the local shops. Pulling the double buggy backwards through the slushy grey snow on the pavements, Matilda and Daisy took in the new view all around them. Manoeuvring the double buggy through the door of the local butcher's shop was a struggle and immediately there was silence and all eyes were on me. There were four women standing at the counter. The first lady nudged the second lady who nudged the third and so on. If they were dominoes they would have all fallen flat on their faces.

I had no absolute clue why they were staring at me in this way.

My northern roots were just about to get the better of me so I counted to ten and pressed my lips hard together to ensure a flippant remark didn't escape from my mouth then I asked for a pound of back bacon and four faggots. I didn't have a clue what faggots were but I'd overheard the woman at the front of the queue order a couple as I walked in so I thought I would give them a try.

The second lady in the queue was trying to whisper but certainly wasn't making a very good job of it.

'That's her, you know that's her. She looks a lot younger than I expected.'

I actually wondered what my crime was. All I wanted was a piece of meat for tea. The kind butcher intervened.

'Good morning,' he piped up. 'How are you settling in? Did the kids get off to school OK? What time are the removal men arriving?'

Standing back in surprise my mouth fell open.

Did everyone know everything in this village? He carried on, addressing the small crowd in the butcher's shop.

'This is the young lady who has moved into the headmaster's house overlooking the valley.'

I did want to make it absolutely clear I hadn't moved in with the headmaster but for the second time in my life I was genuinely speechless. The first time was when Mrs High School Musical turned up at parents' evening wearing her fishnet stockings and a mini skirt, her ploy clearly to impress the male teacher so he would promote little Troy on to higher level reading book. Goodness knows what that woman would do to move little Troy on to free reading? Everyone in the queue was eyeing me suspiciously. One lady spoke; she must have been the gutsy one as she spilled out the question they all wanted the answer to.

'How many children did you say you have?' she enquired.

'I didn't,' I replied.

'Is it three?' she continued.

'No I have four.'

'All the same father?'

'Of course all the same father.'

She gave an approving nod to the rest of the queue.

'That's unheard of these days,' she muttered as she turned her back to me and proceeded to order some sliced tongue.

This was supposed to be the good life. The heating was broken, we were squeezing ourselves into the Shack and the orange and brown swirly carpets were giving me blinding headaches. There was nothing good about it so far.

Tossing the faggots into the net basket underneath the buggy I dragged the pram a little further along the slushy pavements towards the post office. On a Monday morning, it turned out, this was not a good idea. The coffin dodgers were out in full force, queuing up for their pensions. It appeared that this was their weekly outing when they stood in the queue and had a general chit-chat about absolutely nothing.

A couple of excited pensioners stood before me and I had no choice but to listen into their conversation. They were excited that Pearl appeared to be missing from the queue – according to them this usually meant there was a possibility that she had passed away.

This was a positive outcome for them and the rest of the queue-dwellers usually because it meant they had a funeral to look forward to, which generally included free food and drink at the wake. 'Rent-a-mourner' sprang to mind.

I glanced over to a couple of women chatting to the side of me, who were perusing through the paltry birthday card assortment. Hearing the postmaster shout 'Camilla Noland', the woman next to me immediately looked over, waving in acknowledgement when she realised she had forgotten her book of stamps at the counter. I watched her plod over to the counter and back again to carry on her conversation with her friend.

Camilla Noland was not an inch over five foot three. Her hair was ginger and she was well-groomed with a blunt fridge in a bob; she definitely had a look of Janice Battersby about her. It was difficult to tell her age but my guess would be probably late thirties. Her leathery tanned skin aged her, making her appear older than her years, and was probably down to the overuse of sunbeds.

I didn't need to be a detective to identify that Camilla more than likely owned horses. It was clear she was a woman with determination, squeezing into her size 12 jodhpurs when clearly she was nearer a size 16. She was what I would class as a big unit, substantial rear-end probably a dead ringer for the Welsh cob she more than likely owned. Her matching navy blue quilted jacket topped off her outfit to perfection.

The queue was moving slowly. Inching the buggy forward, and being careful not to clip the ankles of the customer in front, I could now hear Camilla's conversation clearer.

The pair of women were gossiping about a child-minder who allegedly spent most of her day playing games on her phone, updating her Facebook status and chain-smoking whilst ignoring Camilla's child, Rosie, who she was paid to look after her.

Camilla was shooting from the hip, she was taking no prisoners, and continued to tear into the reputation of the child-minder, Penelope Kensington. According to her version of events Penelope had ruined a brand new pair of Rosie's trainers and Camilla was furious, she was going to demand that Penelope replaced the trainers or refunded her back the cost.

The woman she was talking to seemed to have lost interest in the conversation, her eyes were glazed over and she occasionally responded by tipping her head from side to side like a puppy waiting for a treat. When I finally escaped from the post office I tried to establish on a scale of one to ten who was worse; Camilla Noland or Mrs High School Musical? Chuckling to myself I couldn't decide so I made an executive decision, I allocated them both the first two seats on my bus, the bus to be driven over the cliff never to darken my door again. There were eight seats remaining.

The day flew by without any hiccups and it was already approaching school pick-up time.

Matilda and Daisy were participating in an afternoon sleep but I managed to lift the pair of them gently and strapped them safely into their car seats without a murmur from either of them.

Eva and Samuel had been on my mind all day and I was anxious to collect them both and listen to their exciting tales of their first day at their new school. The school wasn't too far away but with the children still asleep my plan was to park as near to the school as possible and let them snooze a little while longer before the school bell rang.

Driving slowly past the school gates my eyes were rapidly searching up and down the road trying to locate a convenient parking space. Quickly indicating to the left I couldn't believe my eyes: as luck would have it there was a vacant space straight outside the school gates. Quickly pulling the car into the empty space I parked the car.

Resting my head against the back of the seat I closed my eyes for a couple of minutes. Then feeling my head tilt forward

I shuffled down in my seat and leaned my head against the window and closed my eyes again.

I must have dozed off for a moment and with only a few minutes to spare before the bell sounded I quickly bolted upright. In super-fast speed I strapped the children into the double buggy and eagerly pushed them through the school gates to wait for Eva and Samuel.

Standing at the back of the playground I closely observed all the doors because I wasn't sure which ones Eva and Samuel would escape from.

I was alerted to a group of mothers that were standing in front of me, they appeared quite agitated. One mother in particular was hopping from foot to foot, her arms folded across her chest and was continuously looking in my direction. There was no mistaking the disgruntled look on her angered face. I glanced behind me to catch a glimpse of who she was staring at but there was no-one standing behind me.

How very strange.

Intrigued, I watched the woman from afar, her shoulders were raised, her chest thrust forward and she was nearly hyperventilating. I wasn't sure if I should go over and suggest she take deep breaths or ask her friends to call an ambulance but the group of mothers didn't seem concerned or look that friendly so I made my decision it would be best to let her collapse on the spot if needs must.

Their mutterings were becoming louder and now the whole group were staring at me from over their shoulders with raised eyebrows. I was beginning to feel very uncomfortable and my nutter radar started beeping incessantly in my head but I knew they couldn't be looking at me. All I had done in the last ten minutes was park my car. I looked around for reassurance but there was nothing from anyone, just stares of resentment.

Straining my ears to listen, the only words I could identify were 'Penelope' and 'parking space'. This was the second time today I'd heard the name Penelope; I wasn't sure which of the mothers she was or maybe she wasn't here. I watched the woman with the disgruntled look on her face turn around and prance off down the playground in her skinny jeans and Ugg boots but not before she glanced back over her shoulder in my direction one last time. She had definitely been under the surgeon's knife; there was no mistaking that her chest was artificially constructed and her wrinkle free forehead suggested her dabble with Botox.

I was beginning to realise this village life wasn't quite what I expected and everyone seemed to be well and truly into everyone else's business. This Playground Mafia were even more high maintenance than the ones I had left behind if muttering over a car park space was the norm. I considered giving this Botox Bernie – with her artificial chest and disgruntled wrinkle free face – a seat on my bus. I couldn't believe I had lived in the village for less than a few days and already had three candidates for the bus. I would need a double decker at this rate.

Camilla Noland was cutting it fine when she arrived at the school. I watched her saunter up the playground towards the group of displeased mothers that were still muttering amongst themselves. This woman seemed familiar to me and since I noticed her this morning in the post office I had racked my brains all day to why.

Suddenly it dawned on me. One afternoon a month or so ago, Matt and I had arrived in the village to view the Shack for a second time and make a visit to the local school. Before heading back up north we stopped by at a quaint pub on the outskirts of Tattersfield for lunch.

Realising that's where I'd seen her before, I remembered that Camilla also had a lunch date that day in the very same pub. She was seated at the table next to us. The man Camilla had been dining with was built like a string bean, very tall and very skinny with overgrown messy blonde hair that hid his unusually long ears. I remembered him because Matt had made me laugh when he commented that he was the spitting image of one of those Quentin Blake illustrations from the Roald Dahl books.

That lunchtime in the pub the two of them were very cosy, very cosy indeed. They had situated themselves right in the far corner of the pub, their legs were entwined under the table and they were holding hands, looking deep into each other's eyes. Camilla was constantly tutting because the man's phone was repetitively beeping with text messages – they were coming through thick and fast. The phone was lying on the table next to the man and every time it beeped he strained his neck to read the display.

'It's her again.'

'What does she want now?' Camilla gave the man a withering glance.

Removing his hand from Camilla's grasp the man buried his head into his hands. The beeping continued.

Matt and I looked on in amusement.

'Have you seen the size of her to him?' Matt whispered over to me with a chuckle.

Sneaking a glance over at the pair of them I knew exactly what Matt was thinking.

'Behave! They will hear you.'

Camilla at the time was dressed in horsey attire, riding boots, jodhpurs and the same quilted navy blue jacket she had been wearing in the post office.

'She must ride him like a bucking bronco. Quick, check his legs for any marks, do you think she uses a riding crop on him?' Matt hooted loudly.

'Stop it, stop laughing,' I hissed. 'They will notice us.'

Looking over in their direction, Camilla and her lunch guest were glaring at us.

'I'm sorry,' I spluttered apologetically. My face blushing from embarrassment. Kicking Matt under the table I raised my eyebrows at him.

'Don't worry, I'll rein it in!' he chortled.

Casting my mind back, I had been mesmerised by Camilla and her gentleman friend. Matt had wandered over to the bar to order our food then disappeared off to use the loo. I pretended to be preoccupied with my phone but their conversation was proving to be more interesting than my Facebook feed.

'Penelope wants to know where I am,' the man whispered to Camilla.

'Where does she think you are?'

'I'm not sure but she is asking some very awkward questions, the texts are coming through thick and fast.'

Camilla leaned forward and looked down at the message on the phone.

'What am I going to say?' he asked with genuine concern written all over his face.

'You aren't going to say anything, we are going to enjoy our lunch without your wife disturbing our precious time again,' Camilla responded loudly, clearly annoyed.

Listening into the conversation I rapidly concluded that they must be having an affair.

Quickly tapping on my phone I sent Matt a text message. 'The couple at the table next to us are having an affair!'

Matt had been a while now and I knew exactly what he was up to – he was sitting on the toilet playing with his phone and trying to secure the next level of *Candy crush*. It didn't matter as there was plenty to amuse me at the table next door.

'I do know Penelope is getting a little suspicious; she does think you may be having an affair.'

'What? How do you know that? Why haven't you told me?' The man was clearly agitated.

'Sshh keep your voice down, someone might hear you.'

'Don't worry, it's all under control,' Camilla reassured him. 'Penelope is my friend and she confides in me. I'm cleverly keeping her off the scent, she has no idea.' She smirked with satisfaction.

The little minx, I thought to myself whilst sending Matt another text to get his backside off the toilet because the food had just arrived.

'Remember that dalliance you had with the farmer's wife?' Camilla mused, trying to lighten the mood. 'You didn't get busted then, did you? I saved your neck that time too.'

From their mutterings I surmised that this wasn't the man's first affair.

A smug smile spread across the man's face, he must have cast his mind back to the incident whilst Camilla continued whispering over the table. Little did she know I could hear every word.

They upped and left the table just as Matt finally returned.

'Did I miss something? I just got your text.'

'Miss something, *miss something?* Those pair were having an affair and it's not his first one! Apparently the man had an affair with a farmer's wife and was discovered by the farmer when he returned home to find that man sat there "at it" on the kitchen table. No doubt the farmer wanted to cut off his tail with a carving knife but instead filled his trailer and dumped two tonnes of fresh horse manure onto the man's drive at home. That woman sat opposite had saved his skin by occupying his wife whilst her own husband helped to shift the manure.'

'And now she is having an affair with him?' Matt enquired.

'It appears that way and it sounds like her husband must know him too … what tangled webs they weave and the wife was none the wiser!'

Finally hearing the school bell ring I shook myself out of my reverie. The children started to filter out to the playground from their classrooms. Pushing the pram across the yard I made my way towards the furthest door. I wanted a quick update from Eva and Samuel's teacher to check how they had coped with their first day at school. I spotted Botox Bernie again; she had now accosted another group of mothers who had gathered around the netball posts. She was spouting on about her latest shopping spree and the purchase of a designer coat that cost her in the region of £400. I suppose it made a change from the relent-less reading book conversations at the last school. This group of mothers appeared not to be entertaining her self-indulgent ways and after a few eye rolls the group soon dispersed, leaving her standing on her own.

For the second time in fifteen minutes Botox Bernie seemed unhappy but I could only assume this by the look in her eyes as there was absolutely no movement from her forehead. The children came out from school quite happily and the teacher confirmed that only a few tears had been shed by Eva earlier in the day. She'd gotten a little upset during the lunchtime break because she missed sitting next to her old friends. The teacher soon buddied her up with a lovely girl and she seemed much happier as the day went on.

When we got back to the Shack, Matt had arrived home. There was a huge pot of chilli bubbling away on the stove and fresh bread had been baked. If nothing else, the bread masked the musty odour of the wood-chip wallpaper and the torrid smell coming from the avocado toilet. Kicking off their Wellington boots the children skipped up the long corridor towards the back door, once inside they grabbed a mug of hot chocolate and settled themselves down comfortably in front of the telly.

'Come on then, you pair, tell me about school. Did you enjoy it? Have you made any friends?'

Samuel was first to reply.

'A boy asked me what football team I supported but I didn't have time to answer before he asked me what level reading book I was on.'

'What was his name?' I enquired.

'Everyone calls him Little Jonny for some reason,' he responded.

Eva told us that there was a girl in her class with the same name as her, a smiley girl who seemed nice and friendly.

I was relieved both of them had survived their first day of school, it couldn't be easy adapting to a new house and school all in one day. After washing our hands we all huddled around the table. I scooped ladles of chilli onto everyone's plates whilst Matt tore the fresh bread and placed it in the basket in the middle of the table for us all to share. Just as I sat down at the table the doorbell rang and the dog, finally realising that this was now his house, started to bark. Opening the front door I peered all around but there was no-one was there.

Strange.

Then I heard that noise again, the shuffling sound, closely followed by the back door being flung open with Mr Fletcher-Parker standing as bold as brass in my kitchen again.

'Good evening, all, I've just popped in to see how you are all settling in.'

He had popped in all right, right through my back door again and was leaning himself against my prehistoric free-standing cooker.

Matt looked up in amazement.

'We are all OK, thank you, Mr Fletcher-Parker,' I managed.

'Please call me Fletch,' he insisted.

'Where do you live?' Samuel enquired.

'We live just a few doors down but we haven't spoken to your neighbours for over fifteen years, they aren't the friendliest of people. We like to keep ourselves to ourselves where they're concerned.'

The conversation continued on and Matt was introduced to our omni-present pensioner.

He carried on to inform us that if there was anything at all we needed we must not hesitate and let him know. I thanked Mr Fletcher-Parker, politely. I wasn't quite up to calling him 'Fletch' just yet!

At this point I hadn't actually clapped eyes on the other next door neighbours and now I was feeling reluctant to pop next door and introduce myself if they weren't the friendliest of people.

Overnight the silent snowflakes fell thick and fast from the night sky leaving a pristine, untouched fresh blanket of snow covering the ground the following morning. After dropping Eva and Samuel at school I again dragged the double pushchair along the pavements through the snow in the direction of the post office to purchase some milk.

Turning around, I leant against the post office door and hauled the pushchair in backwards over the step before spinning it round and heading towards the far end of the shop to retrieve the milk from the fridge. It was like déjà vu: there was Camilla again standing in exactly the same spot, wearing exactly the same attire as yesterday but talking to a different woman.

Joining the back of the queue I could hear every word of their conversation and was quite surprised about their lack of discretion. Camilla was happily chatting about Penelope Kensington again and was confirming to her fellow gossiper that the rumours were indeed true about Penelope's husband, Rupert.

The next minute my jaw fell open as I continued to listen.

'How did he manage to pull that off?'

'It was all down to my quick thinking. I roped in my husband, the farrier, to help him shift the tonnes of manure whilst I occupied Penelope.'

'Gosh, that must have taken ages.'

'It did, two hours to be precise.'

'What's happened to the farmer's wife?'

'The farmer took her back for the time being but I'm not sure how long that relationship will last.'

Shuffling forward in the post office queue, the penny suddenly dropped.

The man that Camilla was sharing her lunch date with in the pub was no other than Penelope Kensington's husband.

Scrutinising Camilla's face I couldn't believe she was standing there as bold as brass confirming the rumours to the other woman regarding Rupert's affair when indeed she had also been playing away with her child-minder's husband. She didn't even look guilty, not even for a brief moment.

As the queue moved forward I strained to listen to the conversation and definitely decided I was Team Penelope for the time being. The poor woman had taken a slating for two mornings running.

'Keep this to yourself, don't say it's come from me,' Camilla remarked as they ended the conversation and the women parted company. Shaking my head, the only thought that crossed my mind was who needs enemies when you have friends like Camilla.

I spent the rest of the day trying to organise our furniture, clothes, toys and games into a house that was half the size of the one we had left behind. Matilda spent most of the day watching DVDs whilst Daisy gurgled and kicked her legs from the comfort of the Moses basket. The day flew by and glancing up at the clock I couldn't believe that school pick-up time was fast approaching again.

Wrapping the children up warm in their coats and strapping them securely into the car we headed off in the direction of the school. The road outside the school gate was lined with cars, mainly Range Rovers I noted, and numerous mothers were already heading through the school gates.

I couldn't believe my eyes: the same space was vacant, how lucky was I? For two days running I had found a parking space directly outside the school gates.

Manoeuvring into the space I almost jumped out of my skin. Hearing a loud screech followed by the incessant beeping of a horn I slammed my brakes on.

Looking up I came face to face with an outraged woman glaring at me from behind the wheel of her Fiat Panda who was trying to park her car in the same space.

I quickly in my mirrors to ensure the children were OK. Luckily they were none the wiser.

How bloody stupid, the woman driving the other vehicle could see I was nearly parked in the space.

'Let the battle commence,' I thought to myself edging forward into the space. I was now parked securely in the space but feeling the other woman's eyes burning fiercely in my direction I avoided any further eye contact. The car sped off leaving the other mothers wandering through the school gate turning around to see what all the commotion was about.

Securing the children in the pushchair I made my way towards the gates. Feeling a tap on my shoulder I looked round to find a pleasant-looking woman facing me.

'Are you new here?' she enquired with a warm smile.

'Yes second day here,' I responded.

'I heard the beeping and noticed where you had parked.'

'Is there a problem parking there? I couldn't see any double yellow lines?'

'That's Penelope's space. She has parked there for years. I don't think she was very happy.'

Hearing the bell ring I wandered towards the back of the playground leaving the pleasant-looking woman making her way to the other end of the school.

It was at that very moment I realised that I had laid eyes on Penelope Kensington for the very first time: she had been the angry woman fighting me for that parking space.

She wasn't what I was expecting, in fact on first impressions I would have never put her and her husband together at all.

Penelope Kensington was a very masculine-looking woman; she was tall but by no means feminine and resembled a Russian female weight-lifter. She had jet black, shoulder length bobbed hair and a fringe that acted like a curtain hiding a deep furrowed brow. I gave her the once over and immediately concluded she was a smoker. Her fingers were stained and her nails painted, probably in an attempt to disguise the yellow colour from the nicotine.

I noticed Botox Bernie was still lording it about at the bottom of the playground exercising her vocal chords again. The price of her designer coat was yesterday's fish and chip paper but she was still insistent on telling anyone that would listen. Bring back Mrs High School Musical. She was shallow but at least she didn't pretend otherwise.

I was holding on to the handle on the pushchair, rooted to the spot. I scanned the playground observing the little groups and cliques that were apparent. These cliques never survive when one member's child overtakes another with their reading books. The mothers are fickle and will then shuffle on to the next friendship, choosing a friend whose child is usually a little less intelligent than their own to ensure their offspring are never out-shone. The new friend's child will then be invited for tea, providing an opportunity for the mother to rifle through the child's book bag looking for evidence of their reading stage. While tucking into their sausage, beans and 'smiley faces' the child is subjected to 'Spanish Inquisition' style questioning to determine which table they sit at during literacy and numeracy lessons.

There is one major problem with Planet School – the mothers. If mothers didn't exist, the school would run incredibly smoothly. Primary school children just want to skip, play hopscotch, run around and kick a ball to each other. It doesn't matter to them who is higher up the *Oxford Reading Tree* scheme. It's the competitive mothers who relentlessly push their children that cause all the rifts on Planet School. These mothers are in and out of the school building on a daily basis, complaining about anything and everything. As soon as the door is open, they hover outside the staff room waiting to accost the teacher who can usually be seen running to take refuge in store cupboards or even hiding in the toilets until they are saved by the bell. The worst thing about being a teacher is the mothers. These mothers think they know more than the experts, they think they know what's best.

What do they do when they think their child is not being pushed to their full potential? Let me tell you – they invest in the dreaded workbooks that every child detests. Their poor kids, after spending a day at school, are faced with yet another textbook before tea.

'It's for your own good, Troy. You want to grow up and be a brain surgeon, don't you?'

Actually all little Troy wants to be is a train driver. He wouldn't even mind working in McDonald's as long as he was entitled to free burgers. This is when these kids have had enough. They start finding mischief as respite for their over-worked minds and begin to bully their classmates and become generally unpleasant. No doubt they will progress to stealing cars and mugging old ladies in a few years' time.

These types of mothers all belong to the PTA – the dreaded Parent Teacher Association. The PTA in my opinion stands for the 'Petty Tedious Army', 'Particularly Troublesome Army' or even the 'Pathetic Tampering Association', take your pick. They make you believe they take part in these groups for the good of the school and the community but, as you look around the village, you begin to notice that the same mothers turn up everywhere. They are involved in absolutely everything ranging from Knit and Natter at the village hall – that's Stitch and Bitch to the likes of you and me – to making the tea at clog dancing in the church hall on a Friday. They're not doing this out of the goodness of their hearts, they are doing it to find out everyone's business and they don't miss a trick.

In reality, think about the children you went to school with. How many of them grew up to be a brain surgeon or an inventor or a rocket scientist? The majority of people end up with a bog standard job and a family, pay a mortgage and never let the *Oxford Reading Tree* scheme cross their paths again. None of these mothers would pass the seven-year rule of friendship. Step away from the staff room, step away from the workbooks, let kids be kids.

In the playground on the second day no-one spoke to me at all, which wasn't such a bad thing but, on the third day, the thing I was dreading most happened – Samuel was invited to another child's house for tea.

Margaret's words of wisdom rang through my head. 'The first person who invites your kids for tea – AVOID!'

Well I suppose someone had to be first.

Samuel skipped over to where I was standing on the playground and excitedly told me that he had been invited to Miles Lawrence's house for tea. I didn't know who Miles was or who his parents were.

Penelope Kensington was loitering not far from where I was standing. Witnessing the look on her face, she seemed a little put out when she overheard Samuel's excited chatter; she looked across in our direction.

'Good luck with that,' she muttered before quickly turning back and facing the other way. Samuel pleaded with me, he wanted to go and pointed to where the child and his mother were standing. They were both staring in my direction so I thought it was only polite that I ventured over to them for a chat.

Imogen Lawrence appeared a nervous character. She barely made eye contact while talking to me but when she opened her mouth to speak, out came a booming voice which I wasn't expecting.

Imogen gave me directions to her house along with her telephone number and I agreed to drop Samuel off in half an hour.

Arriving home, Samuel quickly changed out of his school uniform and into his playing out clothes.

Luckily for me Matt arrived home early from work due to the continuous bad weather which meant I didn't have to drag all the other children out again whilst I dropped Samuel off.

Imogen's house was easy to find from the directions she had provided. Parking the car on her gravel drive we walked towards her front door and rapped on the knocker.

Imogen very kindly invited us both in and Samuel ran off to play with Miles while she made me a cup of tea.

She appeared very friendly and shared with me that she too had once been a newcomer to the village. It had taken her a while to feel settled and to make friends. She knew how difficult it was for the children as she too had been an outsider. I thanked her for her kindness and arranged to pick up Samuel after tea. So far so good, nothing at all to suggest she might be a nutter. No mention of reading books and, having a quick scan around her living room, there were no workbooks in sight. Maybe, just maybe, I was reading too much into Margaret's comments and I began to relax.

I left Samuel for a couple of hours. The snow was beginning to thaw so I decided it was about time I went in search of the local supermarket as we really didn't have much food.

Earlier in the day I'd bumped in to Mr Fletcher-Parker after my morning visit to the post office and he had provided me directions to the local supermarket. He was turning out to be a very lovely neighbour indeed and always made me feel extremely welcome.

After placing my pound coin in the supermarket trolley, I set off amongst the aisles of hell. I wasn't sure whether I had actually died. Everyone I saw – and I do mean everyone – was around seventy years of age. The aisles were narrower than usual and they were filled with wrinklies shuffling their feet and pulling their fabric shopping trolleys behind them. They were clearly in no rush to get home, dilly dallying in the middle of the aisles they stood discussing the funerals they had attended that week and debating which wake had provided the better food. They had preferred the thinner-sliced loaves at Fred's wake to the thicker slices used to make sandwiches at Betty's. The larger

slices of bread played havoc with their dentures. I heard conversations about grave plots, the new woolly slipper boot which
was now a bargain price down at the market and the scandal
surrounding the discovery that the sherry was watered down at
Knit and Natter.

I turned the corner to the next aisle and did a double-take.
There were Camilla Noland and Rupert Kensington in the flesh,
having a rendezvous amongst the Andrex quilted toilet rolls
which were on special offer. They stuck out like a sore thumb,
cavorting like a young couple on honeymoon. They must have
figured out that no-one under eighty visited this supermarket
so they were quite safe, unless Penelope's great-grandmother
needed to pick up some ginger biscuits. Staring down at my
watch I panicked; I'd lost track of time and it was nearly time
to pick Samuel up from Imogen's. Managing to grab only a few
essentials I paid quickly and threw the couple of carrier bags of
food onto the back seat of the car before trundling back along
the high street towards Imogen's house to collect Samuel.

I arrived at Imogen's, still a little flustered from the lack of
food I'd purchased on my shopping trip. We chatted on the
doorstep whilst Samuel was putting on his shoes and grabbing
his coat from their cloakroom. Telling Imogen I was disappointed with the lack of variety in the supermarket down the road
and that I hadn't managed to purchase a lot of shopping, she
laughed.

'No-one goes to the coffin-dodger supermarket; there's a
more upmarket one a few miles up the road.'

I am useless at directions so Imogen did a very kind thing
and offered to take me to the other supermarket later that evening. Well, to be exact I would take her, as her husband, Steve,
was using their car to ferry Miles to football training. I loaded
Samuel into the car and headed home, spotting Camilla and

Rupert returning to the village in separate cars. I wondered if they had taken advantage of the 'buy one get one free' offer on Andrex quilted toilet paper. It was a great offer; I wished I'd picked some up.

We arranged to go to the classier supermarket at 8pm. I pulled up outside Imogen's house and pipped the horn. She appeared with Miles' younger brother, Thomas.

'I hope you don't mind me bringing Thomas?'

Thomas hadn't wanted to watch his older brother play football and screamed until Imogen had agreed he could stay with her and come shopping.

I didn't mind at all, I just needed to do a shop and fill those avocado green kitchen cupboards with food. As we approached the supermarket I sighed with relief. This looked more like it, it was twice the size with a petrol station to boot and it was only a mile in the opposite direction. I was sure I would be able to find this place again.

Imogen sat Thomas in her trolley and we entered the shop to find there was a much wider selection of food on offer. We bustled along, filling our trolleys with fresh fruit and vegetables. The sale racks were full of dressing-up costumes left over from Christmas and Halloween festivities. Imogen picked up numerous outfits and hooked them on to the back of her shopping trolley. I considered buying a few outfits for the children and usually wouldn't hesitate but as I was having trouble squeezing the contents of our last house into the Shack, I decided against it at the moment.

Poor little Thomas was beginning to get very grouchy and tired. Imogen thought there was only one thing for it and handed him a large cup of Pick 'n' Mix. I couldn't believe it – that was just what he needed as the time approached 9pm. His little body would go hyper with all the 'E' numbers. Imogen made sure she filled the cup right to the top. On the plus side, he was soon stuffing sweets into his mouth and had finally stopped whining. I was very surprised at Imogen's actions as the sweets hadn't been paid for and Thomas was gobbling them down at a rate of knots. We continued around the supermarket, manoeuvring our trolleys into the household aisle and, for the second time today, I spotted Rupert Kensington having another toilet roll rendezvous – only this time it was actually with his wife, Penelope. I was impressed; he had obviously spotted the 'buy one get one free' offer after all and decided it was a good deal not to be missed.

Imogen and Penelope made eye contact and then totally ignored each other. I thought this was strange as they had children in the same class but I made no comment. I was getting tired myself now and just wanted to return home as quickly as possible.

We loaded our items onto the conveyor belt and when the Pick 'n' Mix cup reached the cashier, she removed the lid.

'Excuse me,' she pronounced. 'You need to fill these cups right to the top otherwise you don't get your money's worth. These sweets are very expensive.'

Imogen smirked, collected the cup and headed straight back towards the Pick 'n' Mix.

'Works every time, free sweets,' she winked as she passed me to shovel another load of fizzy cola bottles, white mice and strawberry laces into the cup, clearly following the cashier's advice to the letter. By the time he had got through that lot, Thomas would have eaten his own body weight in sugary treats.

I spotted Rupert and Penelope at a cashier's till further down the supermarket. I concluded that Rupert had definitely spotted the toilet roll offer as six packs of quilted rolls were loaded onto their conveyor belt. I paid for my shopping and we headed towards the doors that led to the car park. I felt like I had stepped into Dr Who's TARDIS as a loud beeping noise started, followed by a deafening alarm which hurt my ears. I glanced at Imogen's trolley and spotted the dressing-up outfits hooked on to the back – which she clearly hadn't paid for.

I was just about to suggest going back to pay when Imogen shouted 'RUN!'

I am a law abiding citizen – most of the time – and I don't know what possessed me but instinctively I followed her lead and ran like hell. We drove home in silence. Within a few days of arriving in the village I had rattled Penelope's cage over her alleged car parking spot, rumbled Camilla and Rupert on more than one occasion and had been shoplifting with a woman who was a virtual stranger. On a positive note though, Thomas was now asleep. In fact he was completely comatose, no doubt induced by a top-up of fizzy cola bottles and white chocolate mice.

Finally arriving back home I slumped down into a chair, not quite believing what had just happened. Matt asked how successful the shopping trip had been.

'Andrex toilet rolls are on special offer. If you buy one, you get one free,' I replied, exhausted.

The next day I completed the morning school run without making eye contact with anyone. I managed to make it in and out of the playground in less than ten minutes and park safely with no arguments, which surely has to qualify for an entry in the *Guinness Book of Records*.

Arriving home from the school run, I kicked off my shoes and headed straight towards the kitchen and switched the kettle on. Hearing the sound of the doorbell ring, the dog launched himself at the swirly glass panes in the aluminium door. Opening the door I found Imogen standing in front of me. I invited her in and to be fair, even before she had placed both feet onto the swirly orange carpet, she apologised for the mad shopping trip and explained that she didn't know what had come over her. I knew exactly what had come over her – three free dressing-up outfits and a cup of Pick 'n' Mix. I wouldn't mind but she had completely missed out on the Andrex offer. However at this moment Imogen was the closest thing I had to a friend, so I didn't judge her. I needed all the friends I could get.

Imogen sat down with a brew and began to tell me a little about village life. Her two closest friends were Meredith and Lucinda. They also had children at the school and were proper villagers. They had lived in the village all their lives and their parents and grandparents had lived here too.

Imogen had met them at a toddler group and they had bonded well. I think her exact words were, 'We never really socialise, we just sort the kids out together.'

Mainly that meant taking them to football practice, swimming lessons and after-school clubs, etc.

I plucked up the courage to question her about Penelope. I was surprised they hadn't spoken in the supermarket, especially as they had children in the same class at school. I could see from Imogen's reaction – no Botox in sight at this point – that there was a story to tell so I waited in anticipation.

'We were once good friends but Penelope falls out with everyone. And I mean *everyone*. She is incapable of having more than one friend,' Imogen revealed.

As she talked my mind was preoccupied with all the jobs I needed to carry on with that day. The wood-chip wallpaper needed stripping off and the carpet from the kids' bedrooms needed a clean. Before I could stop myself my mouth opened and I spoke.

'How about you save that story for Saturday night – why don't you all come round to the Shack and I'll prepare some food and you can enlighten me about village life?'

So that was that, a dinner evening had been arranged. Our first proper guests at the Shack!

All the children were settling in well, and I was really busy making the Shack into some sort of habitable state. I'd also taken part in a small amount of exploring around the village and had located the bank and the local garden centre all by myself.

My fondness for garden centres has grown over the years. I'm fascinated by that fact that they don't just sell plants and gardening tools. There is all sorts of tat to buy, books to read and the huge strawberry cream tarts that they sell in the cafes are to die for. I decided one morning to have a quick trip to the garden centre as I was on the hunt for a plant that would grow quickly and cover up our hideous garage. Mr Fletcher-Parker shared his knowledge that a clematis would do the job just fine.

I'm not the best gardener and every time I purchase a plant I somehow manage to kill it but it was worth a try. I searched through hundreds of plants and had no real idea what I was looking for. I headed towards the trees and shrubs that were located at the back of the garden centre and stopped in my tracks. I couldn't believe my eyes – there again was Rupert Kensington holding a woman's hand – but the hand belonged to neither Camilla Noland nor his wife.

This woman had a lovely figure and fantastic legs and was overall very feminine. She and Rupert were laughing and giggling and both looked like they didn't have a care in the world. It certainly looked like Rupert wanted to plough her furrow and plant his seed in her lady garden. It took me by surprise when a male member of staff approached me and asked if he could help. I was still slightly flummoxed after spotting Rupert again so I answered him by saying I was looking for a clitoris. The assistant gave a loud embarrassed laugh and Rupert and his mysterious woman glanced over in my direction. The member of staff informed me politely that I wouldn't find one of those in a garden centre.

'Clematis, I mean clematis,' I stuttered, trying to rescue myself from the situation.

'You're a bloke anyway, you'd have no chance of ever finding a clitoris,' I muttered as I walked off quickly, leaving all my dignity amongst the potted plants.

This was the first time Rupert had made eye contact with me. I wanted to ask who had dumped who. Had he dumped Camilla or had she dumped him?

Saturday night had arrived and our first dinner guests, Imogen, Steve and their children, would soon be arriving at the Shack. The house was so small that at present we didn't have a dining room table, we couldn't fit one in. My genius plan was to throw a tablecloth over the patio table and move it into the freezing cold conservatory where we could all quite comfortably fit around it to eat. The doorbell rang, signalling that our dinner guests had arrived. Miles and Thomas said their 'Hello's and ran off to play with the other children, not to be seen again for the rest of the night. Before I'd even poured the first glass of wine – well Imogen's first and my fourth – she brought up the subject of Penelope.

Two hours and two bottles of wine later, Imogen finally finished talking about Penelope. The men had taken themselves off into the warmth of living room and were spending their time chatting about cars, golf and anything remotely blokey.

Imogen appeared exhausted; it was like a therapy session for her. She did look better for getting it off her chest and at that point my thoughts turned to Rupert Kensington. I wondered whose chest Rupert would be rolling off later.

Imogen enlightened me that she and Penelope had once been friends. Good friends, friends that socialised with each other most Saturday nights. They shared barbeques in the summer and occasionally had days out together. Imogen said that their friendship had blossomed from the start. They enjoyed each other's company whilst shopping, dined out for lunch and even participated in the odd bit of exercise together. The friendship lasted approximately four years – so they never made it to the seven-year point – but it all went wrong when the children started school.

Penelope and Rupert have two children – Little Jonny and Annabel – who were in the same classes as Miles and Thomas. Imogen claimed that as soon as Miles and Little Jonny started school, the situation changed. Apparently Penelope became materialistic and incredibly competitive too. Little Jonny always had to have the most expensive football boots, was given the latest football kit the day it was released and he was always dressed in the latest designer coat. Penelope must have a thing about coats because every time I saw her she was wearing a different one.

Imogen claimed it wasn't the fact that he had all this gear; it was the fact that Penelope never shut up about it that drove her mad.

Poor Annabel never got a look in, she was cast aside and it was all about Little Jonny.

'Little Jonny this, Little Jonny that.'

Little Jonny could name every single dinosaur at the age of three. According to Penelope, when he grew up he was going to be a philanthropist. She probably meant palaeontologist – if Imogen was right about her materialism I couldn't imagine him being encouraged to donate large sums of money to charity. Penelope didn't shut up about Little Jonny until poor Imogen couldn't take any more.

Little Jonny had the best designer school bag to carry his reading book in; the reading book that became the catalyst to the deterioration of their friendship.

Miles had been invited for tea at Penelope's and Imogen claimed that she had never even mentioned to Penelope that Miles had started reading. In fact he was so good at reading that he had skipped the first level and started on level two. Little Jonny was still on the first stage picture books which don't contain any words. You are supposed to discuss the story portrayed in pictures with your child to gradually introduce them to books. During Miles' visit for tea, curiosity got the better of Penelope and she rifled through Miles' bag to discover that he had started reading. Penelope nearly passed out when she realised Little Jonny was not the cleverest in the class. Miles was – by far.

When Imogen collected Miles later that evening, she could see that Penelope's face was like thunder. Imogen was immediately bombarded with questions.

'When did Miles start reading?'

'How long has he been on that level?'

'Why didn't you tell me he was on reading books?'

Imogen wanted to reply, 'Because quite frankly it's none of your business,' but instead she scooped Miles' coat off the peg, laced up his shoes and took him home.

That night Penelope had a sleepless night trying to work out how Little Jonny was going to up his game. There was only one thing for it; Penelope needed to invest in the *Oxford Reading Tree* books. As a part-time child-minder she could claim the cost of these back through her tax and pass it off as an educational tool for all the other children she looked after. Genius!

Imogen arrived in the playground the next morning to find Penelope already inside the school, bending the teacher's ear and complaining that she wasn't pushing Little Jonny enough. According to Penelope, Little Jonny was way too intelligent than the level of the books he was reading. She demanded the teacher either send home three books a week or move Little Jonny up a level. The teacher – who is a teacher because she is qualified and knows what she is talking about – refused. That poor teacher would be haunted by Penelope for the next school year as she challenged her assessment of Little Jonny's ability on a daily basis. Miles had completely overtaken Little Jonny on the reading scale and Penelope wasn't having it. Poor Little Jonny, all he wanted to do was make mud pies in the garden and annoy his little sister by teasing her with the worms he had pulled out of the ground with his fingers. Little did he know that over a hundred *Oxford Reading Tree* books had just been delivered to his house and he was going to spend the whole summer reading them all. But I suppose it made a change from Penelope forcing him to learn the names of those flippin' dinosaurs Imogen joked.

Two days later, Imogen and Penelope's friendship totally broke down when Miles became ill with the 'flu. Imogen had decided to send him to school but he was sent straight back home again by the teacher. Penelope was fuming and sent a text message to Imogen inferring that she was a bad mother for sending him to school in the first place! I think Penelope was put out because Miles had been sent home with numerous reading books to study while he was recovering, which would make it even harder for Little Jonny to catch him up. Imogen kept her dignity and didn't reply. They never spoke again.

I topped up Imogen's wine glass while she described how she was relieved the friendship had finally come to an end. Penelope was too intense for her. She would text every day inviting her to pop round for coffee and when she did, she would have to endure endless stories and anecdotes about Little Jonny. Imogen claimed that every Saturday night was taken up socialising with Penelope and Rupert. Rupert worked shifts at the local factory and if he was working nights Imogen still got lumbered with

Penelope. Imogen was thankful she would never have to listen to the relentless dialogue about Little Jonny again.

Imogen wasn't the only one cleansing her soul that night. The Shack was finally hooked up to the Internet and once Imogen and Steve had sauntered on home with their children I logged straight into my Facebook account. Immediately spotting that my news feed was full to the brim of Mrs High School Musical's antics I shook my head. Even with the distance between us she was still having a detrimental effect on my life. Facebook to me had become all about quality, not quantity of friends. It wasn't a popularity contest. Last year Mrs High School Musical spent her entire birthday on Facebook reading 'Happy Birthday' messages from people she used to go to school with and who she didn't actually like or remember. The whole world was going mad with social networking. I implemented my motto 'don't pretend, just un-friend' and hit the delete button, catapulting Mrs High School Musical and her gang from my life forever. She was no longer in my gang but I had most definitely allocated her a seat on my bus!

CHAPTER 2

February

The move to the village was going smoothly. We were settled in the Shack, Imogen was my friend and life was ticking along happily. Until I got a bee in my bonnet about chickens that is.

This move was all about the country life. I wanted chickens and ponies. I wanted to spend my days baking cakes and cookies. The Shack had plenty of land and there was definitely enough room for chickens. I had never seen a live chicken up close, never mind cared for one or kept one as a pet. I informed Matt that I was going to buy some livestock. Matt thought this was a ridiculous idea and reminded me I didn't know one end of a chicken from another. For at least an hour he kept telling me what a stupid idea it was. He was getting more and more irate and I could tell I had ruffled his feathers. You would have thought I had suggested that Penelope and Rupert should join us on a family holiday or that I was planning on having a lesbian affair with Camilla Noland. There was no need for him to get his wattle in such a twist; I had only suggested getting half a dozen chickens.

I decided to keep my beak clean and pecked around the Shack until Friday when I eventually decided I was going to purchase some chickens. I obtained the phone number of the local poultry farmer and gave him a ring to arrange the delivery of my new feathered friends. I was careful to arrange this at a time when Matt was away on business.

A burly, friendly man turned up and pulled onto the Shack's drive in his tractor. We hit it off straight away. He was hilarious, making fun of me as he passed the chickens over to me feet first, squawking and flapping their wings. I didn't have a clue what to do with them but Reg the farmer soon settled them in for me. He told me to ring him straight away if I had any problems, then left me to it. Maybe I had pecked off more than I could chew and I was flapping more than the birds. The children thought it was brilliant and spent the next hour watching the chickens to see if they laid an egg.

After tea, I rounded up the kids to help me catch the chickens and place them in my newly constructed coop for the night. If anyone had videoed this ridiculous scene they would have made a fortune – well, maybe two hundred quid – on *You've Been Framed*. We chased the chickens round and round in circles, tried to divert them with patio chairs and threw linen baskets over the top of them in a vain attempt to catch them. One had flown to the highest branch of the tree to roost and we were covered from head to toe in muck. We hadn't caught one single clucking chicken.

I was beaten. Matt was right for once – this was a stupid idea. Even the dog stared at me as though I had totally lost the plot and then settled back down to sleep. There was no way I could waste this amount of time every evening running around after birds – that was Rupert Kensington's job.

Telephoning Reg in a panic, I panted down the phone in sheer exhaustion. He must have thought he had a heavy breather on the line.

'I can't catch the chickens, Reg. I'm knackered.'

Reg was bewildered and didn't have a clue why I was even trying to catch them.

'I need to get them in the coop so if I don't catch them how do I get them in?' I quizzed.

At this point Reg was in the pub with his cricket mates and unknown to me had put my conversation on speaker-phone. I could hear the whole pub erupting with laughter when Reg announced I was a complete turkey and informed me that at dusk the chickens would strut into the coop one by one in readiness for the night. By the time I had hung up the phone, the chickens were all tucked up in bed. Thank God Matt wasn't here to witness any of this.

Luckily for me when Matt returned home from his business trip the chickens had settled in nicely. They were like a part of the family, clucking around and laying fresh eggs every morning. It felt like Christmas when the first egg was laid – it was a miracle! Matt sat at the table with the children for breakfast and I presented them all with dippy eggs and soldiers. All except Matt, that is.

'Where's mine?' he enquired.

'What do you mean?' I replied.

'My egg?' he spluttered.

'Well because you threw all your eggs out of your basket and had an eggifit, we only bought five chickens. You haven't got a chicken and no chicken means no egg!'

I thought it was eggceptionally funny. He looked like he was about to eggsplode! Three weeks later Matt ventured out and bought three chickens of his very own and was proud of the fact that he had his own supply of eggs.

School was relatively quiet so far this week. I continued to park in a space without any further altercations. Until Wednesday that is, which was going to be a day to remember.

I was taken by surprise when Penelope wandered over towards my space in the playground. I'd never ever spoken to her or made eye contact with her since the car parking dispute out-side the school gates.

'It's Little Jonny's birthday party on Saturday. Would Samuel like to come?'

I was a little shocked as I absorbed this information but was impressed that the car parking incident hadn't meant that Samuel would be excluded from the party celebrations.

I wasn't a fan of kids' birthday parties to be honest and these days the parties seem all about the parents not the children.

I could imagine Penelope and Botox Bernie spending all year planning their child's next birthday party. Of course, they would have to outdo the rest of the Playground Mafia and their previ-ous parties. Their parties were way over the top, featuring luxu-rious cupcakes, expensive balloon displays and not forgetting the designer party bags.

When I was a child, you were lucky to have a birthday party at all. Any party you did have involved a simple buffet at home and games such as Pass the Parcel, Musical Statues and Pin the Tail on the Donkey. You were grateful for what you got. I could bet my life Botox Bernie and Penelope would spend at least four hundred pounds on their children's birthday parties. Birthday parties were a status symbol and a power trip to these mothers.

I suppose the only positive thing about the parties were that the children could actually play with their friends without their book bags being rifled through. Or so I thought. According to Imogen, Little Jonny wouldn't have a say in his party guest list. Penelope would do the inviting based on specific criteria. She would write and re-write the guest list many times, taking into consideration how well she liked the child's mother, the intel-ligence level of the child and the apparent wealth of the parents. Well, she wanted Little Jonny to receive prestigious presents.

Imogen had first-hand experience of this as Penelope had neglected to invite Miles the previous year due to their personal differences, but it was awkward as the boys were still good friends at school. To top it all, Penelope used Facebook in a vindictive manner to publish a public post of details and photos of the party just to alienate Imogen. Imogen didn't rise to it and hit the delete button. Sometimes it was like being back in the school playground ourselves.

I would rather spend my children's birthdays with them as a family and treat them to a day out. The four hundred pounds wasted on a magician or a bloke who brings reptiles to your house to entertain the Playground Mafia's children – while they slope off to have their nails painted – is just not for me.

Imogen had been unlucky in the past and had endured three of Little Jonny's birthday parties when she was good friends with Penelope. She had recounted the story of the last party to me. As Little Jonny excitedly tore at the wrapping on the presents from his classmates, Penelope stood over him taking the presents from him one by one. She organised them into three piles. When Imogen asked Penelope why she had organised the presents into piles her response was priceless.

The first pile was for the expensive presents that she – not Little Jonny – didn't want. These were to be sold on eBay which would help to pay for her next new coat. The second pile went into the unwanted present cupboard at home; these were the presents that weren't worth much and could be recycled. She would pass them on to children that invited Little Jonny to their parties in the future. The third pile was the pile Little Jonny could keep. So out of nearly thirty presents he would usually end up with approximately six.

According to the conversations held with Imogen the night they came for the dinner at the Shack, it was alleged that Rupert

Kensington had confided in Steve about his love of children's parties. He encouraged Penelope to organise the most lavish parties and to attend all the parties their children were invited to. You may think this was strange but there was a method to his madness. The reason he loved children's parties so much was because it meant Penelope was out of his hair for a few hours, leaving him free to let off his party popper with his latest woman. Penelope would be preoccupied for weeks before a party which meant the house was empty for Rupert to play his own party games.

I accepted Penelope's invitation, thanked her for her kind offer and stood and wondered which dinosaur I could buy Little Jonny for his birthday. I also considered cutting out the middleman and handing some cash directly to Penelope for her new coat – it would save her listing the present for auction on eBay – but I'd only got Imogen's take on previous events.

That evening two things happened in the Shack. Firstly Matt had become quite ill of late, he was spluttering and sneezing and had continuous headaches. I packed him off to the doctor to investigate what was wrong. He arrived home two hours later clutching his allergy test results. I couldn't quite believe what I was reading. The poor bloke was allergic to chickens.

The second was a visit from Imogen. She looked like the cat that had got the cream and was beaming from ear to ear. Imogen had just visited the post office to post her eBay parcels – probably unwanted expensive presents from Miles' last birthday party – when she had literally bumped into Camilla.

Camilla had been in full gossip mode and couldn't hold her water; in the strictest of confidence she enlightened Imogen that Penelope Kensington had uncovered evidence that Rupert was playing away from home. She had no qualms in spreading the gossip of Rupert's new affair to Imogen – or anyone else for that fact – as she was a woman scorned.

Camilla wasn't coping well with her rejection by Rupert Kensington now she had been cast aside for a newer model. Imogen knew about Camilla's affair with Rupert; she too had spotted them in the local woods together while she walked her dog. She found it very amusing that Camilla used to pay Penelope as a child-minder to look after her child whilst she was off riding her husband in the back of her horse van.

This information was second-hand to Camilla as she had already prised the news of Rupert's latest squeeze out of her babysitter, Wendy Barthorpe's daughter. Imogen couldn't help smiling to herself. In her opinion it couldn't have happened to a nicer person. As she continued to relay all this information to me, I started to feel a little sorry for Penelope. How would she face everyone at Bingo on Friday? This was becoming a frequent event for her.

According to Imogen, when her friendship had broken down with Penelope, Penelope moved on to a lady called Wendy Barthorpe. Wendy was mother to three girls and her eldest often babysat for Camilla while she was mucking about with Rupert in the back of her horsebox. As Wendy was also one of those people that looked after children, this friendship was made in heaven. Wendy had the utmost respect from everyone in the village; she was a down to earth, hard-working woman that would put herself out for anyone. She was a very energetic lady; her days were filled to the brim with activities for the children. She was always taking them swimming or entertaining them in soft play areas and frequently visited the park. She would put the average mother to shame. This was a huge change for Penelope who spent most of her child-minding days seeking attention, updating her Facebook status every two minutes while chain-smoking, before nipping off to Home Bargains to stock-up on anti-nicotine air freshener that she sprayed religiously before the children were collected by their parents.

Wendy had another good friend – Annie Carter – who was the sole carer of her ill mother. They had been friends for many years – since school in fact – and Penelope had met them at various social events around the village over the years. Annie's mundane life – the majority of which had been spent looking after her mother – had shaped her personality into an easy going character. She was a kind hearted and wonderful woman who saw the good in everyone. Her sense of humour was infectious, she was full of fun and she smiled and giggled from the time she woke up in the morning to the time she fell asleep at night. The three of them became inseparable, spending every minute of the day together, constantly chatting on Facebook at night and enjoying frequent nights out to the pub, cinema and theatre.

Since we had arrived in the village I been shoplifting, bought chickens, hosted a dinner party and witnessed Rupert Kensington with two different women. Now I was about to come face to face with Camilla Noland.

My daughter Eva had needed a little persuasion to move from the north. She was a fantastic horse rider and her obsession with ponies had stemmed from an early age. At the present time money was a little tight for us but my parents offered to buy the children a pony; it was a little extreme but these are the lengths one must go to in order to escape from the likes of Mrs High School Musical. It wasn't a top of the range thoroughbred, more like an old oversized donkey that only cost a couple of hundred quid.

What we needed now was a saddle and other leather paraphernalia – I believe the proper term is 'tack' in horsey circles. Being new to the area I enquired at the post office as to the whereabouts of the nearest saddlery. The postmaster was very knowledgeable and pointed me in the direction of the nearest saddlery which was situated a few miles away in the next town and was owned by Camilla Noland!

Driving to the saddlery I wondered if Camilla would remember me from her lunch date in the pub but, thinking about it, she hadn't recognised me from the post office queue on the last couple of occasions. Taking a deep breath I approached the shop door, which was ajar, and I could hear voices. I was just about to stroll through the door when the conversation suddenly became very interesting and I stood still. It wasn't my usual style to skulk around corners – that was Rupert's speciality – but I was frozen to the spot, listening intently. Bloody hell, the conversation was crystal clear: they were discussing Rupert the stallion and his latest dalliance.

Camilla was spreading her gossip again, this time with another woman whose voice I didn't know. Peering through the crack in the door, I didn't recognise her either. After already hearing the same story from Imogen who had heard the story from Camilla, I still stood outside, taking it all in and waited for a good time to enter.

As the story went, apparently a few Saturday earlier Wendy Barthorpe had hosted a poker game at her house. Rupert was there – no wonder, he would poke anyone – and so was Annie. While Penelope had been smoking outside, Rupert and Annie's eyes met over the faded green felt of the poker table. Allegedly Annie was in admiration of Rupert's full house. She was fun; Penelope was not and Rupert became instantly attracted to her.

Inconspicuously Rupert and Annie arranged to meet the following day. Rupert's day was already planned; he was due to collect and rev the engine of his new car, a car he had dreamed about owning since he was a little boy. It would sport his own personal number plate, alloy wheels, fog lamps and leather seats

– complete with seat warmers. He wanted to test out that suspension and who better to invite along than Annie.

The next morning, luckily for Rupert, Penelope was due to attend a children's birthday party with Little Jonny. Rupert had managed to squirm his way out of going again, clearing the way for him to take Annie for a ride in the new car. Penelope was miffed as Annabel hadn't been invited to the party, so she would have to spend the whole time with her. Penelope droned on and on to Rupert that he should look after Annabel but nothing was going to spoil Rupert's plans. Penelope was not pleased. If only she knew.

Rupert raced along the country lanes with Annie and they giggled and screamed in his new car. He had instantly connected with Annie and this was a far deeper connection than he ever had with Camilla Noland – which wasn't hard, as from the conversation I was overhearing, Camilla appeared to be as shallow as a midget's Jacuzzi. He had grown distant from Penelope, thinking she was lazy, boring and self-interested. Day in, day out, it was all about her and the amount she constantly spent on coats was driving him insane. Rupert was falling for Annie. He did fall for Annie, that very morning in Penelope's bed while she was enjoying her cupcakes and checking out the latest craze for party bags.

Rupert was happy for the first time in a long while. The other women he had been messing about with had merely helped him survive his boring daily routine with Penelope. This was different, Annie was different. He was falling in love with Annie and he had never considered leaving Penelope before, until now. Rupert and Annie continued to see each other at every opportunity – usually on a Friday night while Penelope was off with her dabber playing Bingo at the local hall with Wendy. It also helped that Rupert mostly worked nights; well that's what he told Penelope. He was actually a regular guest in the premium suite at a local hotel, which he shared with Annie. His discount card was safely tucked away in the glove compartment of his new shiny motor.

This was all according to Camilla Noland and the other woman. I was still standing at the saddlery door like a flippin' lemon. I still hadn't found the right time to enter.

The other lady continued. Penelope had been woken up in the night by a vibrating noise. Rupert was lying fast asleep next to her when she noticed that his phone had lit up. The display on his phone read 'Hot Legs' and Penelope's heart began to race as she opened the message. She was devastated to read a text from a woman thanking Rupert for showing her his royal flush. Not sure that Penelope wanted to shout 'Bingo' at that particular moment.

I couldn't stand there any longer so I walked through the saddlery door. They stopped talking immediately and glared at me; you would think they had never seen a northerner before. Although they both nearly jumped out of their skin, they didn't appear to be too concerned as to whether I had heard their gossip or not.

'Can I help you?' Camilla asked curtly looking me up and down.

Her manner was very stand-offish but that's her all over, Rupert must have had a hard job trying to loosen her up.

Camilla made a gesture to the other woman that she would only be five minutes. I would have liked to give them both a gesture but I needed a saddle and needs must. I started to make polite chit-chat, not because I wanted to but because I knew it would aggravate the hell out of her. I started off with the weather, followed by the pony I had just bought. I was friendly; in fact I made myself feel quite queasy I was being that amiable.

I piped up, 'Nice place you have in the village.' Camilla's farmhouse was surrounded by acres and acres of land with the most breath-taking scenery.

There's one thing Camilla liked doing and that was talking about herself. She whined on and on and on about her manor house, how she loved having acres and acres of her own land and how convenient it was attached to the house. She droned on about her thoroughbred horses and her successful, booming business that she had built from scratch. I was beginning to get bored now listening to her self-indulgent drivel so I brought her off Planet Self with a bump and announced I was there to buy a saddle.

'A saddle? A saddle?'

She raised her eyebrows in the direction of the other woman she had been talking to on my arrival.

'Yes, a saddle,' I responded politely.

Camilla opened her eyes wide and made no attempt to disguise the fact she had just looked me up and down.

'Um I don't think so.'

'Excuse me?'

'My saddles are way too expensive for you,' she announced.

Did she really just say that? The cheeky mare! You know when you've just had a *Pretty Woman* moment, I was expecting Richard Gere to walk in and rescue me at any moment. Big mistake, Camilla Noland – big, big mistake!

I was a believer of karma and in time Camilla Noland would no doubt get her comeuppance.

After listening to the gossip regarding Penelope and failing to purchase a saddle, my inbuilt satnav told me to do a 'legal U-turn' and that's precisely what I did, never to gallop on her land again. I headed straight for a beautiful equestrian shop only a few miles up the road and bought the pony the most beautiful second hand saddle with barely a scratch on it.

Every cloud.

The chicken situation at the Shack had gone clucking mad. I originally acquired five hens and Matt had his three. He spent most of his wages on anti-histamines and never went near the chickens but made sure he ate his fair share of the eggs. The chickens that Matt owned all of a sudden became broody so we sat them on a clutch of eggs and let nature take its course. Three weeks later there were fourteen of the species pecking around. Matt's pill-popping of anti-histamines doubled in intake. We were overrun with eggs; we ate scrambled eggs, boiled eggs, poached eggs, fried eggs and egg custard. I was clucked off with eggs. So there was only one thing for it – I made myself a sign which read 'Fresh Eggs for Sale'. I hammered the sign into place in the middle of the front garden and waited. Matt thought I had OCD – obsessive chicken disorder. I thought it was a great way to make a few quid. Within twenty minutes – no word of a lie – we had the first knock on the door. We ran to the door with our best box of half a dozen only to find it was some bloke making sure we had managed to find God. I was lucky to find my Wellington boots in the morning, never mind bloody God!

Good old 'Fletch' – that's Mr Fletcher-Parker to you and me – became a regular visitor to the Shack on a Friday for his fresh eggs, clutching a pound for his finest half-dozen. He was turning into a lovely neighbour; every time I turned round he was there giving me a little wave most days or shouting a friendly 'Hello' from somewhere in the lane. I still hadn't clapped eyes on our other next door neighbours, the ones Fletch didn't speak to, but that was all about to change.

The eggs were flying out of the coop right into the hands of the local pensioners in the village. The eggs were fresh and a bargain and the old people couldn't get enough of them. The dog was launching himself constantly at the door as the doorbell never stopped ringing. I began putting all my eggs in one basket and taking orders before the eggs had even been laid.

Sunday mornings were the busiest time. Unfortunately for the customers I'm not the best morning person, so 9am on a Sunday morning, when I've got the hangover from hell and the orange and brown swirly carpets are really not helping, is not the ideal time to visit. Matt's new pastime was snoring and not only did he snore but he clucked at the end. I could have sworn I had seen every hour of the night and I must have dozed off just as the doorbell rang.

I bolted upright in bed, clucking hell I'd had enough. I opened the door and was about to be very short-tempered when I was taken by surprise; there standing in front of me was a woman holding in her hand what looked like a drowned rat. I did a double-take, how wrong was I? She was holding my cat by the scruff of its neck and it was dripping wet with water. I thought I was still dreaming, but no, she handed me the dripping wet cat and went into an angry dialogue of how my cat was chasing her rabbit around her garden. Stupid as this may sound, I apologised and told her I would have a word with the cat and she would be grounded – I would make her stay in her room all day! She looked at me as though I had just escaped from the local funny farm. I wish I had – I bet you get more sleep there – maybe I'll check myself in. Then I came to my senses and asked the lady why my cat was dripping wet.

'I've dunked it into a bucket of water,' she responded angrily before turning around and stomping off back up the path.

'Who the hell are you?' I shouted after her.

'Your next door neighbour,' was the muffled response I heard whilst she disappeared behind the hedge.

Just great, absolutely great! Not what I needed – a wet cat flung at me in the early hours of a Sunday morning. Looks like Mr Fletcher-Parker was right about those neighbours.

CHAPTER 3

March

March was the month of Little Jonny's birthday party. Rupert was not fond of his own kids' birthday parties, as this generally meant one thing – he had to attend. Matt dropped Samuel off at the party (which was football themed) only because Little Jonny had been boasting that a Premier League footballer was attending. He must have been the bowler-hatted office worker Mr Benn in real-life because after he had finished being a footballer, he reappeared as a magician, then he became a DJ before finally emerging as a bouncy castle owner. If the party had continued much longer, no doubt we'd have seen him appear as a spaceman, a Red Indian and a pirate!

Penelope kindly offered to drop Samuel back home at the end of the party and this is when our friendship started to blossom – or so I thought.

On Samuel's return I invited Penelope in for a brew. I felt sorry for Penelope, she looked sad behind her bright blue eye shadow and her orange foundation. Did she really know anything at all about Rupert's affairs? It wasn't a question I was going to launch into during our first cuppa – maybe I'd wait until the second one. So instead I asked her when the baby was due. Penelope started to cry. Not only did she cry, she cried some more. I started to panic as her orange foundation began to streak. It was a good job I was fully stocked up on the two for one Andrex toilet paper from the supermarket. So there I was, sitting in the Shack with a woman I barely knew who was crying hysterically. Maybe the baby wasn't his? Maybe she had been having affairs like her husband. Her cry turned into a wail and I had to ask her to tone it down as I knew the dog would start howling. I didn't do crying and I certainly wasn't about to do howling.

Matt popped his head around the kitchen door, just to check that the International Sex God hadn't tracked us down despite us being very careful not to leave a forwarding address. The look on his face suggested he thought the big orange guy from the 'You've been Tangoed' advert had called in for tea but he was relieved to find it was just Penelope.

'Is she all right?' he mouthed at me.

'I haven't got a bloody clue,' I mouthed back at him.

He popped straight back out of the kitchen again.

I decided to change the subject fast so I asked how Little Jonny's birthday party had gone. I thought this was a good move, especially as Imogen had informed me how much she liked talking about him.

'I'm not pregnant, I'm just fat!' she shouted.

Have you ever had the feeling when you want to instantly die with shame; to find a spade and bury yourself extremely quickly? This was one of those moments. I genuinely thought she was pregnant. Lucky escape though if you ask me.

What do you do in a situation like this? How do you respond to that? I asked her about a birthday party and she informed me she was fat. I knew she was fat because she wasn't pregnant but I didn't want to dig my hole any deeper!

'I'm fat because I eat too much,' wailed Penelope.

'No shit, Sherlock!' I wanted to reply but instead I offered her more Andrex toilet roll and a chocolate digestive biscuit – they are always good in a situation like this.

I was a little narked as she continued to munch her way through the packet of biscuits – their 'buy one get one free' offer had expired last week. Just my bloody luck.

'I need to discover who "Hot Legs" is,' Penelope cried.

If I hadn't have been ear-wigging at Mrs Noland's saddlery door, I would be thinking she was Rod Stewart's stalker and assigning her a seat on my bus because I could and because she was nuts. It was nearly the kids' bedtime and even the chickens had clucked off into the coop, so I suggested – and this was the point where I shouldn't have suggested anything because it mapped out my life for the next twelve months – that maybe she should go home, put her children to bed and come back for a glass of wine. Penelope left the Shack, only to return within the hour.

The bizarre thing was that from the time Penelope had left the Shack to her return my phone had beeped. It was Facebook notifying me of a new friend request – from Penelope Kensington! Not quite sure how I felt about this. In my opinion I did owe Imogen some loyalty but at this moment I really didn't have any issues with Penelope. I suppose it would have been a bit petty to hold against her the amount of toilet roll she had wasted while she was wailing in the Shack. Almost immediately after I had accepted, my phone beeped again. I had another request, this time from Wendy Barthorpe. I had never spoken to Wendy before or even met her. I postponed accepting that one for the time being although it crossed my mind that this was all very odd.

When Penelope returned, Matt shuffled up the freezing cold corridor clutching his beer and blanket with the dog in tow. He was banished out of the main Shack to the even more freezing cold conservatory while Penelope used up the last of the Andrex and cried some more. I was just hoping the two for one offer was still on.

I thought this Saturday would be an average day in the village but it was about to go down the pan. I felt like I was in a Jeremy Kyle episode. I now had an Oompa-Loompa sitting in my living room. The orange foundation had been washed away leaving a very purple stain-faced Penelope, who after one glass of pinot grigio couldn't hold her water. More Andrex was needed!

I tried to make the mood light-hearted, after all it couldn't be that bad – she wasn't pregnant and she still had all the presents from Little Jonny's birthday party to sell on eBay. That would keep her busy this week, in between her part-time child-minding duties which allegedly consisted of chain-smoking and sitting on Facebook.

This woman knew nothing about me but I knew more than enough about her. I was an average mother praying for the quiet life in my new country Shack. I had escaped from the clutches of the International Sex God and Mrs High School Musical but now, by request of Penelope, I was being bundled into my own car on a mission to follow Rupert to see if it would lead us to uncover the identity of 'Hot Legs'. Just what I didn't need!

Only seconds before, Rupert had notified Penelope by text that he had unexpectedly been called into work and her mother was babysitting the children. Matt was relieved that we were going out as he had started to freeze in the conservatory and had been forced to cuddle the dog for warmth. At least now he could return to the main Shack. At this point Matt was on the verge of hypothermia, his lips were turning blue and his beer was frozen solid. He needed to thaw out.

On a snowy Saturday night in freezing temperatures, when any normal person would be enjoying the warmth of a log fire while drinking a beer, some strange villager was making me play at being Dempsey and Makepeace.

With four children I had a bus for a car, which certainly wasn't inconspicuous as I spun and slid it all the way down the icy lane. We parked around the corner from Penelope's house which was a medium-sized detached property on a new-build estate. She made me abandon my car and crouch behind some bushes just in time to witness Rupert leaving their house. My feet were sopping wet; I glanced down to the frosty, snowy ground and realised I was still wearing my monster feet slippers! This wasn't a good look, a woman crouching behind a bush wearing monster feet slippers, accompanied by an Oompa-Loompa. Not only could we be arrested for lurking in the bushes, but even worse we could be arrested by the fashion police.

'Nice car,' I whispered, as Rupert climbed into his pride and joy.

Apart from being a very expensive car, it had its very own personalised number plate. The thought crossed my mind that my first encounter with Imogen had ended with shoplifting and my first encounter with Penelope – well goodness knows where that one was going to end up! Then it hit me, if my guess was correct I knew exactly where he was going. He was off to Annie's house, Penelope's best friend, and probably for his usual game of poker.

So Dempsey and Makepeace were on the trail to find 'Hot Legs'. At this point I have to say my own legs weren't bloody hot, the car temperature was just not rising. The only thing I could see rising was Penelope's blood pressure.

It wasn't a long car journey – Rupert pulled into a street at the top of the village and parked his car on the drive of one of the houses. Penelope remarked that this house wasn't anything to worry about, as this was Annie's house. I wasn't worried; I just wanted warmth with any sort of alcohol thrown in.

Crouched behind a bush for the second time tonight, we watched as Annie opened the door. I was surprised that on such a frosty, snowy night she wasn't wearing much clothing. Rupert kissed her and entered the house. Her house was definitely more upper class than Penelope's but again this was probably not the best time to say 'Nice house.' Instead I just prayed to God the feeling in my feet would return.

Before I knew it, Penelope was up and running towards the front door, she looked like a cartoon character with steam gushing out of her ears. I found it difficult to keep up in my monster feet slippers; well actually I found it difficult until I slid on the icy path straight past Penelope and hit my head on the front door.

Ouch.

Penelope glared at me and hissed, 'Get up.'

It wasn't my fault. I didn't want to be stalking Rupert on a freezing snowy Saturday night. In fact I didn't want to be stalking Rupert full bloody stop.

Penelope hammered on the door as I stood behind her. I felt like a reprimanded child, looking down at my feet even though I was actually making sure they were still attached to my legs. It took Annie quite a long time to make her way to the door and open it, no guesses why. I was hoping she would invite us both in for a brew but in reality that just wasn't going to happen. Finally as she opened the door Penelope slapped her very hard straight across the face. Marvellous, I think I preferred a night of shoplifting with Imogen.

Rupert must have heard the kerfuffle and he tripped and fell down Annie's stairs while trying to put his pants back on. In all honesty I actually smiled to myself. It was like something out of a comedy sketch.

After spitting out a mouthful of carpet Rupert was the first one to speak.

In fact, I was quite amazed that he didn't come out with the usual man spiel of 'It's not what you think, I can explain.'

Actually after being dragged out on a cold Saturday night I wanted to hear his explanation and wondered how he intended to dig himself out of this hole. After all, he was showing his ace and a pair to Penelope's best friend.

But no, his first question was directed at me.

'Who the hell are you?'

This question took Penelope by surprise. She looked at me waiting for an answer.

'Who the hell am I? Who the hell am I? Me? I am just some woman, who has moved from up north for a quiet country life. But no – I've been dragged out stalking men and now I'm on the trail to find "Hot Legs" and my favourite slippers are wrecked.'

At this point we all looked down at Annie's legs – yep I can confirm Rupert was right, Annie did have hot legs but maybe this wasn't the best time to side with Rupert! Penelope dragged Rupert to the car by his ear and threw him onto the back seat while Annie closed the door behind us. The atmosphere in the car was a little frosty to say the least, just like my bloody feet. I was the first to break the icy silence by suggesting maybe Rupert should drive his own car home.

'No chance,' was Penelope's reply. Annie's husband was due back in the morning and Penelope wanted Annie to explain to him why Rupert's car was there. I wasn't aware she had a husband. I glanced at Rupert's personalised number plate which read 5TUD 1. I smiled to myself maybe, just maybe, he should think about changing it to BA5 TARD!

I drove them back to their house and opened the car door to let them out before driving home. It certainly wasn't Bonfire Night but the amount of fireworks that were going to explode in their house tonight was unimaginable. Unfortunately for Rupert it was a different type of bang than he was originally expecting. I was so glad I wasn't there.

I arrived back at the Shack to find Matt completely thawed out, still cuddled up to the dog, both fast asleep with *Match of the Day* playing out from the television. I left them both where they were and climbed into bed in the hope I would feel my feet by morning and there would be no need for any sort of amputation.

In the morning I was woken by the sound of Samuel screaming, 'Mum! Mum! I'm on the loo and I've run out of toilet paper.'

Great, my stocks had completely diminished as a result of Penelope's crying. For a moment I just lay there thinking. It appeared I was settling in well to village life, everyone I had met so far was a complete and utter lunatic and could fill an asylum all by themselves. The only positive thing to come out of last night was that I didn't have a hangover; after all I hadn't had much of an opportunity to get drunk.

Poor Samuel was screaming even louder now so I finally decided to venture out of bed and pass him some toilet paper. Then I went in search of Matt who must have spent the night with the dog as he had never made it to bed. Matt was hugging his mug of tea and nursing a hangover. In my opinion there was no need to show off just because it had been a sober Saturday night for me. It wasn't fair.

'You'll never guess what happened last night,' I exclaimed.

I was just about to divulge all the details to Matt when the back door flew open and Imogen was standing there grinning from ear to ear.

'Come on in why don't you,' I sighed and handed her my mug of tea.

'You'll never guess what?' remarked Imogen.

'Go on, enlighten me,' I replied.

Then it all came spilling out. Apparently Rupert had been caught red-handed by Penelope having an affair with her best friend Annie. I could feel Matt's eyes locked in my direction but I managed to discreetly shake my head towards him. He knows this is the code for 'Keep your mouth shut and play dumb,' which is not hard for Matt. The last thing I wanted to do was to deny or confirm anything. If Imogen had known I was present at the time of the discovery, I would have to explain why I was out with Penelope – her arch enemy – and why I ended up stalking Rupert in monster slippers. I didn't care how she had got her information; she was not hearing any of it from me.

I was intrigued to know how the whole village had found out about the sordid affair while I was sleeping. I couldn't imagine Penelope broadcasting the fact that Rupert was showing his full house to her best mate.

'Where have you heard this from, Imogen?' I enquired.

Her answer took me by surprise.

'Camilla Noland.'

Camilla Noland? How the hell did she know? Had she been stalking us while we were stalking Rupert? But no, Annie is friends with Wendy, Penelope's other best mate. Last night Annie had taken refuge round at Wendy's house. She needed to come up with an explanation to why Rupert's car was parked on her drive. They both enlisted Camilla's help and the three women pushed the car to the end of the road and rolled it into a hedge. Unfortunately Camilla is not the soul of discretion but it was drastic measures at drastic times. She took every opportunity to bad-mouth Penelope and this occasion was no different. That morning in the local newsagents while buying a newspaper, Mrs Noland had already been spouting off about the affair in earshot of Imogen.

I felt really sorry for Penelope, she really didn't need the whole village knowing her business.

Just at that moment I received a text message from Penelope: *Can I come round?*

That was all very well but Imogen was standing in my kitchen filling me in on last night's adventure that I had been slap bang in the middle of. I'm sure old Rupert had been slap bang in the middle of getting his ace high as Penelope hammered on the door. Dempsey and Makepeace lived another day!

Imogen was in full gossip mode and informed me that Rupert had been up to no good before. I already knew he had been up to no good on more than one occasion. Imogen went on to reveal that again, according to Camilla, Rupert had already had a fling with another one of Penelope's friends called Stephanie. Shaking my head in disbelief I thought to myself it may just be easier if Penelope had no friends, or even easier to name the friends he hadn't had an affair with. Camilla still failed to let everyone know that she had previously shown Rupert the back of her horsebox on numerous occasions. So while trying to be diplomatic and suggesting we shouldn't gossip – actually I wasn't gossiping, Imogen was – my kitchen had been invaded and all I wanted was breakfast and a peaceful day. Already this looked like it wasn't going to happen. I was beginning to think it had been easier living next door to the International Sex God.

Stephanie's affair with Rupert had lasted six months. It had been easy for them to conduct an affair because Stephanie only worked one day a week. She was an attractive woman, and quite quietly spoken but, as the saying goes, the quiet ones are always the worst. Luckily for Rupert, Penelope never discovered this affair. Eventually Stephanie and Rupert drifted apart when Penelope fell out with her. According to Camilla – via Imogen – the rumour was that they argued over Annabel's christening because it fell on the day that Stephanie was working. Penelope had begged her to phone in work and take the day off sick but this was against Stephanie's moral ethics.

I wasn't quite sure where playing with Rupert's king and pair of jacks scored in Stephanie's morals. Rupert just liked to score full stop. Stephanie assured Penelope that she would be there for the evening do but, as Penelope needed to get her own way, it was all or nothing. Stephanie called her bluff and opted for nothing and even gave up Rupert without a fight. Rupert was devastated by this decision; she was the first of his many women and the first one to dispose of him!

I was bloody intrigued as to what Rupert actually had to offer and what everyone saw in him. I didn't get it and had no intention of getting it. I did my best to dodge weekly amorous acquaintances with my Matt, never mind getting it elsewhere. I replied to Penelope's text telling her I was free in an hour which would give me enough time to eject Imogen from the Shack and to jump in the shower. I needed to get myself mentally prepared for the day ahead. Once washed and changed I checked on the children. Eva, Samuel and Matilda were occupied and snuggled up watching a DVD in front of the telly upstairs, and Daisy was still fast asleep after having a restless night.

Matt was banished back to the conservatory with his new best friend, the dog.

It seemed that Penelope wasn't very successful at keeping her best friends. She seemed to rotate them in a two-year cycle and for whatever reason she no longer spoke to Imogen. Two years after that she had driven Stephanie away and now Annie had decided her relationship with Rupert was more important than her friendship with Penelope.

On arrival at the Shack Penelope looked dreadful. Making her a brew I wondered whether to offer her a biscuit, even though there were no chocolate ones left, or should I offer her a stick of celery? In the end, I opted for the safe option, I offered nothing.

For the next two hours – yes two hours – and seven fags later I had her life history. It was two hours of my life I will never get back. But I nodded and tilted my head in the correct places just so Penelope was aware I hadn't slipped into a coma.

Penelope confided in me how she'd taken the texts from 'Hot Legs' to a close neighbour, because she needed a shoulder to cry on. This neighbour was also a mother at school. Penelope made it clear she liked being friends with her as Little Jonny was way more intelligent than her son. I was astounded by her attitude and would have been amazed if that friendship lasted either. Her name was Josie. Josie was good friends with Stephanie and often shared lunch or shopping dates with her. She was already aware of Rupert's affair with Stephanie and knew exactly what he was like.

Penelope had confided in her that the affair was all Annie's fault. Rupert had somehow managed to convince Penelope that physical contact never took place. Who was he trying to kid? They were at it every Friday night while Penelope trundled off to Bingo with her mates. Didn't she think it was strange Rupert never got paid for his overtime at work? Oh and why was he lacking his pants when we busted him at Annie's house? I would have loved to have been a fly on the wall to watch that Oscar-winning performance. How naive was Penelope?

We all knew Rupert had been enjoying regular rendezvous in the local hotel with Annie. Not only had he taken Annie joy riding in his new car but he'd enjoyed afternoon sack games in Penelope's own bed with her and let's not forget his rendezvous with Camilla in the back of her horsebox – not a euphemism by the way! Biting on my bottom lip I kept quiet, which was very difficult for me; being a northerner, I usually have no qualms in saying what I think at the best of times but on this occasion I never said a word.

I was beginning to see that this local village was weaving some very tangled webs. Goodness knows what the gossip was like at Stitch and Bitch this week once they had hit the sherry.

Penelope steered the conversation round to Wendy Barthorpe. In my opinion this poor woman was stuck in the middle of it all. Penelope blamed Wendy for hosting the poker game at her house in the first place. I wanted to suggest that maybe it wasn't Wendy's fault, she couldn't have ever imagined Rupert was actually going to poke Annie. I couldn't understand why she was blaming anyone else, it was Rupert who hadn't been loyal, and he was the one married to her.

At this moment I mentioned that I had received a friend request from Wendy on Facebook. Penelope wasn't best pleased. Penelope drivelled on about how Wendy wasn't prepared to break her friendship with Annie. I wasn't sure why Wendy would, unless we had been catapulted back in time twenty-five years to the school playground. Penelope thought it was outrageous that their mutual friend was trying to steal her husband. If this was me, I would no longer have wanted to be friends with my husband and probably would have wanted to shake Annie's hand for revealing the type of bloke he was. I did think about pointing out that maybe if she wasn't so interested in Little Jonny and his climb up the *Oxford Reading Tree* and paid her husband a little more attention, none of this might have happened. But I didn't, as I only had Imogen's take on how Penelope worshipped Little Jonny.

Penelope begged me not to accept the Facebook friend request, claiming Wendy didn't like her having new friends and she was the jealous type. For the time being the only reason I hadn't accepted the friend request was because I wasn't acquainted with the woman. 'Quality not quantity' was my motto and I was sticking with it. I wasn't yet convinced that accepting Penelope's request was quality over quantity but I supposed time would tell.

As a friend – maybe that was pushing it a little as I had only known her forty-eight hours and as a result of this friendship I had frostbite, had had my first sober Saturday night in years and had just thrown my monster feet slippers into the open log fire to cremate them as they hadn't survived the previous night's adventure – unfortunately I needed to tell Penelope that actually she may not be able to keep the village from discovering Rupert's antics. Half of them had already overheard Camilla spouting her mouth off in the local shop while buying their morning paper. I decided not to rub Penelope's face in it – by also letting on that Camilla and Wendy had helped Annie to roll Rupert's car away from the house, therefore buying Annie some more time before she was busted by her husband.

Penelope stared at me wide-eyed.

'How do you know this?' Penelope asked sternly.

I wanted to say that what I hadn't learned about Tattersfield over the last few weeks probably wasn't worth knowing. Instead, as I had nothing to lose I just replied with the truth that Imogen had passed on the morning gossip to me from the newsagents. Apart from the shoplifting I did quite like Imogen. She was very witty and with her dry sense of humour I thought she would fit in well with my friends up north. But in the next ten minutes Imogen's right ear must have been burning – right for spite – as Penelope verbally tore the poor woman limb from limb.

Penelope started by slating Imogen's 'annoying' kids; Little Jonny was much cleverer than her lads of course – well according to her. She then suggested Imogen's husband, Steve, was a sandwich short of a picnic and the only thing he was good for was circulating the latest chart CD rip-offs or hooky Xbox games. She suggested Imogen was clingy and Meredith and Lucinda only put up with her because they felt sorry for her. I thought about giving Penelope Mrs High School Musical's address and suggesting they could become pen pals. Planet School was enough to deal with but now Planet Village seemed to be taking over.

I ventured into the kitchen to make Penelope yet another cup of tea. Matt popped his head around the kitchen door, which was becoming a bit of a habit. His lips were turning blue and I realised the poor bugger had been stuck in the conservatory for over two hours in freezing cold conditions. Being the kind wife that I am I let him back into the main Shack and suggested to Penelope that maybe I would be arrested for Matt cruelty if he had to stay in there any longer. Penelope took the hint and reluctantly ventured back home.

Before I knew it, it was Monday morning again and I was sitting in the car with the children parked in the space outside the school gates. I had nine years left of this routine, nine years left of my primary school sentence. Watching the playground from afar whilst the mothers trundled in to the yard, I realised I'd only been present for a few weeks and already there had been numerous shuffles around the playground. Mothers appeared to jump from one clique to another, usually because another child had become more intelligent than their own.

Botox Bernie had taken a step to the left in the playground over the last couple of days. According to Imogen she had apparently fallen out with another mother over a recycled birthday present. Two weeks ago, Botox Bernie had given a book as a birthday present to a child and penned a personalised birthday message at the front – only to receive it back for her own child two weeks later. The moral of that story is to make sure you check all the pages of the book before you wrap it back up and give it away.

This particular Monday morning the gossip was rife in the playground. Everyone had heard the Rupert story, thanks to Camilla Noland. The Playground Mafia were like vultures flapping around whilst waiting for Penelope to enter the playground, I felt sorry for Penelope. Botox Bernie seemed to live for gossip. She got high on other people's news and this morning was no different. She received a blow by blow account of Rupert's infidelity from Camilla herself.

Botox Bernie was an unsavoury character. She used the playground like a big chessboard, attempting to dominate the mothers ranking top in playground feuds. Botox Bernie – the white queen – moves first by targeting the mother she wants to displace. She makes her latest grievance known in the playground within earshot of any mother willing to listen. The rest of us on-lookers are simply pawns in the game; occasionally, one of us makes a wrong move after being given little time to think and we make an ill-judged remark, placing ourselves in a position where we appear to have taken sides. Usually the best thing to do is not to think and stay out of it but that is easier said than done. The mother that has then been dragged into the argument – the innocent party – is then a trapped pawn, unsupported by the other pawn mothers and unable to advance as they are dumped after sticking up for the original pawn. I flippin' detest chess – and playground mothers.

I'd had a more than eventful weekend and was hoping the quiet life would soon return. My morning was planned out – a morning of cake baking followed by cleaning out the coop and checking on the ponies, which now had increased to two. Matilda toddled after me everywhere and Daisy would be strapped in her buggy happily gurgling whilst sucking on bread sticks. The weather was warming up a little and it was starting to feel like spring. I had just switched on the kettle when there was a knock at the door.

Opening the door I found Penelope on the other side. Sometimes I envy people with those peep holes in their door; this would have been one of those occasions when I could have peered through and pretended I wasn't at home. Penelope seemed excited, she had an idea that she wanted to run past me. Grabbing her a mug, I poured her a cuppa and we sat down at the kitchen table. Penelope had been thinking, she'd decided that Rupert had only fancied Annie because she was thin. Shaking my head in disbelief I had no idea where Penelope was going with this but I continued to listen. The only thought that crossed my mind was maybe Rupert fancied Annie because he was simply fed up with Penelope and Annie was fun. She told me that it was her fault Rupert had been attracted to Annie because she no longer was taking care of herself and had let herself go. I couldn't believe it. There was only one way this conversation was going and I was correct, Penelope had let Rupert off the hook! She'd thought about it long and hard, well for approximately forty-eight hours and made the decision to save her marriage to Rupert because she didn't want Little Jonny and Annabel coming from a broken home; they deserved better. Penelope was hoping she could forgive Rupert in time. Her master plan was to lose weight. She felt everywhere she turned in the village everyone was whispering about her, so she had decided to get her act together and start to lose weight by walking. And that's where I came in: she had come to the Shack to persuade me to be her walking partner as she felt that I would motivate her. She was so keen she wanted to start walking right that very minute.

Why me? Surely she had other friends in the village that could walk with her. Then again, sitting back and thinking about it, she had already fallen out with most people, so maybe I was the only one left daft enough to go walking with her.

Wrapping the children up in their coats I strapped them into the buggy. Grabbing the dog's lead and my own boots and coat we set off walking.

We had set off towards the canal. Popping my head over the buggy, I saw that Matilda and Daisy had drifted off to sleep. Ambling along nicely and enjoying the scenery, I couldn't believe it when Penelope dropped into the conversation the infamous question.

'What reading scheme did you have at the last school?'

I just knew that the next hour or so was going to be living hell. That was the only time my input was required over the next hour, as the remainder of the walk was filled with Penelope going on and on about Little Jonny. I felt like throwing myself in the canal rather than walking beside it.

I was starting to realise that Penelope was obsessed, not only with her own voice, but more so with her pride and joy – the golden child – Little Jonny. I had to endure every detail of the pregnancy: the days she was sick, her cravings, the description of the first outfit they had bought him, her labour and finally her pain relief. I would have loved a tank of gas and air or an epidural myself at this particular time, just to numb the pain of this conversation. Then thankfully he was finally born! I wasn't sure how much more I could take of this. I felt my eyes starting to glaze over. I was beginning to understand why Rupert strayed; in fact I would have probably encouraged him myself. Rupert thought the grass was greener and he was probably right.

The torture wasn't over.

Next I had to endure the story of Little Jonny's first day at pre-school. I felt as though I had been alongside Little Jonny every step of the way. He was the first baby from the post-natal group of friends to smile and the first one to speak – unbelievably his first word was dinosaur! I imagined Little Jonny was the first one out of his friends to walk; Penelope confirmed this a second later – he was. Penelope was bursting with pride as she told me all about her Little Jonny.

Surely Penelope would change the subject soon. We were half an hour into this walk and I had started to up the pace, pushing the buggy faster just to get home quicker and hopefully never hear the name Little Jonny again. No such bloody luck. She carried on and on. I heard how Little Jonny had stood out from his peers on his first day at school; he was so gifted and talented. Little Jonny could add tens and units at age five. He could recite all his times tables by the age of six and by the time he reached seven, he could write joined up and already he knew he was going to be a palaeontologist. And he could spell it as well! I guessed Penelope must have locked him in his bedroom and didn't allow him out until he could spell it. Penelope was beaming, informing me that Little Jonny could name every dinosaur that existed and could name up to five facts about each of them. I could name one fact – they are all extinct. I wished Penelope was a dinosaur. I wasn't a violent person but I did consider giving Penelope a short, sharp slap to knock her back down to earth. She had bigged him up so much that there was only one way for Little Jonny to go in the future and that was down, hitting his head on the floor as he fell off his pedestal.

Only time would tell. Little Jonny was going to Oxford. Little Jonny was going to be rich and famous. Little Jonny was going to have a beautiful family.

'Let's hope Little Jonny doesn't take after his father then,' I managed to whisper under my breath.

It was Little Jonny this and Little Jonny that but no mention of the golden child's sister, Annabel. I was so thankful to arrive back at the top of my lane. I greeted Mr Fletcher-Parker as he popped up from behind a bush to give me a wave. I'd had enough, a bloody belly-full to be precise. I wondered if Rupert was an alcoholic too – I definitely needed a drink. I had missed Knit and Natter so there was no sherry for me today, I would have to take out my frustrations later at clog dancing.

I continued up the lane when Penelope called after me.

'Same time tomorrow then.'

I couldn't wait.

For the next week I pushed the buggy and walked alongside Penelope every morning without fail (she didn't work mornings – her child-minding duties always started in the afternoon). During this time, in between singing Little Jonny's praises of course, she came up with a plan. This plan was to monitor our weight loss. I wasn't walking to lose weight – in fact I didn't have a clue why I was walking. Her plan involved Fridays. I was hoping the plan would involve Friday lunch at the pub as this was the law up north – and Monday to Thursday too! Unfortunately not though; her plan was to weigh ourselves at her house every Friday, record it and add up the pounds of fat lost each week. My plan was definitely the better of the two; I was certainly the brains of this outfit. Oh, and the thinner one too, well at this moment in time.

Every week I spoke to Fay, my best mate in the world ever. I updated her on my new friends in the village.

We were of the same opinion; none of these people would pass the seven-year rule.

In her words: 'Get them on the bus!'

The first Friday big weigh-in arrived. We walked our walk and Penelope talked her talk, reeling off the achievements Little Jonny had made that week. This kid was amazing – according to Penelope. He was the top striker and top defender in every game for the local football team. I don't profess to know too much about football but it sounded like he was already better than Eric Cantona. Penelope suggested the rest of the team were useless, they were nothing without Little Jonny.

I wanted to scream, 'One lad doesn't make a team,' but no matter how loud I screamed she would never have heard me or taken any notice. So I just didn't bother.

That Friday morning, once we had finished the walk, Penelope invited me into her house. Following her into the kitchen I pushed the buggy to the side of the kitchen table. I noticed the weighing scales were already positioned on the floor, on a particular square tile. Penelope informed me that in order to give an accurate reading the scales had to be placed on the same tile each week. I wasn't sure why I was doing this, I wasn't sure I had even agreed to do this.

Penelope disappeared, muttering about needing to get changed. I didn't have a clue what she meant. Rupert sauntered into the kitchen while I was standing staring at the scales. Glancing up in his direction I did a double-take. He was dressed in a flowery apron and was holding a bright multi-coloured feather duster in one hand and pushing a Hoover with the other.

I had to do everything in my power to stop the lyrics of the famous Queen song 'I Want to Break Free' flying out of my mouth.

Annie had had a lucky escape if you ask me. Poor bloke – this must have been Penelope's way of making him pay for his indiscretions.

'Nice apron,' were the only words I could muster up.

A few minutes later Penelope reappeared and that's when I did my second double-take of the morning. Was this for real? Penelope looked like she should be a plus size model in *Climber Weekly*. She was dressed in clobber that would not be out of place on an expedition about to climb Mount Everest. This woman was barmy, end of discussion. She approached the scales dressed in a hat, ear muffs, ski jacket, salopettes, numerous thermals and massive snow boots. I was fascinated by her madness. I was mesmerised. This was a photo opportunity, evidence for when the men in white coats came to take her away – and in my opinion, the sooner the better. I thought we were meant to be losing weight, not adding it on. She looked ridiculous. Surely they had mirrors in this house? She stepped onto the scales and took her reading. There was a muffled sound escaping from under her balaclava. I was hoping she had suffocated but she was simply informing me that it was my turn to stand on the scales. I removed my coat, hat and boots and stood on the scales. The display flashed and my weight was revealed.

The next moment Penelope opened a kitchen cupboard door – which was a bizarre green colour but a step-up from avocado – and out it came. After taking off her ski gloves she was clutching a little black book. It wasn't just any old little black book – it was THE little black book. I thought she had uncovered more evidence and was about to show me detailed records of Rupert's misdemeanours, but no. She bent back the cover revealing the first page. In the first column was written the word NAME, in the second column was written WEIGHT and scribbled in the third column was a plus and a minus sign. This was serious stuff. Every Friday, Penelope was going to record the weight loss – hopefully not a gain! She was in charge of this little black book and all evidence would be recorded in it. This was all very well but I weighed in at nine stone – Penelope uttered something under her breath when my weight was revealed but I didn't challenge her to repeat it as it didn't sound very complimentary. I wasn't over-weight in the first place and I wasn't bothered about losing any more. Then it hit me, I was just here to make her feel good about herself.

I had already planned my excuses to leave as soon as the weigh-in was over and I couldn't stay for a moment longer. Quickly wheeling the pushchair towards the door I said my goodbyes and returned home to the Shack. I made myself a warm, milky brew and scoffed half a pack of chocolate digestives and thanked God I wasn't Penelope.

At the same time next morning, Penelope was waiting for me for our now daily walk. She was getting herself into a little routine, just like Mr Fletcher-Parker who was still spontaneously appearing from behind hedgerows at different times of the day to give me a wave. I had never spent so much time in anyone's company before. I was beginning to tire of these walks, I was so desperate to block out her dulcet tones that even Gina G's 'Ooh Aah, Just a Little Bit' song on my iPod was more appealing than another hour of Penelope wittering on. I was losing the will to live. Penelope took care of all the talking on our walks, I just nodded in what I thought were the right places.

However, this morning was different, had Christmas come early? Surely it had as there was actually a change in the topic of conversation. Hallelujah! Flipping heck, Little Jonny had been relegated and was kicked off her agenda for this morning's torture. This morning was all about Wendy Barthorpe.

Penelope spluttered with great pleasure that Wendy Barthorpe wasn't at all happy with me.

Gosh, I felt awful, what had I done?

There was no stopping Penelope this morning or any other morning for that fact.

Apparently Wendy was a little upset that I hadn't accepted her Facebook request. Obviously, Penelope was such a good friend of hers that she hadn't told Wendy she was the one who demanded I didn't accept her request.

'I thought Wendy was a good friend of yours?' I enquired innocently.

A stupid question on my part and I wish I had bitten my lip because Penelope then spent the next hour slating her so-called best mate.

Firstly Penelope prattled on about Wendy's dress sense. According to Penelope, Wendy dressed herself in drab dark colours, over-sized t-shirts and jeans that were worn out, faded and had seen better days. Her trainers were so old that they had come back into fashion. Her hair hung around her face with no shape whatsoever and hadn't been cut for years. It was never high on my agenda to notice what clothes Wendy was wearing. When I looked myself up and down I realised that Penelope had just described me – that was exactly what I looked like! I couldn't even remember the last time I'd had my hair cut. I was a little taken aback that Penelope was talking about her friend in this manner; goodness only knows what she was saying about me behind my back.

I only had Penelope's word that Wendy was narked because I hadn't accepted her friend request, yet it was Penelope that had caused this upset by begging me not to accept it in the first place. I didn't get the logic behind any of it.

From what I could gather, and it didn't take a genius to work out, Penelope was trying to influence what I thought about Wendy but I wasn't going to judge Wendy on someone else's opinion and especially not Penelope's. As far as I was concerned it was nothing to do with me.

Penelope continued. She claimed that even though Wendy was paid as a child-minder – to educate and stimulate other people's children – she actually spent her day on social networking sites, cultivating her make-believe farm. She would wait in anticipation for her phone to *ping* with the latest comments that made her feel wanted and important and in between, she constantly posted status updates, made frequent cups of tea and scoffed numerous chocolate brownies.

I had to listen to this character assassination for over an hour. The amusing thing about this conversation was that I had heard this conversation before; this is exactly what Imogen had said about Penelope! I knew none of this was true. Wendy was always out at the park or swimming baths and stimulating the children she looked after – and Penelope had accompanied her on many occasions! Wendy was the salt of the earth; this was the general opinion of Wendy in the village. She had three children and would work every hour to give her children what they needed. Wendy was the type of woman that would give you her last pound and would never think about putting herself first.

I agreed with Imogen and got the impression Penelope was describing herself rather than Wendy and this was quite evident as I kept receiving farm game requests via Facebook from her. She was the one feeling insecure in case I made another friend in the village – heaven forbid! I was too busy with my own life, family and friends to waste time commenting on Penelope's fake statuses while she sought constant attention on the World Wide Web.

This particular morning was not a good one for me. I had the dreaded women's bug; you took your life into your own hands if you even breathed the same air as me. The medicine to cure this monthly bug was any form of chocolate or, failing that, custard creams. I had PMT! I wanted to stay home, drink tea and eat three thousand calories of sugary snacks. I'm not sure how Penelope survived the next hour as she continuously belly-ached about Wendy. I blocked out her words from my mind and started to fantasise about gagging her. I ventured into the deep, dark depths of my coat pockets grabbing at anything, praying for just a hint of chocolate. Even the smell of a chocolate wrapper would help anaesthetise the suffering of this monthly pain. Luckily for Penelope she escaped my clutches and was unscathed and lived to walk another morning, which was unfortunate for me.

The month of March had seen me observe Penelope's vicious jealous streak on two occasions. One occasion would have been enough for anyone. Day after day I persevered with the mental torture of her conversation, Little Jonny this and Little Jonny that. Little Jonny appeared to be the only positive thing in her life. The rest of the time she oozed negativity. It was the world's fault she hadn't won the lottery, it would have flippin' helped if she had bought a ticket in the first place. It was 'the scrubber's' fault her husband had been enticed away.

Recently Penelope had fallen out with her mother too. Penelope thought it was unreasonable that her mother spent her own money taking herself off on foreign holidays in her retirement. Penelope thought this money should be saved up to send Little Jonny to Oxford. Penelope had also fallen out with her father – her parents were separated – because last Christmas Penelope had requested that he buy Little Jonny and Annabel a five hundred pound flat screen telly EACH for their bedrooms. Penelope claimed her dad owed her. He had split up the family when she was a kid and she was going to milk him for all he was worth. Well clearly he wasn't worth much as he told her that two five hundred quid tellies were excessive and instead he sent her a pen with the name 'Penelope' on it. She wasn't happy to say the least. At this point she cut him right out of her life. No flat screen tellies in their house that Christmas.

The first hint of her jealousy reared its ugly head on a Friday, the day of the weigh-in. I remember this day well – in fact even when I have dementia and am sitting in my rocking chair, pissing my pants in the local nursing home, I will remember this day.

Two could play Penelope's game – the weigh-in game that is. She had stood on the scales the first time wearing every item of thick clothing she could find from her wardrobe. Not this week, this week Penelope was wearing next to nothing. She'd put on leggings, a skimpy black top and no bra. Poor Rupert having to put up with those – I could tell that there wasn't much fun in those cushions. A smug smile crept across her face. She then opened the little black book.

'Last week I weighed sixteen stone,' she piped up. 'Oh my gosh, oh my gosh, I've lost eleven pounds!' she squealed with delight.

No shit, Sherlock! Would that be because your whole outfit last week weighed approximately eleven pounds? But if she wanted to kid herself, who was I to argue? I wouldn't have got a word in edgeways anyway.

Next it was my turn. Like any sensible person I wore the same clothes that I had been weighed in the previous week. I'm no scientist but clearly this would give me an accurate reading of any weight loss or gain. I stood on the scales. Penelope thought that there was no way I had lost much weight, if any.

As Penelope peered down at the display, a flush of anger could be seen creeping up her neck towards her face.

'No way, the scales are broken, the battery must be going flat,' screeched Penelope, flabbergasted.

I glanced down at the scales and saw the evidence for myself. I was five pounds lighter.

Job well done, Rachel, giving myself a pretend pat on the back.

Flippin' hilarious!

Penelope spun round in horror and demanded to know what I had eaten all week.

I answered her calmly.

'On Monday, I ate a burger and chips. Tuesday, I had chilli and rice. Wednesday was curry and Thursday steak, chips and salad.'

She raised her eyebrows and her head looked like it was about to explode off her shoulders.

'You liar! There is no way you've eaten all that and lost five pounds. Get out!' she hollered. 'Get out.'

I was completely taken aback by her reaction. She threw the little black book across the room in anger. What a drama queen, she would have won an Oscar with that performance.

'Are you serious?' I asked, grasping at the pushchair and headed towards the door. Shooing me forwards she slammed the front door shut behind me.

I think that was a 'Yes'! She was serious. If anyone could have seen this it was very comical, side-splitting entertainment. I smiled to myself as I did feel ever so slightly sorry for Penelope because in all honesty I had lied – I was bloody starving! Hardly a morsel of food had passed my lips that week; I had barely eaten a thing. There was no way Penelope was getting the better of me.

I did three things in the next ten minutes. Firstly, I walked to the bakers, bought the biggest cream cake and went home to enjoy every mouthful. Secondly, after logging on to the computer I accepted Wendy Barthorpe's friend request and thirdly, I rang Fay, my best mate in the world ever, to update her on how I was settling into the village. She thought so far so good, I was settling in very well!

So that was the first time I'd felt the wrath of Penelope's jealous streak.

We've established my move to the village was for the quiet country life, even though this was not quite going to plan. The only thing going to plan was the purchase of my chickens and my ponies.

I was missing some of the gang back home. Although it goes without saying this didn't include the International Sex God or Mrs High School Musical. I needed a catch-up with normality and decided the time was right to invite them to the Shack for a small get-together. My friends were excited too and they booked themselves into a hotel in the nearest town. The date was set for the following Friday. I also invited Penelope, Imogen, Lucinda and Meredith. Even Josie said she would pop in for a glass or two of wine.

The night was a great success. The north and south brought together with no major hiccups. My old friends joked that I was the new Felicity Kendal – they couldn't believe I was clucking around with my chickens and galloping around the countryside on my ponies. They were happy for me, genuinely happy for me. Just like real friends should be.

Penelope's behaviour puzzled me, one minute she was kicking me out of her house and then tonight she resembled a limpet, clinging to my every move and listening to my every word. Penelope was full of herself, introducing herself as my new best friend. I'm not a gambling man – obviously I'm not a man at all – but the odds on this friendship surviving a year weren't brilliant. In fact it was odds on in my opinion – it just wasn't going to last.

After lots of drunken laughter, chilli and rice it was time for everyone to vacate the Shack. There was only so much Matt and the dog could take of the conservatory. My friends ordered a taxi and after numerous hugs and a lovely catch-up they headed off towards their hotel. Penelope had ordered a taxi for herself along with Josie and another friend she had invited. On the way out of the door Penelope turned and faced me and thanked me for a wonderful evening.

'You are the best thing to happen in this village for a long time,' she gushed.

I felt myself flush. I'm not sure if this was the wine or the embarrassment of the compliment. She said that she was glad she had finally found a genuine friend.

Standing on the doorstep we arranged to walk again the following morning, followed by a quick lunch session because Matt was home to look after the children. I still felt a little sorry for Penelope. She was having a difficult time at home coming to terms with Rupert's affairs and she was still getting over the fact she didn't own a flat screen telly. Little Jonny's Oxford fund was also diminishing fast, as her mother was currently sunning herself on the beaches of Barbados. So I thought it was only fair of me not to judge her mood swings and to be a supportive friend in such difficult times.

As I watched Penelope climbing into the taxi at the bottom of the path my phone rang and flashed with Penelope's name on the display. Promptly I answered the call but soon realised Penelope must have accidently pressed the buttons on her phone. I was astounded, shocked to the core. I couldn't believe what I was hearing through the open line. This woman was like Jekyll and Hyde; what the bloody hell happened to change her from the lovely Penelope – my apparent new best friend that had ambled down the path – to the venom-spitting Penelope climbing into the taxi? The green-eyed monster reared its ugly head again, that's what happened. The taxi pulled away from the curb and I witnessed Josie and her friend sitting on the back seat open-mouthed. They looked speechless. Penelope launched into a vicious verbal attack on me when I wasn't even there to defend myself.

'She is a complete liar,' she proclaimed. 'She pretends to be someone she isn't. She doesn't even own her own horses; she just pretends she does to make herself look important and rich. I can't believe she stands there claiming she has horses when she doesn't.'

What was Penelope's problem? Penelope needed a slap, a bloody hard slap! A slap to knock her into next week, ideally to land on a day beyond Friday so I didn't have to witness her pathetic weigh-in antics. If she wasn't careful I was going to be the woman to do it – my northern roots never let me down. So what was I going to do about this? I decided to do absolutely nothing. I didn't need to explain myself to the likes of her. I knew I had BOUGHT my horses with my own money and I didn't give a neigh what she thought!

CHAPTER 4

April

Camilla Noland had been pretty quiet of late, which was a blessing in disguise for Penelope. She must have been in arrears on her rent in the parking space she usually occupied outside the school gates because she hadn't been there for a while.

The only bonus for Camilla's bearing a child was the monthly collection of her child benefit money. Which it seemed she used to pay to get rid of her kid at every opportunity.

Penelope bleated on about Camilla's 'poor daughter'. Rosie was constantly dumped at the before- and after-school clubs, so Camilla could secure some free time for herself.

Biting down on my bottom lip was beginning to become a habit. I wanted to say, 'She has more time to herself now she isn't rolling in the hay in the back of her horsebox with your husband,' but I refrained on this occasion.

Penelope had an opinion on anything and everything and even if you didn't want to hear it, you got it. Penelope thought it was outrageous that Camilla never attended a school concert or a sports day and usually had to be reminded that she even had a daughter. I did wonder if Penelope would have an opinion of Rupert and Camilla if she knew about their little indiscretion.

I hadn't really spotted Camilla for a while, that is until she was suddenly standing in front of me in the local chemist. Looking flustered she quickly stuffed some nit lotion into her carrier bag. I could only assume this was for her daughter and about time too as her school class was rife with lice. How did I know this? Well unlike Camilla Noland I did attend Mother's Day assembly and had witnessed her daughter constantly itching her head. When the school notified us of the nit outbreak Penelope apparently telephoned the local education authority reporting her for neglect. According to her version of events the nits could actually be seen crawling in Rosie's hair. I wonder if Camilla ever reported Penelope for neglecting Rupert.

Imogen was no longer talking to me. She would now pass me in the playground without even making eye contact.

Each day this did lead to a slightly uncomfortable fifteen minutes in the playground while I dropped off Eva and Samuel but compared to the hour's walking with Penelope on a daily basis, it was bearable. The joys of the school playground.

I had no real idea why suddenly all communication broke down; my only thoughts were that it was something to do with Penelope. I think Imogen made a conscious decision to stay away when Penelope took up all of my time and to be honest I didn't make any effort to save the friendship. Imogen was never likely to pass my seven-year rule. I decided not to give her a seat on 'the bus' because deep down I did believe she was a decent person.

With all the exercise I'd lost over a stone in weight now and looked hot to trot. Penelope had lost weight too but now had a huge upper body and stick thin legs. A weird body shape like the majority of villains in the animated Pixar movies. Apart from telling me how great Little Jonny was – still no mention of poor Annabel – Penelope's new pastime was tearing apart Wendy and Annie.

Maybe I'm disillusioned; if Matt was having an affair, why would I blame the other woman, friend or not? My normal way of thinking, not that I am always right of course – although I usually am where Matt is concerned – would be to blame the husband. Rupert has a brain. I'm not quite sure how intelligent he is but he knows the difference between right and wrong. He was a married man and married men shouldn't be sleeping with other women. Yet he did, it was his decision. In all honesty if I was Rupert married to Penelope, I would probably have had affairs as well. She must have driven him insane. She was driving me mental and I only had to put up with her for an hour a day walking. Not a week went by without her buying a new coat or the latest electronic gadget. She claimed that they never had any money – no bloody wonder with her constant spending. She was so materialistic it was unbelievable.

Penelope fell out with Rupert on her last birthday and didn't speak to him for two whole days because he bought her an expensive bottle of perfume and flowers. She threw the flowers at him and burst into tears. What was wrong with the woman? Penelope wanted an iPad. She had hinted and hinted for ages. Rupert had noted the hints but thought this was a test to see if he would spend the money and if he did she would make his life hell for being so extravagant. So he didn't buy her one and she still made his life hell. It was a challenge Rupert was never going to win.

One particularly cold morning in April I was left speechless. It's not very often I'm speechless but on this occasion I was definitely lost for words. The knock on the door in the morning usually meant Penelope was waiting outside ready for our walk. The children were already strapped into the pushchair and waiting patiently. I collected my coat from the cupboard, and headed out the door, straight into the arms of Mr Fletcher-Parker – and I mean STRAIGHT INTO THE ARMS.

He held me in a headlock under his sweaty armpit, completely trapping me.

'This village is a much better place since you arrived,' he spluttered and then grasped my face in a tight vice grip, planting his horrible lips onto mine.

This was unexpected and way too touchy-feely for my liking. It was way too anything for my liking. By the time I had caught my breath he had gone. I felt sick. Had I just dreamed that?

I rang Matt immediately, explaining what had happened to make sure I was still on this planet and I hadn't ventured through a *Doctor Who* wormhole – whatever one of those is – into another universe without knowing. He was no use whatsoever. I could hear him in hysterics at the end of the phone. He thought it was the funniest thing ever. I wondered how funny he'd find it when I put a stop to his marital rights for a while. A long while.

I scrubbed the insides of my mouth red raw like a mad woman, trying to eliminate Mr Fletcher-Parker's – from this point now known as Frisky Pensioner or 'FP' for short – sterilised milk taste, a taste I recognised from having a cuppa at my gran's house.

UGH.

I headed out to find Penelope with Matilda and Daisy who were still strapped into the pushchair and probably wondering what all the commotion was about. This definitely wasn't my morning and hurrying down the path with the pushchair in tow I was hoping not to be jumped upon again. This time I nearly took the ankles off the next door neighbours whilst running slap bang into them with the pram. Luckily for me, I hadn't clapped eyes on them since the day they nearly drowned my cat. I knew that I should have stayed in bed today.

I hadn't been thrust through a wormhole – more's the pity – and I hadn't imagined Frisky Pensioner's advance, which was even more of a pity – but the neighbours had witnessed it through their front window and shot right round to the Shack. I sacked Penelope off – she was probably out buying a new coat anyway – and pushing the pram back through the front door I invited the neighbours in for a brew. Plonking the children down in front of the television again I certainly wasn't going to win any mother of the year award but it would keep them entertained for a while. Inviting the neighbours into the kitchen they sat down at the table whilst I flicked the kettle on and made them a brew.

Then it all came spilling out – the truth, the whole truth and nothing but the truth. What they were about to tell me made for very interesting listening.

It turns out I wasn't the only one Frisky Pensioner had tried to get frisky with. Don and Edna – our next door neighbours – had lived in the village for over forty years, the same length of time as Frisky Pensioner. They had all been good friends until the summer of 1969, when it turned out Frisky Pensioner – known as 'Filthy Pillock' back in the day – had taken quite a liking to the number 69. Frisky Pensioner worked the night shift at the factory, which left him skulking around during the day while his wife was putting people behind bars in her day job. Frisky Pensioner thought he was God's gift to women. He was a flirtatious man and everything that came out of his mouth was an innuendo, a suggestion with a motive.

Don had worked days, leaving Edna at home by herself. One summer's day in particular it was extremely hot and Edna was lying on the sun lounger in her garden, topping up her tan. She had the feeling that someone was watching her and as she looked up at Frisky Pensioner's back bedroom window, a shadow appeared to move behind the curtains. It wasn't unusual for his curtains to be closed while he slept in the afternoon before heading off to work. But Edna was convinced he was up and had been watching her through the gap in the curtains. She told me that this had unnerved her so she moved her sun lounger to a part of the garden which wasn't overlooked. After a while she removed her bikini top – strap marks weren't a good look in those days either – and dozed off, with the sun beating down on her. She was suddenly woken by the sound of rustling so she grabbed her top, placed it back on and standing up slowly, convinced she could hear some faint panting. The sound was filtering through from the other side of the fence and was louder towards the middle panel. She crept along the fence line, head bowed and ears tuned in to the sound, slowly homing in. Then she saw it – an eye looking back at her. Frisky Pensioner had been spying on her topless sunbathing through the peep hole in the fence, a manmade hole that he must have drilled on a previous occasion.

This certainly wasn't the story I had heard from Frisky Pensioner regarding the neighbours' hostility. The story didn't stop there. Edna took herself back into the house and clambered into the shower. When she had finished showering she wrapped herself in a towel and returned to the bedroom. She was just about to remove her towel when she suddenly had the feeling of being watched again. She hurried to close the curtains and spotted Frisky Pensioner standing in the garden with his pants around his ankles, exposing himself.

When Don arrived home he didn't hesitate to march round and give Frisky Pensioner a piece of his mind. They never spoke again. I was so relieved I had confiscated the key from him when I arrived in the village because I may not be a farmer's wife but

I would have definitely chopped it off with a carving knife if he had pulled that trick on me.

At this moment I felt like a complete idiot. Even though Don and Edna had nearly drowned my cat – not quite as bad as my previous cat perishing in the tumble dryer – for which they sincerely apologised, I should have never believed Frisky Pensioner. Not only had he snogged me on my own doorstep, he also had history of peeping through fences and exposing himself. Never judge anyone based on someone else's opinion; in future I will always remember there are two sides to every story. Not sure what other side there was to the story of Penelope slagging me off in the taxi – only time would tell.

This advance – if that's what you call it – from Frisky Pensioner happened on a Wednesday. That meant one thing – it was Friday in two days' time, the day Mr Fletcher-Parker routinely bangs on the door to collect his fresh eggs. I was not looking forward to that; in fact I was dreading it. I thought about moving house quick. I thought about closing all the curtains and pretending someone had died – a bit extreme I know, but there was no way on this earth that Mr Fletcher-Parker was getting near any of my eggs again unless he wanted to end up being scrambled.

Matt had decided it wasn't hilarious after all; his only hysterics were now regarding not getting his leg over. I thought he would have learnt his lesson by now and would remember that I meant business after I failed to purchase him a chicken when we first arrived in the village.

Thursday morning Matt was up – not literally, due to the sex ban – and out early in the morning. Even the cockerel was fast asleep and hadn't yet cock-a-doodle-dooed. I couldn't sleep and ventured downstairs to make myself a brew. I was standing in my kitchen in my nightie, looking out of the aluminium framed kitchen window on to my large garden at 5.30 in the morning hugging a mug of tea, when unexpectedly the back gate flew open and Frisky Pensioner strolled into my garden. What was he doing lurking in my garden at 5.30 in the morning? I was like a rabbit in headlights, rooted to the stone kitchen floor. I was literally frozen to the spot – frozen being the operative word – as after all I was wearing next to nothing. He must have seen Matt leave. He must have been watching. The wicked side of me took over and I considered staying there pretending I hadn't noticed him and granting him a flash of my chest, which would hopefully result in a heart attack. I certainly wouldn't be giving him the kiss of life. But no, quickly crouching down, I hid behind the kitchen units, spilling a mug of hot tea all over myself. Well at least that warmed me up. What the clucking hell was he doing in my garden at this time in the morning?

I remained crouched down, peering over my kitchen cupboards trying to see what he was up to. I couldn't believe I was hiding in my own Shack wearing nothing but a nightie! I tracked him as he sauntered towards the bottom of the garden. I felt like I was playing a game of Twister, placing my hands and feet on the floor in an attempt to manoeuvre myself into a position where I could see him. He suddenly reappeared so I quickly ducked back behind the cupboards. Cupping his hands around his eyes he gawped in through the window – Frisky Pensioner versus the woman in the nightie. I stayed where I was, completely still with my heart pounding in my chest, desperate not to be spotted. Eventually, he pulled away from the glass and strolled straight back out through the gate again. I was fuming. This village life was definitely different from back home. If you entered anyone's back garden in the early hours of the morning up there, you would be taking your life into your own hands, literally. But round here, the villagers clearly thought your property was open to anyone – at any time. Well not my back garden. My back garden was my back garden. I immediately went to Matt's tool box – not a euphemism – and screwed – again not a euphemism – a lock onto the back of the gate. That would put a stop to any unwanted early morning garden creepers. I was now freezing, bloody burnt and much drained. I telephoned Matt before I returned to bed. He definitely wasn't in hysterics this time. In fact he was quite supportive. By the end of the conversation he was hinting that maybe it was time to end the bedroom ban. No chance, I thought, as I returned to bed. I would keep Matt sweating a little while longer! Unfortunately, this was not going to be the last time I saw FP – Frisky Pensioner or Mr Fletcher-Parker – this week.

The next day it all went nugget up in the coop. My clucking good hens were fast becoming clucking dead hens. I suppose where there is life there is always going to be death. My hens were dropping dead one by one. I didn't have a clue why or how, it was a complete mystery. So far that week I had lost six. I was bewildered and it was very upsetting to say the least. This particular Friday morning I ventured into the coop to find that Daphne had departed to chicken heaven. I picked her up with a tear in my eye. Suddenly I heard BOOM, BOOM, BOOM. That could only mean one thing; it was Friday and there was no mistaking FP's knock on the door. I actually chose to ignore the door and wandered round to the back of the Shack to find a suitable box to place Daphne in. BOOM, BOOM, BOOM – he wasn't giving up today. I really wasn't in the mood for FP any more. He had changed from a friendly granddad-type character into a creepy old guy that was way too friendly for my liking! Quite frankly I really could do without him.

I could imagine him in his day – many, many years ago – being just like Rupert. A womaniser, having numerous affairs behind his wife's back. He probably thought he was God's gift and I wondered if he was related to the International Sex God. Everywhere I went in the village he popped up – and I mean popped up. If I was walking down the lane he would appear from behind a hedge. If I was in the post office he would be loitering behind me in the queue. It was as if he knew where I was going to be, and everywhere I was, he was too – like some kind of geriatric ninja. I had unwittingly acquired my own pensioner stalker. Why couldn't I have a fit, young thirty year old stalker? Or Gary Barlow, he would be the perfect stalker. But no, not me. I was only able to attract those over the age of sixty-five. I didn't like it and I didn't like him.

There was only one way to get rid of FP quickly that morning and that was to open the door holding the dead chicken so he would notice that I was up to my armpits in death. Unlocking the front door I didn't even crack the smile that I usually forced. This morning, to put it bluntly, I really couldn't be bothered. I was fed up of being nice.

Holding dead Daphne I stared at him and curtly said, 'I'll just get your eggs.'

I left the front door of the Shack ajar behind me and wandered down the hallway towards the kitchen while juggling dead Daphne and placed his eggs into the box. I turned around to head back to the front door and crashed straight into FP! The cheeky pensioner had let himself in the front door and followed me through to the kitchen without even being invited. What happened next was unbelievable and, unfortunately for me, holding a dead chicken in one hand and a box of eggs in the other didn't leave me with any free hands to defend myself.

'Are you upset?' he whispered.

Was he for real? I was holding a dead chicken. I looked at him with an expression that should have questioned his intelligence but it had no effect on him.

With no expression on my face I replied, 'Here are your eggs' and I stretched out my hand with the box. His grubby, fat-fingered hand went to grab the egg box, or so I thought. Quick as a flash, the dirty Frisky Pensioner swiftly slung his arm around my shoulder and pulled me into his neck as his other arm went around my waist and straight up my top. If I could have vomited on demand, that's exactly what I would have done.

'Get off me, what the bloody hell do you think you are doing?' I shouted.

I swung the dead chicken and clouted his podgy, repulsive face with her cadaver – sorry Daphne.

'Get out! Get out now!' I shrieked.

I couldn't believe what had just happened and the only witness I had was a dead bloody chicken! Clucking hell, to say the least. FP skulked out of the Shack with his feathers ruffled and his eggs broken.

I sat down and had a swig of sherry, while I put this into perspective. So far, I'd been shoplifting, played detective, got chucked out of a friend's house and been touched up by a bloody frisky pensioner all in the space of twelve weeks. Marvellous! Could my year get any worse? I rang Matt and filled him in. Straight away he joked how lucky Frisky Pensioner was as he hadn't copped a feel for weeks. But realising this was probably not the best time to be saying this he suggested he could go round with his shotgun. But there was a major problem with that idea – he didn't have a shotgun. There was no way FP would have the cheek to come back for eggs next Friday, was there?

I hoped Penelope was now calm after her outburst in the taxi. I just carried on like nothing had happened. Obviously it had happened as I was looking really good; the weight was dropping off me. Penelope had actually been very sheepish that week – I just assumed she was bloody embarrassed. I, on the other hand, was still fuming over the slating she had given me in the taxi. But deep down I knew Penelope was unlikely to become a seven-year friend – to be honest, I couldn't see her becoming a two-year friend. Paddy Power would have given me favourable odds on that.

Penelope and Wendy's relationship had become very strained since Rupert had been caught playing poker with the lovely Annie. The three ladies had been good friends. Wendy was still friends with Annie and Penelope was just about still friends with Wendy. Penelope thought Wendy should show her some loyalty and stop speaking to Annie. Wendy thought this was ridiculous as she was entitled to be friends with whoever she wanted. Annie hadn't done anything to Wendy. Wendy would not have minded if Annie had tried to take her own husband as she had been wanting rid of him for years. She never had any luck.

Penelope had got her knickers in a twist (Rupert allegedly preferred his women to go 'commando') over Wendy and Annie's friendship and Penelope eventually gave Wendy an ultimatum – it was Annie or her. Wendy was a sensible woman and didn't really have to think about it. There was no contest; it was Annie all the way.

Penelope and I were still walking every morning. This walking lark was definitely character building. The next morning's walk – you've guessed it – was all about Wendy.

I must have uttered no more than two words on the walk that morning. I managed to nod a few times in what I thought were the right places and I definitely rolled my eyes a few times. According to Penelope, Wendy was a home-wrecker and a traitor. Penelope was all me, me, me.

Actually I felt like saying, 'Shut up, woman, Wendy more than likely has her own problems and her own life to deal with.' But of course I couldn't get a word in edgeways.

Penelope told me she had sent Wendy an email telling her how wrong she was to continue to speak to Annie. I couldn't quite see the logic. Poor Wendy was living her own nightmare at this time. Due to all this mither, she had decided that her own husband was a waste of space and was in the process of removing him from the marital home. Did Penelope care? Of course she didn't. Penelope offered Wendy no support, just hassle about something that was nothing to do with Wendy in the first place.

Penelope banged on for an hour and a half, slating Wendy and calling her all the names under the sun. I'd had enough, to be honest. I could clearly see why she fell out with everyone. So far there had been Stephanie, Imogen and now Wendy – and those were only the ones I knew about. No doubt my time would come. I prayed it was some time soon.

That afternoon, Penelope strolled onto the playground and addressed Wendy.

'Hi Wendy, have you had a nice day? I waved at you while we were walking but you mustn't have seen us.'

She was totally unbelievable. I'm sure Penelope has that condition where you have a split personality – she is certainly duplicitous to say the least. This morning she had suggested that capital punishment should be brought back for friends who weren't loyal. At this precise moment I agreed.

Same time, same walk but the next morning I was left completely gobsmacked. I felt like I had been whacked in the face by a dead chicken – that had been filled with lead first! I even questioned whether I was a drug addict and hallucinating over what I saw before me. Was I looking in a mirror? Penelope was standing on the drive of the Shack wearing yet another new coat. Not only was it a new coat, it was MY coat! It was exactly the same style and the same colour.

My jaw dropped. I was speechless and if it was possible to be more speechless, I would have been when I glanced down at her feet. She was sporting new Wellington boots. Not any new Wellington boots, they were the same colour and brand as mine. We looked like twins. I didn't want a twin.

The first thing I wanted to say and it was on the tip of my tongue was, 'Did you keep the receipt?'

'Morning,' Penelope chirped.

At least she was in a better mood than yesterday. This could only be a change for the better.

'Nice coat,' I murmured. 'Nice wellies,' I continued.

'I so loved your coat, I just had to get one,' she retorted. 'We look like twins, don't you think?'

In my opinion we were nothing like twins.

As we set off on the walk, I prayed no-one would see us. It was like a blast from the past, my memory transported me back to when I bought the same clothes as my mate when we were teenagers. We were going to be a girl rap-group called Fly Tie – it wasn't really a group and we couldn't even rap but we had dreams. Back then, we thought it was cool to wear the same clothes. Now, however, it really was not cool – it was not the 1990s.

Just when I thought things could not get any worse, I spotted Wendy and Annie driving towards us, howling with laughter and beeping and waving. I thought the beeping was a little over the top but I really couldn't blame them for the laughter. Penelope couldn't grasp what they found amusing. She convinced herself it was pretend laughter and they were just trying to make her jealous.

I wanted to scream, 'IT'S NOT ALL ABOUT YOU. You have made me look like a complete and utter idiot.'

But I didn't, I just nodded in the right places and plugged my headphones in. Even Gina G's 'Ooh Aah, Just a Little Bit' was beginning to grate on me now. With all this walking there was only one way to drown out Penelope – plug in my iPod and pretend that I was listening. She wouldn't have a clue if I was listening or not as long as I nodded from time to time. I began to realise that I had a lot of shameful songs on my iPod; if these walks were to continue I would have to update the device, and quick.

Penelope was chatting away as usual and just for a change it was all about Little Jonny. Apparently Little Jonny was keeping his options open and if by any chance he didn't grow up to work with dinosaurs he was going to be the next David Beckham. I wanted to shake her and tell her there was no way on this earth that Little Jonny was going to be the next David Beckham. Instead I just nodded in the right place again – I was getting good at this. Penelope was delusional. I carried on listening to my iPod and smiled to myself as 'Always Look on the Bright Side of Life' blasted through my ears.

Approaching the bottom of the lane signalled we were nearly at the end of our walk. Penelope gave me a beaming smile and said she couldn't wait to tell Rupert and was really looking forward to Saturday night. Taking out my earphones I gave her a puzzled look. What was Penelope barking on about now? Then it hit me, I realised I'd been nodding in the wrong bloody places. Penelope had only gone and hinted it was about time that Rupert and Matt were introduced and I had nodded.

There was no getting out of it. Saturday night was the night we were to entertain Penelope, Rupert and Little Jonny. I did wonder if they still had Annabel because Penelope never mentioned her. All I had to do now was break the news to Matt and the kids.

Surely it couldn't be that bad, could it? Spending a few hours with Penelope, Rupert and Little Jonny? Oh and poor Annabel – I was starting to forget her now like her own mother. Flicking through my recipe books I decided to cook a good old pie. You couldn't go wrong with a pie and lots of fresh vegetables. Leaving Matt with the children I rose early on the Saturday morning to venture out for all the fresh ingredients. As you can imagine, Matt wasn't overly thrilled at the thought of spending his Saturday night with a womaniser. I told him to pretend he didn't know anything about Rupert's affairs. It wasn't as if we would be discussing Rupert's infidelities and asking him for marks out of ten for his time with Stephanie, Camilla and Annie – and those were only the ones we knew about. I bet his little black book was packed with numbers – and maybe scores. I assured Matt that once we got Saturday night out of the way we wouldn't have to entertain them again.

Our usual routine on a Saturday night would be to all curl up in the living room and watch brain numbing television until we fell asleep at a ridiculously early time. My party animal days are definitely over. There was only one dress code in the Shack for a Saturday night, pyjamas or any type of slob out clothes, the comfier the better.

When the Kensington clan knocked on the door of the Shack, I realised Penelope had different ideas regarding the dress code. She was wearing a jumper and hot pants. Yes that's right – hot pants. I had a feeling it was going to be a long night.

Just as the Kensingtons arrived, my phone beeped with a text message from Fay. She was wishing me luck for the evening ahead and couldn't wait to hear all about it. I quickly typed a reply.

Why depress both of us?

Penelope introduced Matt to Rupert and Little Jonny.

'Who's this?' enquired Matt.

As usual, Penelope had forgotten all about Annabel.

'I didn't realise you had two kids,' smirked Matt.

'Neither did she,' I muttered under my breath.

Rupert shook Matt's hand and gave me a friendly punch on my shoulder.

'I've heard a lot about you,' he remarked at me.

'Ditto,' I replied.

I had a feeling this night was not going to be chalked up as one of the better nights of my life.

Rupert handed over a bag of beers.

'Well that's something,' I thought, at least they have some manners and if nothing else I could get trollied. Every cloud and all that.

I reached out to take the other bag from Rupert but this time it was Matt's turn to raise his eyebrows.

'Oh you don't want that bag, it's my slippers. I take my slippers everywhere,' Rupert remarked.

'He's brought his bloody slippers,' Matt mouthed at me. I laughed a little uncomfortably and whispered back, 'I hope he doesn't think he's getting his feet under my table.'

I was just praying to God he hadn't brought his toothbrush and a clean pair of pants.

The children kicked off their shoes and ran off to play upstairs with Eva, Samuel and Matilda. Daisy was already fast asleep in her cot. The problem I had not fully resolved was where to seat everyone to eat? I finally decided to stick with the hosed-down patio table that I had earlier placed in the conservatory. Actually the word conservatory was too posh for this room and I'm not even sure you could class it as a room. It wasn't even attached to the main house. You had to leave the main house via the back door, pass the coal scuttle and outside toilet – very classy avocado green, of course – and continue to the end of the long corridor. It was like being transported back in time via Dr Who's TARDIS. The thought of David Tennant made me smile. I needed something this evening to make me smile.

I led our guests through the house, out of the back door and into the conservatory. I offered Penelope a drink like the marvellous hostess I was.

'I'll have a Malibu, please,' she replied.

A Malibu? Where the bloody hell did she think she was? Some tropical Caribbean island or the sticky-carpeted local Ritzy nightclub in 1987? What would she ask for next, Taboo? I may have been ninety miles south of my roots but I was still a northern bird. The choices were lager, bitter, wine, sherry or Babycham. In the end she opted for sherry.

We started to make small talk around the patio table. There was only person talking and you won't be surprised to hear that it was Penelope. Rupert looked like a fish out of water. In fact he looked like a goldfish on numerous occasions as he opened his mouth to speak only to be spoken over by Penelope. It was quite amusing to watch and it was obvious who wore the trousers in that relationship. Well let's face it, Rupert barely wore any trousers and Penelope should have been wearing some, if those hot pants were anything to go by.

Penelope was clearly unhappy in her relationship – that was plain to see. There was no chemistry between the two of them, no glancing moments and every time poor Rupert managed to get his opinion out there, Penelope shot him down in flames and belittled him at every opportunity. Rupert was clearly unhappy with the relationship too, otherwise why the other women? I placed my homemade pie and fresh vegetables proudly on the table and have to admit that it smelled good and looked absolutely delicious. Penelope's face was a picture.

'Have you made that pie?' she enquired.

'I certainly have,' I replied smugly.

'I can't remember the last time we had home-cooked food,' Rupert butted in, only to be given one of Penelope's best withering looks.

Penelope started to shovel the pie from the dish onto her plate in a massive mound. She was like a woman possessed. I always thought that if you were unhappy, you generally had a loss of appetite and stopped eating. But not Penelope – in her miserable state of mind she was comfort eating. Next Friday, when her weight loss was actually a gain, I guess she would blame it on my cooking; it would be my fault entirely.

Matt started to witness what I had to endure day in and day out from Penelope. Every time Matt tried to steer the conversation away from the marvellous Little Jonny, Penelope would steer it right back on to him. The alcohol was beginning to kick in which was a blessing in disguise but somehow I maintained my decorum and self-control. I was smiling to myself as ironically the bottle of sherry we were drinking had been donated by Wendy at the last school fair. I'd pulled the lucky ticket from the tombola and won the bottle and was now using Wendy's sherry to dull the pain of listening to Penelope. I retained my human spirit, pouring Penelope another tumbler full.

Unfortunately the more alcohol Penelope consumed, the greater Little Jonny became. Even Rupert had lost the will to live and started to roll his eyes. The conversation had now moved on to football. Little Jonny was the best footballer for his age apparently, not just in the village but in the world. Penelope sat at my table large as life and informed me that there would be no point sending Samuel to train with the same football team as Little Jonny because he would never get a game. He just wasn't in the same league as him.

My decorum and self-control were slowly departing and staring at Penelope I asked her to explain herself. She was sitting in my Shack, eating my home-cooked pie, drinking my sherry – well Wendy's technically – and slating my son. Penelope needed a reality check. If Little Jonny was such a fantastic footballer, why hadn't he been scouted by one of the big clubs? I let Penelope dig her hole a little deeper while I sobered up quickly, listening intently to her every word to ensure she didn't defame any more of my children. I wanted to knock her over the head with a blunt instrument, any heavy object that was close to hand would do.

Penelope lived on a different planet. She had now moved on to Little Jonny's intelligence. Little Jonny was going to set the world on fire. The only time Little Jonny would be setting the world on fire was if he grew up to be an arsonist – or dropped a fag butt under the local Scout hut and accidentally burned it down. Or would Little Jonny end up being a cheating bastard like his father after marrying someone like his mother? I cruelly imagined Little Jonny getting Annie's daughter up the duff in the future years. It was a known fact that Penelope was already planning different high schools to Annie's kids, as heaven forbid they were educated at the same establishment. I rolled my eyes at Matt.

Matt tried his best throughout this torture to engage Rupert in conversation, any conversation that wasn't about the children. To be precise any conversation that wasn't about Little Jonny. I did contemplate putting a Little Jonny swear box in the middle of the table. I would have been quids in by now if I had. Matt steered the chat on to cars.

'Cracking car you have, Rupert. How long have you had that beauty?' he asked.

Rupert looked relieved and his face beamed as he told us of the proud day he went to pick up the car.

I sat back wondering where this conversation was heading, knowing full well that Rupert had had Annie in tow when he went to collect his new car.

I kicked Matt under the table and mouthed, 'Change the subject,' but there was no stopping Rupert, he was in full throttle.

The excitement on Rupert's face was clearly visible, reminiscing about the day 'they' went to collect his pride and joy. The copious amounts of alcohol he had consumed had loosened his tongue a little too much and stopped him in his tracks when the word 'they' left his mouth. He knew full well he had practically ordered Penelope that day to attend a children's birthday party with both children so he could share that moment with Annie.

Unfortunately for him Penelope was hanging off his every word and clocked the word 'they' as soon as it left Rupert's mouth.

'Cake, anyone?' I piped up, quickly trying to diffuse the situation but by that point it was too late. Rupert had had his cake and eaten it that day and most probably on the back seat of his new car.

If tonight's experience was anything to go by, it really wasn't a million dollar question why Rupert had affairs. I didn't need to ask the audience or phone a friend. Even the Playground Mafia knew the answer to that question as it was allegedly discussed at length at the last Petty Tedious Army meeting. If you need to know anything about anyone, just sit next to Botox Bernie at a PTA meeting. Let's be honest here, the time at these meetings isn't spent discussing fundraising for the school, the time is spent gossiping about whose husband or wife was having an affair with who.

The night concluded with The Verve's 'Lucky Man' blasting out from the iPod. Penelope turned to Rupert and curtly reminded him this was his song. He was the lucky man being married to her. I couldn't work out if Rupert had developed a nervous twitch or if he was simply rolling his eyes in our direction. I didn't think Rupert was a lucky man. I thought he should have escaped from the marriage a long time ago.

From that moment I decided I quite liked Rupert. His behaviour and demeanour suggested he was a man up for a laugh, he was a joker, and Penelope squashed his personality. Where she was concerned he never laughed and who could blame him, being stuck with her since the age of eighteen. The poor bloke had had enough.

And on that final note I raised my glass to a lovely evening and toasted Wendy for donating the bottle that helped the evening along.

Penelope and Rupert left shortly after the cake.

'I'll see you Monday morning for our walk,' announced Penelope.

We shut the front door behind them just in time for our giggles not to be heard.

'I wouldn't like to be in his slippers tonight,' said Matt.

'And I'm glad I'm not in the back seat of his car or honking his horn,' I replied.

The Lucky Man was definitely in for a long night.

CHAPTER 5

May

On Monday morning I was greeted by an eager and enthusiastic Penelope. She had a plan. I like a good plan but joining Penelope for a coffee in the local cafe after our walk didn't seem like much of a plan to me.

We began our walk on the usual route along the main road of the village. Anyone that passed us in the car couldn't miss us. We wore the same coats, same shoes and, as of this morning, now carried the same bags. Penelope couldn't thank me enough for Saturday night. She gushed about how well everything had gone. I was beginning to doubt we were even at the same dinner.

A small, black bubble car raced past us and beeped. I glanced up but didn't recognise the vehicle.

'I don't recognise that car,' I muttered. 'They must like your new bag.'

Penelope didn't cotton on to my sarcastic tone. I loved my bag. I had never seen another one like it until now. Penelope must have trawled the Internet for weeks trying to find a matching bag.

'That was Rupert,' she replied.

'What was Rupert?'

'In that black car.'

I had to assume he was driving a courtesy car and maybe his mean machine had recently seen too much action. It was probably due a service or an MOT.

'Is his in the garage then? I'm surprised Rupert can fit in that car, he looks way too tall,' I babbled on.

My phone beeped announcing the arrival of a text message from Matt. Matt is a busy man and never usually texts me during his working day; according to him there is money to be made in his business world. I knew it must be important.

DO NOT MENTION RUPERTS NEW CAR X, it read.

I couldn't remember any mention of Rupert buying a new car less than forty-eight hours ago when they were sitting around my patio table eating my pie. The ample amounts of alcohol must have clearly been more intoxicating than I recalled because I didn't remember a thing about Rupert buying a new car.

'It's his new car,' spluttered Penelope.

Her face was that blotchy shade of red again and I was lost for words. According to Matt I wasn't to mention it but it was already too late.

Fumbling with my phone I quickly typed a message back to Matt.

I have just seen Rupert in a ridiculous small black bubble car! What is going on??!!! (SHOUTY CAPITALS ARE NOT NEEDED) X

Beep…

PENELOPE HAS MADE HIM SELL HIS PRIDE AND JOY! ANNIE WAS THE FIRST ONE TO HAVE A RIDE IN THE SPORTS CAR. LITERALLY! SORRY FOR CAPS, PHONE PLAYING UP X

Trying to hold on to my laughter I bit the inside of my cheeks and pretended to have a coughing fit.

Penelope glared at me.

'Sorry I don't know what's come over me. Was the new car an impulsive buy? I wouldn't have Rupert down as a bubble car man?' I feebly spoke.

After it came to light that the attractive Annie had accompanied Rupert on his first drive in his new sports car, Penelope had given him twenty-four hours to dispose of the car – together with his private number plate – or she would dispose of him. Rupert was gutted and heartbroken when he chugged off in his pride and joy, complete with heated leather seats and firm suspension, to webuyanycar.com. On his way to the local branch he switched on the stereo and for the second time in forty-eight hours heard 'Lucky Man' blasting out. There was nothing lucky about Rupert; he was under no illusions about that. Rupert's instructions were to return with a car that wasn't a status symbol and wouldn't attract women. I personally thought he would be better suited to a scooter; he wouldn't be able to give anyone a 'backie' on one of those without being spotted! In all honesty his new bubble car did fit the criteria she had given him – you couldn't argue with that. According to Penelope, there was no way Annie would recognise this car around the village. I begged to differ as the new car was hilarious. Eat your heart out, Mr Bean! Little Jonny would be a laughing stock when his mates clocked the new car. I felt sorry for Rupert again. He had worked hard for the sports car. It was the only thing that was his.

After the walk and a quick change of clothes we ventured into the local town for coffee. I don't even drink coffee but I went along as I felt responsible for Matt changing the conversation to cars on Saturday night. Penelope was feeling better since the car was removed from her life. I wanted to enquire when the house would be going up for sale. Rupert and Annie had spent many a children's party entertaining themselves while Penelope was off hob-nobbing with the PTA mothers at school. But let's face it; it wasn't my problem. Approaching the local shops I quickly changed the subject.

'Lovely bag that, Penelope. Where did you get that from?' I enquired.

I wanted to nip into Home Bargains, which was on our way to the coffee shop, for some toiletries. Penelope reluctantly followed me in.

'TART,' Penelope suddenly shouted at the top of her voice. 'You TART.'

There was no need to call me a tart, everyone who knew me knew I wasn't a tart, I was a one-man woman and my clothes were certainly on the conservative side.

I was just about to protest when Penelope suddenly raced off like the Bionic Woman.

'TART,' she continued screaming.

Everyone stopped and watched her as she bounded past the fellow shoppers like a wounded gazelle. They were all thanking their lucky stars she wasn't shouting at them.

Then I spotted her. She was standing in a pretty, bright-coloured summer dress weighing up this week's special offers on cat food. She had slim, toned, tanned calves and as she reached up to one of the higher shelves, her dress lifted slightly to reveal a recurring theme – she had amazing thighs too. Again, I could see why Rupert had named her 'Hot Legs'.

To be honest, if I was gay I probably wouldn't have said 'No'. Rupert must have thought he had the winning poker hand when he'd first met her but this was perhaps not the time to bring that up in conversation. I'm pretty sure no-one was interested in anything I had to say at this moment anyway.

So there I was, standing in Home Bargains in my mid-thirties – and let's just get this straight, this was not on my list of things to do before I was forty – watching Penelope push Annie into the shelf of cat litter which was now spilling all over the floor. This gave a whole new meaning to cat fighting.

Annie was now face down in the bargain bucket of the cheap, own-brand cat food. The bystanders started to gather round them in a semi-circle which reminded me of my high school days and the kids gathering round in a similar fashion whenever a scrap broke out on the school field. Well there was only one thing for it; I squeezed through the crowd, leaned across the bodies on the floor, bent down and picked up some reduced cat biscuits and carried on walking, pretending I didn't know either of them. I suppose technically I didn't know either of them. I just had the unfortunate pleasure of walking with one of them on a daily basis and allegedly the other one was a tart.

Apart from the fracas in Home Bargains, the week was pretty quiet until Thursday when my eyes were opened to the wicked ways of the Playground Mafia and a way of making money out of other poor mothers without them even knowing.

The scheme was very clever and rewarding and identifying the victim took a genius but somehow Penelope had got it down to a fine art. When I witnessed it happen, I naively thought she was being friendly and paying someone a compliment. How wrong was I?

It was quite a chilly Thursday afternoon. The school bell rang and all the children ran out to greet their mothers, still wrapped up in their winter coats. However, you got the feeling that the weather was about to get warmer and the days of wearing these bulky coats would soon come to an end.

Penelope identified her victim as he ran to the arms of his mother. She wandered over and positioned herself right in front of the mother, who was chatting away to her son about his day at school.

Her timing was impeccable.

'What an absolutely lovely coat your son is wearing. I've admired it for a long time and would like to get my son one. Can I be cheeky and ask where you bought it from?'

I glanced over at the mother who I had never seen before and took a glimpse at the boy's coat. Yes, it was a very trendy coat and looked very, very expensive.

'Thanks very much,' the mother replied beaming from ear to ear.

'At last a woman with taste,' she thought.

The designer coat had probably cost the woman in the region of ninety pounds and right at the end of the season the only person to comment on her son's coat was a stranger in the playground.

'It is this season's and was very expensive. George is growing out of it now but it's in beautiful condition. Your son looks slightly smaller than George so I can pass it on to you when we have finished with it if you like?'

Let's get this straight; Penelope wasn't the least bit offended. She may as well have taken the coat off the boy's back there and then.

'Oh yes please, that would be very kind of you,' gushed Penelope.

By the following morning the mother had packaged up George's coat and handed it over to Penelope in the playground.

'The warmer weather looks like it's finally arrived. Hopefully your son will love the coat as much as our George did.'

To be fair, George did look secretly pleased that he wasn't trussed up like a chicken in his puffed out designer coat any longer. I couldn't quite imagine Little Jonny in this coat either, it just wasn't his colour. It would clash with the colour of his face, which had been permanently red since his mates had spotted Rupert driving his new car around the village.

'Thank you. Thank you so much. This is extremely kind of you,' responded Penelope, in a very over the top sickly voice.

People in this village were so kind, I thought to myself. This woman doesn't know Penelope from Adam yet she has handed over a coat that was probably still worth in the region of fifty quid. Penelope was in a very jolly mood that morning and swung the carrier bag containing her newly acquired designer coat the whole way on our walk.

Then, twenty-four hours later, while I was sitting in Penelope's conservatory – with its matching blinds, cushions and vases – with a cup of tea in my hand, the motive behind the scheme was revealed. Right in front of me, Penelope's laptop was sitting open on her eBay page. I wasn't being nosey – it was just sitting there facing me. There were numerous items listed on her selling page – a couple of Rupert's old jumpers and some worn out school shoes. At the bottom of the page, I spotted the lovely designer coat she had cunningly conned from the woman in the playground with bids at fifty-one pounds already. I couldn't believe my eyes – no wonder Penelope had been swinging that carrier bag! Penelope wasn't interested in the coat for Little Jonny at all; she was only interested in making a few quid. It was one thing selling your child's birthday presents on eBay but Penelope had handpicked that mother in the playground simply to make some money. It was the easiest fifty quid she had ever made. I just stared at the screen gobsmacked. I couldn't believe the underhandedness of it all.

All in all, the month of May was going well and I was starting to feel a little more settled, so the thought of looking for a job crossed my mind. Well, it was only a thought at this stage. I didn't need to rush into anything but it would be the excuse I needed to get out of this walking lark with Penelope. No sooner had the thought crossed my mind when I had landed myself an interview by mistake and it was all the fault of my clucking good hens.

I had grabbed the country life in the village with both hands. I had ponies and chickens. The chicken census revealed that we now had twenty-three and I had eggs coming out of my ears. The children were clucked off with eating eggs. So there was only one thing for it – I put a poster up in the local village hall.

'Clucking good eggs for sale,' it read.

My sign was also still outside the house but not many people ventured past the Shack so sales were slow. I was also hoping to attract customers that didn't sexually harass me like FP. Matt thought my OCD – Obsessive Chicken Disorder – was getting out of hand and wagered ten pounds that I wouldn't sell any more eggs. Within ten minutes of the poster going up, I was sold out and was raking in the money. To add insult to injury, I took the tenner off Matt and invested it in an incubator. I started to receive regular orders and the chickens couldn't produce eggs fast enough. There was a lovely woman who started to purchase my eggs on a weekly basis and this was how I landed my interview for a job, working part time at a mother and toddlers pre-school. This would be perfect because Matilda and Daisy would be able to stay and play whilst I earned a little bit of extra money.

I wasn't sure I really wanted a job but the extra money would definitely come in handy, especially now I needed a different coat – a different coat to Penelope's that is. I made a list of the advantages and disadvantages of taking the job – well that's if they offered it to me. The advantages included extra money, making new friends and, best of all, it might not leave any time to walk with Penelope every morning. The only disadvantage was never being able to enjoy a full free day to myself again until all the children had left home. The interview was to take place the following morning at 9.30am, giving me just enough time to drop the kids at school beforehand.

Matt was working from home on the morning of my interview which I was extremely thankful for because he could mind Matilda and Daisy whilst I disappeared for a couple of hours. I was under scrutiny in the playground. I was wearing a smart black dress with heels. Botox Bernie nearly dislocated her neck when she swung round to stare at me. She was getting scrawnier by the day and the veins in her neck were starting to bulge out. She reminded me of Deirdre Barlow from *Coronation Street*. I felt like telling her to wind her neck in or even wringing it myself but I kept my self-control. I did hear her muttering to herself that I was completely overdressed for a violin concert. Oh no, I had totally forgotten the children's violin concert. I chalked it up on the advantage list for the interview as it would be more like a vile din concert! When the kids practised at home the poodle would howl. I tottered off quickly from the playground before Penelope arrived and shone the interrogation light into my eyes to find out where I was going. It wasn't that I was deliberately keeping it from her, I just didn't have the job yet and was still unsure whether I actually wanted it.

Then the text messages started. Not just one or two text messages but forty-eight! I had never had a full inbox before – but I did now.

My screen was about to explode and the constant beeping was flattening my battery. The display read 'Penelope Kensington (48)'. That was the number of text messages she had sent me and it wasn't referring to her age. I switched my phone to silent as I entered the interview room to be seen by the lovely woman who bought my eggs. She was sitting with Humpty Dumpty and the White Witch of Narnia. I thought Humpty Dumpty was a bloke with his dungarees and bowler haircut and what I assumed was stubble – until 'he' was introduced to me as Davina. I was mesmerised at the amount of spit that flew from her mouth every time she talked and watched it consistently land in her coffee.

The White Witch of Narnia, apparently called Sal, never moved. She just stared at me the whole time, occasionally flicking her blonde hair and I was convinced she was looking down her snooty nose at me. I had a feeling the White Witch was trouble and my gut feelings were usually right. I don't know why but I decided to allocate her a seat on my bus immediately. It was only after I was offered the job that I discovered the White Witch had been roped in as a stand-in because the chair of governors couldn't make it. She wasn't even an employee, just a mother of a child that attended the education establishment – and on occasions a dreaded parent helper who had her fingers in many pies.

I had landed myself a job. I couldn't believe it as technically I hadn't even applied. But in two weeks' time I would be able to paint, tell stories and act as a referee to a bunch of lively little people for ten hours a week. And take Matilda and Daisy to work with me.

I flicked my phone back off silent and glanced at the screen. 'Penelope Kensington (72).'

My, how she had aged in forty-five minutes! Whatever was the matter with her? I could only assume that it must be a major trauma to send seventy-two texts. Maybe Little Jonny had disappointed the Kensington family by no longer wanting to study dinosaurs. Finally reading the messages I couldn't believe my eyes.

Where are you? X
Are you there? X
Why aren't you at the violin concert? X

Why aren't you answering me? X

Have I done something to upset you? X

Well don't answer me then.

So after five texts Penelope had stopped putting kisses.

Why are you ignoring me?

I am worried now.

Then the shouty capitals started.

ANSWER ME.

WHY WON'T YOU ANSWER ME?

And the texts just kept arriving, they went on and on and bloody on. Was this lunatic for real? Unfortunately the answer to that was most probably yes. What was wrong with this woman? Maybe she thought I was out with Rupert, or even worse, Annie.

It was ridiculous. Even if I had wanted to reply it would have proven quite difficult as it appeared a text message had been sent every thirty seconds. I was quite amazed at the speed she must have typed the texts. The stalker tone of the text messages were a little alarming. Maybe it was her time of the month which had led to her behaviour spiralling out of control but then I remembered, we had the same coat, same wellies, same bag and now our periods were in bloody sync!

I was quite taken aback by the tone of the messages. I could suggest a stalker management course to her but I did what any normal, sane person would do in these circumstances and ignored them, well for the time being anyway. It was at this precise moment that I mentally placed Penelope on my bus along with Mrs High School Musical, Mr International Sex God and his plus one Lois, Botox Bernie, Mrs Noland, Frisky Pensioner and the White Witch of Narnia. There were only two seats left.

I took control of the situation and made an executive decision. I wasn't going to let anyone spoil my day so I wandered into the nearest town in search of cake. A big fat cream cake would help me celebrate my job news. However, for some reason I just knew today wasn't going to be a normal day. How I longed for a normal day.

Making my way towards the cake shop I could almost taste the pastry and cream but first I needed to nip to the chemist on my way past to pick up some lady products as I – and therefore Penelope too – were soon due a visit from our monthly friend. Still with cake on my mind, I spotted someone who was clearly having their cake and eating it. Luckily for Penelope it wasn't Rupert this time, it was only Camilla Noland's husband. The farrier was skulking at the back of the pharmacy pondering which flavour condoms to buy with a busty brunette hanging off his arm. Vast improvement on Camilla, I mused to myself. This pharmacy was tucked away down one of the back streets and the farrier must have thought he would be safe away from prying eyes.

I sneaked right up behind them.

I'd only met the farrier a couple of times before in the school yard and in the local newsagent but he always waved or nodded his head in my direction in acknowledgement.

'Hello, fancy seeing you here,' I bellowed, right into his ear. The poor bloke nearly jumped out of his shoes. He went bright red and clearly didn't know where to look. Instead of making another comment I gave him a knowing smile and wandered off to pay for my stuff before finally bagging that cream cake that had my name on it.

Finally arriving home I sat down and chatted with Matt over a pot of tea and we devoured the cream cakes before he promptly had to leave to visit some clients. Sitting on the floor in front of the telly playing Lego with Matilda and Daisy I quietly pondered my next move in the stalker Penelope game.

Over and over again I typed, deleted and retyped replies to Penelope's messages – well obviously not all of them as that would have taken a lifetime – but I couldn't bring myself to send them. I decided to ignore her messages and send an upbeat one instead.

Good news! I've landed myself a job, ten hours a week!

It took less than a minute for her to reply and it wasn't quite the reply I was expecting.

Charming, and you didn't tell me because?

I read and re-read the message. I was looking for the hidden 'Congratulations, that's great news, I'm so happy for you', but it must have been extremely well hidden because no matter how hard I searched through the text, I couldn't find it.

I didn't tell anyone. It all happened so quickly and actually you are the first person I have told.

Technically she wasn't but I thought if I made her sound important all would be OK. How wrong was I?

You didn't tell me about the job because you knew if I'd applied too I would have secured the position instead of you, she insisted.

I couldn't work out whether she had an A* in self-importance or whether she was just a nutter; at that precise moment I concluded it must be the latter. The last thing I wanted to do was hurt Penelope although I was starting to consider putting it on my 'To Do' list. So while maintaining my dignity I Googled 'restraining order' and took my time to reply. In fact Penelope is still waiting for that reply.

I made myself a cuppa and stuffed a custard cream into my mouth and continued to ponder whether Penelope was for real. I started to think – which can be a dangerous thing – and came to the conclusion that Penelope was never going to be a true friend. Fay would never ever even think of sending me texts like those. Penelope had shown her true colours and jealous streak and was now well and truly on my bus, ready to be driven off the cliff, never to send text messages to my phone again. If only. Sometimes I wish fantasy was reality.

My phone beeped again, this time a reminder to pick up Annabel from school.

'Shit,' I thought. I had completely forgotten that I had agreed to collect Annabel from school. Penelope was probably sitting with her feet up, updating her Facebook status for the umpteenth time that day. There was only one thing for it, I had to rise above it, drop Annabel off at home and act as if nothing had happened. And that's exactly what I did.

Penelope answered the door in a very subdued manner and couldn't make eye contact with me. Normally she would ask me in but not on this occasion.

I put on my chirpiest voice and must have sounded like a chipmunk on helium.

'You OK to walk in the morning? I'll see you then.'

What I really wanted to say was 'You're a bloody nutter, full of your own self-importance and you don't give a stuff about anyone else, it's all about you,' but I did the grown up thing and kept my mouth shut for an easy life. Believe me it was hard – very hard to do.

Penelope grasped the olive branch with both hands, which was extremely lucky for her because I felt like whacking the olive branch right over her head.

'Yes that's great,' she said. 'I'll see you in the morning.'

I wouldn't have minded but Penelope was in fact the only one that knew about my new job and look at all the drama she had caused. When arriving home it had completely slipped my mind about the job interview – I was far more interested in revealing to Matt that I'd rumbled the local farrier riding a busty brunette whilst purchasing chocolate ribbed condoms from a chemist.

The previous day's shenanigans would make for a very interesting walk today. I was determined there wasn't going to be an atmosphere. Yes, I thought Penelope was maybe a little insecure at the moment and with everything going on in her home life I wanted to give her the benefit of the doubt and put it behind us.

I couldn't believe the change in her the following morning: she looked sprightly and was beaming like the Cheshire cat. She was grinning from ear to ear and seemed ready to burst. I didn't even have my trainers laced up before she spilled the latest news regarding Camilla Noland and Penelope had heard it straight from the horse's mouth, Camilla herself.

Camilla Noland was having an affair.

I tried to act surprised and didn't like to mention it wasn't for the first time this year. Rupert had seen to that. I decided this wasn't the time to burst Penelope's bubble so I let her have her moment to fill me in on the gossip. It would have been rude not to.

Penelope started at the beginning. I thought this was a very good place to start.

'Camilla has told me this in total confidence so promise me, you swear not to tell a soul.'

Two things flashed through my mind at this very moment:-

Never divulge anything to Penelope that you didn't want repeating.

Why would Camilla Noland confide in Penelope?

Then I realised there was only one reason why Camilla would spill details of her affair to Penelope: she knew Penelope would confide in Rupert, leaving him jealous of her latest conquest. Camilla had a plan, she wanted Rupert back and wasn't willing to share him and the only way for her to achieve this was to become Penelope's new best friend. I bet Rupert was squirming in his Y-fronts at the thought of having to share nights out with the new loved-up couple.

According to Penelope, Camilla was getting soapy with the bottle washer at a local eatery. We shall call him Professor Plum because she liked to have him in the library, in the study, in the kitchen – well to be honest anywhere – it didn't really matter. On a Friday night he was the DJ in the restaurant where he worked but I think that was probably bigging him up way too much. In reality he placed a few flashing lights at the side of the sound system and played the latest chart CDs.

On a Saturday night he was an Elvis impersonator and belted out tracks in the restaurant.

This was where the affair had started, when Elvis enticed Camilla onto the dance floor and he warbled to her 'Are You Lonesome Tonight?'

Actually when Camilla thought about it, she was lonesome tonight as the farrier was away on business. Anyone who had the nerve to warble that in my ear would have definitely been returned to sender. The most amusing thing about this situation was that Elvis was alive and kicking in my village and so was his ex, a Marilyn Monroe look-alike. I pictured the pair of them together, it was just so wrong. I couldn't make up my mind who was worse, Camilla or Marilyn.

So both Mr and Mrs Noland were having affairs then? I never mentioned to Penelope that I had seen the farrier with his busty brunette in the back street chemist. The only good thing about this was Penelope was more concerned with Camilla's antics than my new job. I was yesterday's fish and chip paper. Thank God, and Penelope seemed to have got over her strop. Well for today anyway.

CHAPTER 6

June

Penelope still seemed to be enjoying our walks each morning; I, on the other hand, had lost all enthusiasm. They were becoming tiresome and not just because of the exercise. The Friday weigh-ins were painful. We were beginning to get saddled with the Kensingtons' most Saturday nights too as they didn't appear to enjoy each other's company very much any more. Penelope was always keen to get the 'next date' in the diary when they left and it was nearly always the Saturday after. Each weekend they would turn up with a bag of beers and tucked down the side of the bag were Rupert's slippers.

Matt had built up quite a rapport with Rupert and they kept a running joke between them that they might as well have their own coat pegs with their names on in our cloakroom as they were here that often. One Saturday afternoon he ventured off to the local DIY store and returned with four coat pegs which he skilfully managed to fix to the wall just as they knocked on the door for our usual Saturday night get-together. They were genuinely pleased they had named coat pegs in the Shack, not realising that we were taking the mickey in the hope they would take the hint and allow us to spend a Saturday night without them.

Summer was upon us and the warmer days began to creep in. Penelope took this opportunity to suggest Saturday afternoon

BBQs which basically comprised of more of the same antics but starting a few hours earlier. The children usually bedded down in the living room if they were feeling tired and Daisy could sleep for England.

The first Saturday in June was an eye opener for me. This is when I witnessed again Penelope's competitive streak. June was the month – according to Penelope – that Little Jonny was going to win his Olympic medal. To be precise, not any old medal but an Olympic gold medal. This month is the month I pray for constant rain. Why would anyone wish for constant rain in June, I hear you ask? So primary school sports day would be cancelled.

During this annual event, the Petty Tedious Army (PTA) are out in full force, strutting their stuff and attempting to walk in their high heels over the school field. They look totally ridiculous in their floral numbers, big floppy hats and oversized sunglasses. Anyone would think they were attending Ladies Day at Royal Ascot, not the local village school sports day. I am amazed how seriously some mothers take it. I have first-hand experience of how competitive these mothers could be.

Penelope and Rupert were due to arrive at the Shack for a barbeque later that Saturday afternoon. The sun was shining, the chickens were clucking and the new ducklings quacking. I was sitting enjoying the sunshine in the garden, swigging a sneaky beer when I glanced down at the text that had just arrived.

I know we are due round at 4pm but is there any chance I can come at 2.30pm and borrow your garden x?

I was a little dumbfounded; why would Penelope want to borrow my garden? I noticed from the text she was back to putting kisses at the end of her messages so hopefully that meant she was over her strop regarding my new job, which I hadn't even started yet.

I sat in anticipation as the garden gate flung wide open at 2.30pm on the dot and in flounced Penelope. She was dressed in tight, white shorts and a vest top. Strapped to her feet were the shiniest, brightest white trainers I had ever seen.

Penelope threw a stop watch in my direction and shouted, 'Time me,' before bending over to tighten her laces.

At the same time, she let out the most almighty gust of wind that almost ripped the backside out of her shorts. Can you imagine being next to her in a yoga class? Her embarrassed, beetroot-coloured face glanced up in my direction and I tried my best to contain the roar of laughter that I wanted to let out – and the trickle of wee that I didn't.

When I finally composed myself I shouted, 'On your marks, get set,' as she bent over again – no bottom burp this time, thankfully – and placed her feet in the imaginary starting blocks she must have visualised in my lawn.

I was still completely bemused and didn't really have a clue what was happening, so I took a swig of beer and shouted, 'Go!'

Penelope was out of the pretend starting blocks, running around my garden like a demented greyhound. I had seen her run before of course but that was down the aisles of Home Bargains after Annie and, prior to that, when we were out playing at Dempsey and Makepeace.

I had no idea what the purpose behind this was until she collapsed in a heap at my feet.

'Time? What was my time?'

I wanted to shout back, 'Your time is up, you lunatic,' as I secretly hoped the men in white coats would be next through my gate.

Alas, no such luck as the next person to pass through the gate was Rupert.

'How did she do?' he hollered.

Matt's timing was as impeccable as ever as he appeared and handed me another beer.

'What's going on?' he said with an amused tone to his voice.

We both waited in anticipation for Penelope's reply. At this point she lay flat on her back – a position Rupert was obviously used to seeing women in – fighting for breath. I considered phoning an ambulance but after finding a pulse, I helped her up and sat her on a chair. I moved the beer out of the way and handed her a glass of iced water.

'Sports day… it's nearly sports day,' she panted.

I could barely hear her words as her head was squeezed between her knees and I was frightened she was going to pass out.

'Penelope, what are you panting on about, you left school years ago, many years ago?' I asked.

'The mothers' race! The mothers' race! I have to win. I need to beat Wendy and Camilla Noland!' she gasped.

I looked in Matt's direction. He was circling his index finger at the side of his head, obviously inferring that he thought she was a fruit loop. I realised I was shaking my head in disbelief with that strained expression I have on my face when I am absolutely flabbergasted and forced myself to stop. I didn't get it, I just didn't get it. Maybe it was a village thing or just something that these people did.

Penelope got her breath back and pulled herself together. She was ready to go again. I, on the other hand, had already had enough of this caper and ordered the men to do what they did best and throw some meat on the fire. I needed food as I felt a little light-headed at this moment, not sure if this was caused by the beer or the sight of Penelope running in tight white shorts around the garden. On Penelope's impressive third lap she looked like a T-Rex thundering after its prey. The dog sat in the conservatory, clearly amused watching Penelope run round and round. He decided that this must be some sort of game and he wanted to play. So there I was, sitting in the sunshine in my own garden, trying to mind my own business when the standard poodle escaped from the conservatory and started chasing the T-Rex thundering around the garden. I sat open-mouthed, completely lost for words at the spectacle in front of me so Matt took the opportunity and stuck another beer in my mouth.

After a couple of laps the dog suddenly leapt off the ground and launched himself at Penelope, placing his paws on the back of her shoulders. This clearly caught her by surprise and knocked her off balance and she tumbled to the turf, face down in a heap with her backside sticking in the air. Not only was she face down in the turf but her shorts were covered in chicken shit and grass stains that were never likely to come out. Then, to add insult to injury, the dog started humping her.

This was very unfortunate for Penelope to say the least. There was no rescuing those new tight-fitting shorts – or her dignity. The only thought that crossed my mind at that point was the chat I needed to have with the dog about his taste in women.

Rupert looked mildly amused at the entertainment Penelope was providing but also appeared a little preoccupied with his mobile phone. Every time Penelope nipped to the fridge for another beer, his mobile phone was straight in his hand and placed back on the table before she reappeared.

'What's the pile of stuff you've got clogging up your landing area?' piped up Penelope.

I wasn't quite sure why Penelope had ventured upstairs but I answered her anyhow.

'It's just old clothes and games that I need to sort through and decide what we are keeping and what's going into the charity bag.'

'What are you thinking of doing with the dance mat in the pile?' Penelope enquired.

I had visions of this being a new mothers' craze in the playground or maybe Penelope had dreams of becoming a hip-hop dancer. Nothing would surprise me at this moment in time.

'Why? What are you thinking, Penelope?' I asked. 'Would you like it?'

Penelope replied that Annabel would love the dance mat. I was surprised at the unusual mention of Annabel as Penelope continued.

'She is always dancing and singing. She'd love it.'

Penelope thought she was going to have a career in entertainment. I thought to myself, if daughters take after their mothers then on this occasion Penelope could be correct. The entertainment she had provided in the last hour had been hilarious; I wish I had sold tickets. I handed over the dance mat to Penelope as my children had had it for a while and never really played with it so if someone was going to make use of it I didn't mind.

They finally left about two hours later after sinking a few more beers with the newly acquired dance mat tucked safely under their arm.

Once I had cleaned up the empties from outside and washed and dried the dishes I curled up for the rest of the evening on the settee. The children were all tucked up in bed, Matt was watching the telly and I settled down with a good book. Noticing the lid on my laptop was slightly ajar I wandered over to it to switch it off. Just as I was about to close the lid, there before my very eyes was Penelope's eBay home page. I assumed she must have had auctions finishing when she was here and wanted to check how much money she had made. I was just about to slam the lid shut when I stopped dead in my tracks. Listed in the last hour was a dance mat – not any old dance mat but *my* dance mat!

I was absolutely livid. Penelope was trying to make money out of me and was succeeding. The bids were already up to ten pounds. The cheeky mare was trying to make a quick tenner out of our friendship and there was no way she was getting away with it. As rage took over, I placed a bid on my own dance mat. I was going to win that mat back – not because I wanted it but because I was going to make Penelope wish she had never set eyes on the flippin' thing. The bids were now heading towards twenty quid and I imagined Penelope sitting smugly in her conservatory, watching the bids going up and counting her money. I thought I'd see how smug she was when I won the mat and sent her a lovely message telling her that I would collect it to save her posting it. I knew exactly where I wanted to post that mat.

As the auction neared a close a week later I sat in my conservatory fuming. I watched the bids rocket upwards until the highest bid was twenty-five quid with ten minutes to go. I couldn't resist and I decided to send Penelope a text message. It read…

Thanks for a great afternoon/evening last weekend. Did Annabel enjoy her new dance mat?

Her reply was almost instant as I read, *She absolutely loves it! Thank you so much.*

Penelope was none the wiser that I was on to her, she didn't have a clue. The auction ended with me as the highest bidder. I couldn't believe it. Slumping back into the chair, I was the proud owner of a dance mat, my own bloody dance mat. A dance mat that had just cost me £27.31 to buy back.

I wasn't quite sure what I was going to do now. I hadn't quite figured out my next plan of action. Then, almost immediately, I had an email from Penelope via eBay asking me if I was available to pay for the item so she could pop it in the post on Monday morning.

Good job I had an email address she would never know was mine. I knew the email address *attractsnutters* would come in handy one day. Sending a lovely email back I could hear the sarcastic tone in my reply; luckily for Penelope she didn't suspect a thing.

'Thank you very much for listing your lovely dance mat, my daughter will absolutely love this. I live very close to you.'

Little did she know at this point, it was just down the lane and around the corner.

I continued, 'Don't trouble yourself posting it, I will nip round and collect it on Monday morning, if it's convenient for you?'

I knew Penelope would be peeved at the offer of collection because I noticed on the auction she had charged way over the odds for the postage and was probably hoping to pocket a few extra quid that way as well.

I had no intention of paying for the mat but I had every intention of making Penelope squirm. The time of collection was arranged for the same time we would usually start our walk together. Sneakily I had suggested this time purely for the sheer amusement of what Penelope would say to me regarding her inability to walk that day. I actually felt disappointed in myself stooping to such a level but telling myself I could only react to how someone treated me made it seem a little more bearable.

Penelope was a no-show in the playground that Monday morning. Rupert had been roped into dropping the children off at school. I didn't need to enquire where Penelope was because

Botox Bernie was already grilling him, trying to establish why he was in the playground and not his wife. As the story went on, I could hear Rupert relaying the facts that Penelope had been up all night with a stomach bug and was trying to sleep. Poor Penelope, my heart went out to her. Call me cynical but I didn't think there was anything wrong with her. My gut instinct told me I was about to receive a text from her letting me know she was unable to walk this morning, not because she was waiting in for the buyer of her dance mat but because she was feeling under the weather.

And just on cue, my phone beeped and the text arrived.

I'm sorry I'm not feeling very well, I won't be walking this morning x.

My plan of action was simple. I was really worried about my poorly friend so I would pop round just before ten o'clock to see if there was anything she needed or wanted me to do. And that's exactly what I did.

Knocking on Penelope's front door I stood on the doorstep waiting in anticipation without the twenty-seven odd quid she thought she was getting.

Penelope opened the door as bold as brass and didn't appear sick in any way, shape or form. Lo and behold, tucked under her arm was the dance mat.

'Hi, I just thought I would pop in to see how you are feeling. I bet you are exhausted if you've been up all night, go and put your feet up and let me make you a brew.'

If the truth be told I actually barged past her so she had no choice but to let me in and, making my way towards the kitchen, I clicked the kettle on. Penelope was standing before me with a full face of makeup, dressed in her best clothes and not looking in the least bit sick. The one thing she did look though was edgy, continuously straining her neck to peer out of the kitchen window. Penelope was on the lookout for the mystery buyer.

'Just think, Penelope, being sick is always a bonus – think of the weight loss,' I joked. 'You don't look too bad actually,' I continued. 'In fact you look extremely well. What's with the dance mat under your arm? Are you just about to shake your moves?'

'Err, I was just tidying up,' Penelope replied.

We both knew that was a lie.

I sauntered into the conservatory and plonked myself comfortably onto the settee. Penelope looked like she had ants in her pants, she just couldn't sit still. She was up and down peering out of the window every two minutes.

'Is everything OK? You seem a little agitated,' I enquired.

Her laptop was open on her eBay page. She had pocketed quite a few quid that week according to her sales totals.

'I feel a little unwell, a little queasy, I think I've overdone it, maybe I need to go and have a lie down,' she replied weakly.

'Nice try,' was my response.

She looked at me with a puzzled expression on her face.

'Let me make this a little easier for you, Penelope. My guess is you aren't the slightest bit ill. My guess is you sent Rupert to the playground to tell me you were unwell. My guess is you are sat there squirming in your seat hoping to get rid of me sharpish because you are expecting your buyer to collect the dance mat you have sold on eBay. My dance mat, the dance mat I gave you in good faith for Annabel.'

Feeling the rage rise throughout my body I continued.

'But greed has clearly outweighed our friendship, a friendship that you value at twenty-seven quid! I can see the cogs turning while you try to work out how I know it's twenty-seven quid. Well I am your buyer, Penelope, but as we both know I will not be handing over any cash. I will take back my mat and leave you to recover from your illness. You look a little pale. I suggest you go for a lie down.'

I gave her a deathly stare, a stare that told her not to mess with me. Picking up the mat, I left the house, leaving Penelope still catching flies as her chin hit the floor. I didn't even want the flippin' dance mat back. It had been gathering dust in the Shack for quite some time but that wasn't the point. I knew for sure now that Penelope would never pass my seven-year rule. Who needed high maintenance friends like her? There was only one thing for it, I would list the mat on eBay myself and if Penelope wanted the flaming thing that badly, she could bid on it herself.

I wasn't sure how Penelope would be feeling about me reacquiring the dance mat but when I got home I knew her day had the potential to significantly go downhill even more.

Making myself a cuppa I logged on to my laptop. There, staring straight back at me on the right-hand side of my computer screen, was an advert. An advert for a dating website showing pictures of available men, which looped round displaying a new man every few seconds. The image that had just appeared on my screen was a photograph of Rupert Kensington and he was advertising himself as a single man. I had already taken a double glance but it was definitely Rupert. There in bold letters was his profile, or rather the profile of 'Rupert Bond'. The silly sod had even used his real first name but obviously fancied himself as a secret agent with his fantasy surname.

I did what any normal person would do in this situation and clicked on his profile. I was intrigued. Rupert Bond the single man was a professional athlete. I nearly spat out my tea, Rupert was no more an athlete than the likes of James Corden or the dad from Stavros Flatley. The only thing athletic about Rupert was his athlete's foot.

The photo of Rupert showed him standing next to his pride and joy – his ex-wheels – wearing some dodgy leather jacket and a cream scarf. I noticed that he neglected to mention his wife or his new ridiculous bubble car but his athletic career sounded amazing. I was in awe. He'd travelled all over the world and won medals. I knew for a fact he had never left the village and had never been on holiday abroad.

No way! Rupert Bond even had his own boat; Bubble Car Rupert didn't have a bloody boat – he didn't even have a plastic one in the bath. Gosh, he made himself out to be such a catch that I felt like answering his advert myself.

On this website there was an opportunity to rate the women you had been matched to and Rupert was not shy in rising to this task. There was one woman in particular that Rupert had reviewed numerous times. I could only assume that he must have dated her on more than one occasion so I clicked on her photo. She was a pretty woman with blonde bobbed hair. She had a beauty spot on her face and seemed familiar to me but I couldn't quite work out where I had laid eyes on her before. With all this information in my grasp, my dilemma was whether or not to share my findings with Penelope. I pondered while eating another custard cream. Based on previous experiences in these circumstances the messenger is always the one to be shot. I didn't really mind getting shot over this, at least then I would have a quieter life.

As I closed down my laptop there was a knock on the door. I opened it to discover a sheepish Penelope standing in front of me holding a bouquet of flowers.

'I'm sorry,' she said meekly.

I was impressed she had the balls to come round to apologise but I certainly wasn't impressed with the standard of flowers.

They looked more like dead weeds being held together by a tatty peach ribbon.

I let her in – I suppose I had to – she had no other friends and now I knew Rupert was playing at being Mr Bond, flogging himself on dating websites. She was going to need a friend more than ever now but I decided to keep the information to myself, at least until I had a chance to talk it over with Matt.

I knew this week was never going to be quiet, especially since school sports day was less than three days away. Putting on the kettle, as that's what people do in times of trauma, I watched my only friend Penelope running laps of my garden again. This time the dog just glanced at her with one eye out of the conservatory and didn't even attempt to move from his chair. He probably thought he could do much better.

Now though I had yet another dilemma. Not only did I need to decide whether to tell Penelope about Rupert's presence on the dating website but, watching her bound round the garden, I also needed to choose whether to enter myself in the mothers' race on sports day. I decided to sleep on both.

Matt must have longed for the day when he arrived home from work and I had nothing to report. I spilled the beans about Rupert being on the dating website and have never seen him fire up his computer so quickly in my life. Matt didn't believe me until he saw him with his own eyes. Rupert Bond in the flesh.

'It all goes on in this village,' he remarked shaking his head in disbelief.

'What am I going to do about it?' I asked him.

'Absolutely nothing,' he replied.

I already knew that would be his response.

'But if that was you on there I would want to know,' I challenged.

Matt raised his eyebrows in my direction and remarked, 'I would not be stupid enough to enter my details on a dating website, let alone call myself Bond. I bet Rupert likes his women shaven, not furred,' he sniggered, in a crappy Sean Connery accent.

This remark gave us a 'licence to laugh' but Penelope would have a 'licence to kill' when she found out.

The day Little Jonny was going to win his gold medal had finally arrived – the school sports day. When I arrived on the school field dressed in my comfy jeans and Converse All-Stars I felt a little underdressed. Penelope was waving at me from the front row. She must have been there at the crack of dawn to get those seats. She was wearing a chiffon dress and a hat with a brim so large it hit me in the face every time she turned her head. She looked ridiculous. Her heels were so high that she struggled to walk properly and staggered around looking very uncomfortable. I did wonder how on earth she was going to run the mothers' race in those heels. I sat back in the chair and waved at my children as they trundled out from the classrooms, waiting in anticipation for the races to begin.

And they were off. Race after race Penelope shouted at poor Little Jonny; he looked very embarrassed and spent the whole time glaring back at her. After a while he just blanked her in the hope nobody would realise she was his mother.

The PTA women were strutting about selling raffle tickets for items left over from the Christmas Fair. The prizes – if that's what you could call them – were usually shower gels and body lotions that brought you out in a blotchy, spotty, allergic rash. The PTA had already siphoned off any decent prizes for themselves, perks of their commitment apparently. That was a commitment or perk I could definitely do without.

There were two races left. The first was Little Jonny's main event, which was in the bag according to Penelope. She had already prepared her speech for when he was presented with his gold medal. And the last race of the day was the mothers' race.

I could say I was glued to my seat waiting for the next race to start but that would have been a lie. Penelope looked like she was about to wet herself, she was that excited shouting for Little Jonny at the top of her voice. I didn't know any of the kids lining up for the race – I prefer it that way – except my Samuel. Penelope hadn't even noticed Samuel or given him a second thought. I didn't make it obvious my son was in the race but I gave him a cheeky wink and quick thumbs-up to encourage him – and with the promise of twenty-five quid to beat Little Jonny I knew he would give it his best shot.

The whistle went and the kids raced off. Penelope stood on her chair as they sprinted towards the finish line. Little Jonny was in front for most of the race until one boy came from nowhere in the outside lane. He got faster and faster until he overtook Little Jonny and raced through the finishing tape first.

The roar of the crowd was immense and as the cheers died down I could hear the spectators whispering.

'Who is that boy?'

I noticed Penelope was like a deflated balloon, she was slumped over in her chair clasping her head in her hands, mortified that Little Jonny had disgraced the family name. Samuel looked over at me and gave me a thumbs-up on his way to receive his winner's medal. Twenty-five quid well spent in my opinion. That's my boy!

Next it was time for Penelope to restore the 'Kensington' reputation. She needed to show Little Jonny that one of them was a winner.

The headmistress grabbed the megaphone and bellowed, 'Time for the mothers' race.'

Right before my very eyes Penelope stood up and whipped out a rucksack from underneath her chair. Not only did the bag contain her running gear but also an energy bar. I watched as she shovelled it down at superfast speed. I was mesmerised. That bar would have given me energy all right, energy to get off the school field and into the pub as fast as I could. Jesus, she wasn't running a marathon, it was only a hundred metres sprint. She limbered up on the sideline in her new running spikes with some squats and stretches. I waited with bated breath for the sound of her shorts tearing, or her backside rippling.

'Can all competitors make your way to the start line,' shouted the headmistress.

Penelope stood at the starting line in her clean, bright, white running shorts and a vest top that was way too tight. When the whistle blew, she was off, bounding up her lane heading towards the finish line. With all the drama that was going on around me I had forgotten to run the flippin' race myself. What an absolute shame.

I craned my neck in the direction of the finishing line. Botox Bernie was holding the rope. Botox Bernie had lost so much weight that you could hardly see her when she turned sideways. She was getting scrawnier by the day; rumours had it she was on the divorce diet.

It was turning into a day full of surprises. I couldn't believe my eyes – Penelope was actually winning. She was just ahead of another blonde who was vaguely recognisable. I squinted in the hope it would help me see more clearly. Then it twigged, it was only the woman with the beauty spot – the one on Rupert's dating profile. Talk about doing it on your own doorstep. Penelope was head to head with Rupert's new lover, neck and neck, fighting to be crowned mother of the year at the school sports day. I'm sure this is how wars start! Then it all took a turn for the worse. Almost within reach of the gold medal, Penelope tripped in her new running spikes and made a desperate grab for her husband's new squeeze and they both hit the deck, face down in the dirt. Wendy Barthorpe stepped over the heap of mothers to take the winning medal! The crowd erupted with rapturous applause.

It was turning out to be an eventful day but unfortunately for Rupert he had arrived when all the action was over. Well, apart from his wife sprawled on top of his new lover face down on the ground. They had even managed to take Botox Bernie's legs from underneath her, though fortunately for her she had landed on her fabulous chest which had cushioned her fall. I couldn't work out what the white heap was, on the floor next to the pile of women. It looked like hair – surely none of the mothers had brought a cat? I squinted again and realised it was a wig. At the same time there was a loud gasp from the crowd. The women were scrambling to their feet and the spectators could see that the blonde was now a brunette. I knew she looked vaguely familiar; I had definitely come across this woman before. This woman was the brunette hanging off the farrier's arm when he'd been buying the chocolate ribbed condoms. This woman was the same woman having the affair with Camilla Noland's husband. Funnily enough the farrier was also at sports day and hadn't recognised his own lover until this moment. He had obviously never seen her in a wig before. Rupert did the best thing he could possibly do and quietly retreated out of the school gates back to his house, leaving the farrier to question the brunette's transformation.

I scanned the field looking for Camilla. I thought it was odd that the farrier could be in deep discussion with this lady – in the loosest sense of the word – and Camilla was nowhere to be seen. I don't know why I was surprised I couldn't see her; she never went to Mothers' Day assemblies, harvest festivals or any other events for that matter to support her daughter. So why would sports day be any different?

I was just about to leave the shamed Penelope handing the wig back when things started to get interesting. I could hear shouting – shouting that sounded like 'Camilla'. In a strange twist of events I could see her racing across the field after 'Elvis'. She was running so fast that I considered suggesting she should enter the mothers' race herself next year. I didn't have a clue where the pair of them had appeared from – probably the bushes at the back of the field. Elvis was shouting after the woman in the wig – the farrier's and Rupert's lover. Then like a lightning bolt it all fell into place.

The lady in the wig was his ex, the Marilyn Monroe look-alike. Camilla was married to the farrier but she was having an affair with Elvis. The farrier was having an affair with Elvis' ex who was also having an affair with Rupert (Marilyn, not the farrier). Rupert was married to Penelope who quite frankly was the innocent party in all of this. Camilla Noland had once had an affair with Rupert but Penelope was yet to find out about that one. And they were all squabbling on the school field in the middle of sports day with the PTA having a field day – pardon the pun. I think the tight shorts and the figure hugging vest was the least of Penelope's problems as she went in search of Rupert.

CHAPTER 7

July

The sun shone brightly as Penelope and I headed off on our usual morning walk. June had been a rotten month for her. Little Jonny hadn't stepped up to the mark on sports day, Penelope had ended up eating grass during her race while clutching the wig of the latest woman in her husband's life. She had been humped by a standard poodle, made the wrong choices on eBay and Wendy Barthorpe had totally cut her out of her life. Due to the stress of it all, Penelope had piled the weight back on. She put it down to comfort eating. Maybe July would be kinder to her.

Penelope decided she was on a mission to set herself new challenges. I noticed that the challenge this morning was to walk with heavy weights strapped around her ankles in the vain hope of accelerating the weight loss. I had decided to knock the Friday weigh-ins on the head, it was too much hassle. Every week Penelope stomped off in a mood because I was losing more weight than she was. I don't think she quite grasped the fact that we were two different body shapes, which was life.

We headed up the main road on our walk and for a change Penelope and I weren't dressed in the same attire. The previous day I had noticed she was wearing the same strappy sandals as me but I didn't pass comment. I pondered the idea of buying and wearing a ridiculous item of clothing, just to see if she copied. I suppose I should look on the positive side, obviously I was a trend-setter and I should have felt privileged she wanted to copy my style.

We ambled along the fields and streams for quite some time until Penelope suddenly stopped dead in her tracks. I thought that the weights had got too much for her and she couldn't walk any further. There was no way I could carry her back, weights or no weights. We had walked a great distance and there straight in front of us was Camilla Noland's house. Penelope was staring at the property and I followed her gaze. There, right outside her house, was a 'For Sale' sign. I was actually a little gobsmacked myself. I thought back to the conversation in the saddlery, when Camilla was adamant how much she loved her beautiful house and how it was worth a fortune with all her land. It was apparent the grass wasn't greener hanging out with Elvis – either that or she was moving to Graceland.

Camilla and Penelope had been hanging out a little more than usual and Penelope couldn't wait to share the gossip. This proved that they were both as two-faced as each other – in the past Penelope had continuously slated Camilla and Camilla was always the one spreading Penelope's – or Rupert's – misfortune around the village.

Penelope had been spending some evenings in Camilla's and Elvis' company. The local eating establishment that employed Elvis was providing them with not only a little entertainment but a free night out on the house. According to Penelope, she was Camilla's alibi, leaving the farrier convinced she was out with her. Penelope had made up a foursome with a bloke called Tom. Tom was one of Elvis' mates. It was unfortunate for Tom that his surname was Jones but he wasn't Welsh and he didn't have wiry, curly hair or an orange complexion.

However, he did insist on role playing as his namesake and assumed he was hilarious. Tom thought Penelope was a lady and greeted her with 'What's new pussycat?' every time they met. Penelope didn't seem to mind, if there was a free feed involved she was there.

The sports day incident had the whole village talking. Rupert had saved his own skin by disappearing from the scene before anyone cottoned on to the fact that the farrier wasn't the only one who'd had a close encounter with Marilyn. Both Camilla and the farrier had come face to face with each other's love interests and quite frankly what could either of them say? Camilla had never loved the farrier, he was just her meal ticket at the time for a more prosperous life. Camilla no longer had to endure his moaning or his repulsive snorting noises when he awoke each morning. Not to mention his vile habit of cutting his toe nails with one of his farrier tools at the kitchen table. None of these characteristics were the least bit attractive. She was entitled to half his worldly goods, which would be quite substantial given the amount of land that was attached the house.

Once the walk was over, I returned home and made myself a cuppa. Camilla's pad was on my mind and I decided to have a nosey of the particulars on the estate agents' website that was advertising her property. I thought that if it was up for sale at a half decent price it might be worth a look, especially with all that land. Surely my money was as good as anyone else's? I located the house on the website and couldn't believe my eyes. Camilla's house was indeed a bargain and cheaper than the Shack. I knew this for certain because we had only recently had the Shack valued. What an absolute bargain with all that land, a substantial house on the market for buttons. I was so excited I telephoned Matt immediately, who was not the least bit thrilled at the thought of moving house again so soon. My argument was the land; we had horses and it would be ideal. I persuaded Matt to at least have a look when he arrived home.

I waited patiently for him to arrive home at six o'clock and as soon as he entered the house I thrust the laptop into his face to view the details. He made himself a drink while I hopped from one foot to another, willing him to hurry up. Eventually he sat down and looked over the details.

'Great house,' he said, 'it would be ideal for us and the children but there is a reason why the house is so cheap. Have another look yourself.'

He swung the laptop in my direction.

Oh my gosh … it slapped me straight in my face. Camilla Noland wasn't Lady of the Manor or Mrs 'I'm better than everyone else'. The particulars showed only a small courtyard attached to the property, the only land the substantial property actually had. After a quick search on the Internet, it became apparent the acres she claimed were attached to the property belonged to the farmer at the rear of the house. She just rented grazing space for her horses.

I let out a howl of laughter.

'Mrs Noland has NO LAND.'

Her surname suited her completely. She'd had the cheek to turn down my money for a saddle while standing as bold as brass boasting about her land and property. How the mighty have fallen. Some people are not quite who they make out they are.

Mrs No-Land, as I now thought of her, was one of these people. I knew every time I saw her I would have a secret smile to myself. She was no better than me – or anyone else for that fact.

The next day's walk was extremely interesting. Matt was working from home and was quite happy to supervise Matilda and Daisy whilst I trekked out with Penelope. We trekked miles, ten miles to be exact, to a pub along the canal. We were armed with a rucksack full of water, money and toilet roll in case we got caught short halfway there. We picked the pub at random; neither of us had visited this joint before but it was a beautiful day and to be honest I was quite looking forward to a few hours without the children.

We wandered along the canal in the sunny weather. Today, Penelope's choice of subject was Camilla and she was chatting quite openly about all the dirt she had on Camilla.

In Penelope's words, 'It's only you I am telling.'

Camilla was hoping to set up home with Elvis once the house and land were sold. That would be all well and good if she actually had some land to sell. Penelope vouched for Camilla claiming that the land was indeed all hers. Penelope was quite adamant that Mrs Noland had no reason to lie, but I knew different.

The pub was in sight, a welcome view to be honest. Entering the pub we headed straight towards the bar, after ordering our drinks we looked around to locate a table so we could sit and peruse the lunchtime menu. I was ravenous after all the exercise. Immediately scanning the room I clocked the White Witch of Narnia sitting at a table in the corner. She was the woman who had interviewed me for my latest job – or should I say the woman who sat in on the interview and did nothing except peer down her snooty nose at me. She sat alone but had two drinks resting on her table. I assumed whoever her lunch date was had nipped to the toilet. We both eyeballed each other at the same time but she quickly looked away.

I thought this was very rude of her, so when I passed her table I gave her a cheery, 'Hello, how are you?'

My greeting was a little over the top and a few customers sat at the other tables glanced over in my direction. The White Witch looked up and forced nothing but a smile.

We sat at a table not too far from the White Witch.

'How the hell do you know her?' Penelope enquired.

Her voice was a little shaky and I knew immediately from her reaction that there was a story behind this question. Surely Rupert hadn't been poking his wand in her cauldron as well? If that was the case, my opinion of Rupert would hit an all-time low.

'She was on the interview panel for the job I just landed. Well, when I say she was on the interview panel, she was attending to make up the numbers. That's the only time I have come across her. Why?' I replied.

'That witch used to be my best friend,' answered Penelope. That didn't seem a major drama to me as Penelope had loads of people who used to be her best friend. One day I would be one of those people who used to be her best friend.

Penelope shared the story of how she, the White Witch and another friend called Mel were once the terrible threesome. Always out together, having a laugh, until Mel landed a boyfriend. Mel broke away from the group a little and started to see Rob more and more until, eventually, the times she met up with Penelope and the White Witch became very scarce. Mel was very happy and had set up home with Rob and their first baby was on the way – exciting times.

During the last couple of months of the pregnancy, a distressed Mel had contacted Penelope and the White Witch to invite them round for a catch-up. When they arrived Mel appeared to be in a right state, to say the least. She was becoming suspicious of Rob's behaviour and thought he may be having an affair. His routine was changing and more often than not he would arrive home from work later than usual. No sooner had he arrived home he was straight back out again to pump some iron at the gym but Mel never found any gym clothes to wash in the washing basket. Penelope and the White Witch had assured

Mel she was probably imagining it and no doubt the pregnancy was taking its toll. The White Witch decided to be a 'Good Witch' and took it upon herself to follow Rob one evening so she could put her mind at rest. Her findings concluded that Rob was indeed working late and then travelling to the gym so there was nothing to worry about all.

The baby was born and Penelope and the White Witch were among the first visitors at the hospital. The Witch ventured off halfway through the visit in search of the shop to buy Mel some magazines. Penelope went to the toilet five minutes later and busted Rob and the White Witch doing a little more than wetting the baby's head in one of the cubicles. No wonder the White Witch had told Mel that Rob was behaving himself – it was her having the affair with her best mate's bloke behind her back.

Penelope continued with her story. She ran straight back as fast as her legs could carry her up the hospital corridor to Mel and told her everything. Mel had literally given birth just a few hours before. With the baby cradled in her arms, she told Rob to sling his hook and take the White Witch with him. Mel never contacted him again and brought up the child as a single parent. Penelope hadn't clapped eyes on the White Witch from that day until now.

I had decided during my interview there was something shifty about that woman. I had a gut feeling despite her snooty attitude that she was no better than anyone else, and stealing her best mate's husband was just unforgivable. I was right to allocate the White Witch of Narnia a seat on my bus. Always trust that gut instinct. Always.

While Penelope was recounting this tale, we both failed to spot who had joined the White Witch back at the table. Luckily for Penelope, it wasn't Rob as that may have led to an awkward moment. Instead, sat there as bold as brass, holding hands with the White Witch, was Elvis! He looked at us and we looked at him. He quickly moved his hand away from the White Witch but we had already spotted it and he knew we had seen him.

It was no skin off my nose that Elvis was swinging his hips with another woman other than Camilla Noland and her week was going from bad to worse. First the village would find out she had NO LAND and, second, Elvis was clearly all shook up but not over Camilla. Maybe he had decided she wasn't such a good catch after all, especially now her land prospects had diminished overnight.

Penelope was all of a dither and didn't know what to do about the situation. I wasn't going to offer any advice, I wanted nothing at all to do with this business. The walk home was torture. Penelope ran through every scenario of whether she shouldn't or should tell Camilla. Personally I didn't care either way. One thing was for sure, Camilla would need a short stay at heartbreak hotel, however she found out.

'How are Mel and the child?' I dropped into the conversation.

'I have no idea, we fell out years ago,' Penelope responded.

Now why didn't that surprise me? I hadn't come across any long term friends of Penelope yet and I suspected I never would.

Within twenty-four hours of our walk Camilla became single; dumped by Elvis and with her husband now shacked up with Marilyn she was left high and dry. In an attempt to cheer up Camilla, Penelope sent me a text to see if I was free to party with them both this coming weekend.

I'd rather listen to the farrier's repulsive snorting sounds in a morning than spend a night with that pair. I replied, politely declining the kind offer and suggesting it wasn't my thing. There was a silver lining to this cloud, Saturday night was approaching and that meant Matt and I were free of Rupert and Penelope. It would be quite a rare sight for their coats not to be hung on their coat pegs in our cloak room.

Saturday night was upon us, Matt and I ordered a curry and cracked open a couple of beers.

'Knock…Knock…Knock…'

Matt ventured off to open the door and in walked Rupert with Little Jonny and Annabel.

'Is everything OK?' Matt enquired.

'Yes perfect, Penelope is out with her new best friend so I was at a loose end with the kids. I thought I'd come and keep you both company.'

'Marvellous,' I said as I took his coat and hung it on his peg. There was one thing I detested in life and it wasn't just the arrival of unwanted visitors – but sharing my curry with the same unannounced guests. My curry was my curry and I still liked playing at being a student and enjoying the leftovers for breakfast.

Just for a change Rupert had brought his slippers and made himself at home. Apparently Penelope and Camilla had bought tickets to watch an Elvis tribute act down at the local drinking hole. Maybe she was really missing Elvis. It was a hole to say the least, one of those places where your feet stick to the floor and the loos are outside. If you wanted to regain entry to the venue after a visit to the toilet, you had to obtain a very classy hand stamp.

Monday arrived, which was the day I was starting my new job. There were only two weeks left of the school term and this would break me in nicely ready for the new school year in September. Penelope had got her knickers in a twist over that, complaining that we wouldn't have much time to walk. Nothing had actually changed. It wasn't as though I spent the whole day with Penelope, just an hour every morning. We could still amble round on our walk in the morning and I could tootle off to work in the afternoon.

From this moment on Penelope's behaviour started to change towards me. I felt she was jealous of my new job. She didn't want me spending time with anyone else. There was nothing to be jealous of. It didn't change my relationship with her in the slightest. The ironic thing was she was still child-minding every afternoon anyway so I couldn't see any problem at all.

Since her friendship with Wendy and Annie had deteriorated she loathed her afternoon child-minding duties. It was no fun any more. Wendy and Annie were joined at the hip and were always together. Penelope now had to actually child-mind all by herself. Even Facebook wasn't fun any more due to the lack of comments on her continuous status updates. That was an attention-seeking game I had started to avoid.

Penelope sent me continuous text messages throughout the day – usually about nothing – but when my job started, she totally backed off. So much so, that I thought she may have lost her phone. But no, she was behaving like a toddler who hadn't succeeded in getting their own way. I didn't rise to it and didn't even mention it. As far as I was concerned, nothing had changed but Penelope had decided to change the friendship from this point. This was Penelope's choice. I was not going to throw my-self into any friendship that needed to be forced. It was either there or it wasn't.

I didn't even receive a text from Penelope asking me whether I had enjoyed my first day at work. Fay was the first one to text as soon as my shift had finished. That's the difference, a true friend is happy for you no matter what you do and what you have and quite frankly I didn't have the time for meaning-less conversations or friendships that drained me of my energy.

Smiling to myself I remembered my gran's old saying, 'Always surround yourself with radiators not drains'. I let Penelope have her tantrum and later on I sent her a text to see if she was still OK to walk the next morning.

I'm sorry, I can't tomorrow, came the curt response.

That was it, nothing else, short and to the point. I didn't reply, I just left it there.

The next morning I stood in the playground with Matilda and Daisy in the pushchair waiting for Penelope's arrival. She said she wasn't walking so I dressed in my jeans and thought I would take the opportunity to nip to the shops to pick up a few essentials before work to have a browse. Penelope sauntered onto the playground and waltzed straight past me, without even making eye contact. There was no way you could have missed me standing there.

There was no 'Hello' or 'Good morning' and strangely she was dressed in her walking gear. Once the school bell rang I watched her plug in her headphones and set off in the direction we usually headed on our walks. Everyone noticed her behaviour in the playground and saw that it was a deliberate attempt to ignore me.

I felt like saying, 'I've seen your swagger, lady, and if you'd like to have an intelligent conversation about it I'm all ears,' but I left it, what was the point? There was no point, I couldn't make anyone talk or stand with me. It just all seemed a little childish. I thought the adults in the playground were there to set an example to the children. The children behaved better than most of the adults. Penelope in particular was acting worse than a toddler, so I left her to it.

That afternoon at school pick-up time I stood again in my usual spot on the playground, the place where I had stood with Penelope for the last seven months. Penelope arrived and walked straight past me again, deliberately ignoring me. She headed towards the middle of the playground and pretended to be on the phone. You could tell she wasn't and I seriously thought about calling her phone so it would ring and she would look like a complete idiot. But I decided against it; I had four kids of my own and I didn't need to deal with another child.

I remembered the wise words Fay had once remarked, 'You don't need a certain number of friends, just a number of friends you can be certain of.'

This was very true. Those certain friends pass the seven-year rule, not like the pretentious nutters you have to pass the time of day with as you serve out your school playground sentence.

I didn't bother to text Penelope that night. If she could treat me in this way then she was no friend of mine.

The next morning was interesting to say the least. The gossip amongst the Playground Mafia was all about me and what the hell I had done to Penelope for her to be ignoring me. This was the first time I had come under playground scrutiny and I was livid at Penelope for placing me in this situation. My only crime had been to find employment, I hadn't done anything else. Penelope's behaviour was strange and unstable and it was obviously something to do with me as I was the only one in the playground that she was ignoring.

That morning I pushed the pushchair along to the high street and headed towards the local bakery. I was just about to push the door open when Penelope came flouncing out. There was no way she could have missed me but she totally ignored me. Instead she pretended to look deep into the bag of cakes she had just bought and scurried away. How very strange, what a weird woman. We had spent four months in each other's company and there was no need for such strange, uncomfortable behaviour. I decided to send Penelope a text:

Hi, hope everything is OK? Have I done something to upset you? If so I would sincerely like to put it right.

The funny thing was I knew Penelope had read the text as she was only a little further up the road and I noticed that she had taken the phone out of her pocket and was glancing at the screen. However, it took her two hours to reply.

I do not know what you are talking about.

Everyone else knew what I was talking about, the whole playground knew she was walking straight past me, ignoring me and standing somewhere else. It wasn't in my head. I just left the situation again, what was the point? If she wasn't adult enough to discuss it and move on then she could keep her childish behaviour to herself.

This carried on for nearly a week.

Everything in her life was a drama. Her attention-seeking antics were apparent when she thanked some random person in a status update which she made public so I could see, indicating how much of a rock they had been in the last six months, supporting her with her weight loss. This was clearly aimed at upsetting me. I had been the one walking with her in minus temperatures and in the rain for four months while putting up with her drivel, yet there was no mention of me. If she wanted to get her kicks in this way she could go ahead but I wanted to keep my dignity. The next comment she posted was so random, I couldn't quite decide if she was having a nervous breakdown. It read…

The great thing about living in a small village is when you don't know what you are doing, someone else does.

The most amusing thing about this was most of the time nobody had a bloody clue what she was doing! They all thought she needed to be sectioned for her own good.

A week had gone by and Penelope began to stand in the middle of the playground. No-one stood with her; she was all on her lonesome. She appeared to be that paranoid she didn't even trust talking to herself.

Then out of the blue one morning, as she passed me she spoke.

'You free to walk in the morning?'

I decided the best tack was not to judge her as I already knew she was a complete attention-seeking fruit loop. I didn't need to judge that fact. There was no need to blatantly ignore me like she had done the past week, manners cost nothing. I was dubious as I didn't really want to get back into the walking lark with her and I was looking forward to getting my Saturday nights back to myself. However, I decided to give it another chance; I felt sorry for her, her behaviour wasn't stable and she certainly didn't have any other friends to rely on.

The next morning we set off on the walk. Even though the sun was shining and the birds were tweeting, the atmosphere was bloody frosty to say the least. So frosty in fact it could have been the middle of December, not July.

The conversation felt forced and Penelope was being guarded about what she said. I didn't quite understand any of it until she suddenly said, 'How come Samuel got selected as the captain for the school athletics team?'

So that was what all this was about? Samuel had been chosen over the almighty Little Jonny.

As we walked further Penelope started to relax a little and hopefully started to realise that it didn't actually matter who was the captain of the athletics team.

She was starting to behave more normally and I complimented her on her weight loss. It genuinely did look like she had lost a few pounds and I knew bringing the conversation back round to her would please her. She said that she felt a little better about herself and that she and Rupert were trying to get back on track for the children's sake, even though she was finding it hard to spend time alone with him.

I piped up, 'In the bedroom department,' but she informed me that they hadn't even got as far as the stairs yet.

Penelope decided she needed a challenge. She was already providing me with the challenge of being her friend – when it suited her of course. I wasn't sure I needed any more challenges, it had been nothing but a challenge since we'd arrived in the village.

Then Penelope came out with a bright idea.

'Let's climb a mountain!' she proclaimed.

She couldn't even climb up the stairs with Rupert, never mind a bloody mountain. The thing I found strange about this conversation was the word 'let's'. That word is plural so did her plan include me? Did it have to include me? This woman had spent a whole week not speaking to me, probably because my child had beaten her child to the captain's place in the athletics team. I looked at her in complete disbelief but I suppose all the climbing gear she wore on her first weigh-in on that Friday morning needed to be put to use somehow.

There was a method to her madness; if she threw herself into this challenge it would mean spending even less time with Rupert. Deep down Penelope knew Rupert and Annie were the perfect couple. She was convinced they were 'in love' and they were always going to be in love. The sad thing for them, however, was that they couldn't do anything about it.

I could see the desperation in Penelope's face; she needed to climb this mountain to prove to herself that she could do it. When I returned home, I rang Fay.

'Why me, Fay? Why me? Why do I attract these nutters, shoplifters, frisky pensioners, witches, people who want to climb mountains and other folk one wave short of a shipwreck?' I demanded.

Fay let out a howl of laughter and said, 'God put you on this earth to take the crap away from the rest of us "Normaltons" who wouldn't be able to cope with these nutters.'

'Do you think that's true, Fay?' I asked.

'No, do I bollocks – you are just one unlucky sod!' she giggled.

CHAPTER 8

August

Over dinner I informed Matt that I had definitely decided to allocate Penelope a seat on 'the bus' and she would be keeping Camilla company. I was contemplating saving a place for Elvis on the bus too, just for the comedy factor: they'd certainly be 'All shook up' when the bus trundled over the side of a cliff. If only the bus theory was real, it would give me something to look forward to. I'd even pay for the petrol to transport them to the cliff then all these nutters would be driven out of my life forever. Matt pointed out that all these nutters had one thing in common – ME! I reminded Matt there were still seats on my bus if he carried on sharing his daft opinions. He made a conscious decision to quit while he was ahead and before he was banned again from all marital privileges – he had learned the hard way last time.

Frisky Pensioner had been keeping a low profile of late but he was still hard boiled enough to knock on the door every Friday for his eggs. I was ready for him each week. I made sure the eggs were placed by the front door so he didn't have the opportunity to venture into the house. I thought, or rather hoped, he would have ceased coming by now as every time he did I was extremely unpleasant. I didn't smile and I didn't make conversation, in fact I was a very unsociable bugger. But no, I still had to hand over the eggs while he placed his grubby little fingers over the top of mine for a quick squeeze when he grabbed the box from me. Every week, I scrubbed my hands red raw trying to get rid of his grubbiness. It made me cringe.

Frisky Pensioner's wife had recently retired and he appeared to be keeping his head down more than usual. Maybe he was on his best behaviour because she was present all day to witness his antics.

This week they were both walking up the lane – well his walk was more like a shuffle – when Mrs FP bawled a very loud 'Good morning' in my direction.

I glanced around and she gave me a polite wave which she complemented with, 'Hello, how's village life treating you?'

Frisky Pensioner himself looked very shifty and seemed to be in a hurry to whisk Mrs FP away from me.

At that point I wasn't sure whether to reply with, 'Yes village life is great, thanks. I've been touched up by old men who felt it appropriate to put their hands on my breasts while I was holding a dead chicken?' or just to say, 'It's marvellous, thank you very much; especially when I am snogged by pensioners.'

Instead I opted for a frosty glare in Frisky Pensioner's direction and replied, 'It's all been very quiet of late, thank you.'

He looked relieved. In fact his look unnerved me somewhat, as I recalled him spying on the neighbour through the hole in the fence during the summer months. I physically shuddered.

The next Saturday night Penelope and Rupert were due to visit the Shack – just for a change! I decided to cook a curry from scratch which hopefully would give me an hour to myself in the kitchen while Matt had to entertain our dinner guests.

Penelope appeared to be on top form. Hanging her coat on her named peg in the cloakroom she poured herself a drink. I'm not sure if Rupert felt a little embarrassed being here again as he retrieved his slippers out of his carrier bag and mumbled, 'I ought to buy an extra pair and leave them here.'

Rupert looked very subdued tonight. I collected the beers from his hand and he followed me into the kitchen. Matt was left stranded entertaining Penelope and their kids. Samuel was in hiding, he didn't want to see Little Jonny. He had been upset all week at school. Little Jonny had begun to tease him at school about his curly hair and Samuel pleaded with me not to let them come round but what could I do? If you fell out with every parent over a child's argument, you would have no friends left. Gosh I was missing a trick here; that sounded like a plan to me.

'You OK, Rupert?' I enquired. 'You appear a little subdued?'

Pulling the ring pull on his can he looked up and replied, 'I'll be OK after a few more of these.'

He had finished his first beer and was on to his second before I could even remove the cork from the wine. Something was troubling Rupert and I'm sure it wouldn't be long before we all found out what it was – the beers were not even touching the sides.

'Do you find my wife boring?' Rupert unexpectedly asked.

Well that was a loaded question, how the hell was I meant to answer that? I've always been taught to be as honest as I can but sometimes the truth can be very painful, so maybe it would be better to lie through my teeth on this occasion. Rupert looked bedraggled and completely fed up. The kitchen door was ajar so I walked over to it while pondering my answer.

Closing the door I looked Rupert directly in his eyes and I answered him.

'Yes, so boring I would probably have more bloody fun hanging out with dead people.'

I wasn't sure if my answer was a little harsh but I knew I hadn't lied, so my parents would be proud.

The poor bloke went into a spiel about how he couldn't take much more. It was all very bizarre standing in my kitchen with some other bloke – wearing his own slippers, which I always thought was strange – slating his wife who was no doubt boring the pants off Matt in the next room – well not literally I hoped. Don't get me wrong, I wasn't opposed to the slating Rupert was giving her but I was concerned that I was starving and if Penelope could hear him, there would be fireworks and we would never get fed.

Penelope was a smoker but she cleverly hid this secret from her kids. Every smoker I had come across in the past was stick thin, usually because they prefer to stick a cigarette in their mouth instead of food. Penelope was the exception to this rule which proved to me that I should never stereotype people. I wouldn't let Penelope smoke in the Shack so she always nipped out of the back door and stood around the corner, hidden from the children. Unfortunately on this occasion Rupert and I hadn't noticed her and she was no longer boring the pants off Matt in the next room. She was staring straight at us through the open kitchen window and had heard every word Rupert had said. Just my luck when I was flippin' hungry!

Penelope looked livid. She raced through the back door and stood directly in the space between Rupert and me.

'How could you, Rupert, how could you say I was boring? That's an unforgivable thing to say.'

'Gosh,' I thought.

If that was unforgivable Rupert was on to a winner here. He could walk away from the marriage and his previous misdemeanours would have no bearing on the divorce settlement. I wasn't sure how much a judge would award in his favour for putting up with a boring wife for years but I guessed it was probably a lot. I could have helped Rupert out of the sticky situation at this moment by agreeing with him but the look on Matt's face told me we needed to vacate the kitchen quick and leave them to row in peace.

Matt and I were like school kids with our ears pinned to the kitchen door, listening to every word. Penelope was very forceful with what she thought Rupert should be thinking. She was shouting at him then answering on his behalf. He didn't have a chance to speak, she just wouldn't let him. There were no ifs, buts or maybes, Penelope was not boring according to her.

Matt and I were still trying to hold in our laughter when I realised I had left the curry bubbling away on the stove. How stupid was I? Now I was going to have to enter the war zone and turn off the heat under the curry. I manoeuvred in as quickly as I could, switched off the cooker and retreated out of the kitchen even quicker, not forgetting to grab the bottle of wine from the worktop. I winked at Matt – RESULT! We'd had enough of listening to what Rupert should think – according to Penelope – and we sat in the dining room waiting for them to sort themselves out. How long do you let another couple row in your home?

We had to admit this wasn't our usual Saturday night, another couple standing in their slippers rowing in our kitchen; it was like we were the visitors in our own home. Two minutes later, Penelope slammed the kitchen door and ran upstairs. It was all quiet for a minute so I decided to follow her to make sure she was OK; it was my house after all. I found her sat on my bed sobbing her heart out.

Penelope cried out, 'I bet you could write a book about us pair, someone should think about making a movie out of my life.'

I wasn't sure which actress could play Penelope in a film as I wasn't sure who could do her justice.

Matt managed to organise the curry and by the time Penelope's tear-stained face had returned to normal I persuaded her to venture back downstairs and eat some food. We all sat round the table in complete silence. In fact we all sat in silence for nearly thirty-five minutes. This situation reminded me of the couple that position themselves in the corner of the pub, both staring in opposite directions. They have been married for years and only stayed together for the sake of the kids. Now the kids have flown the nest they have nothing left to talk about, they just sit there for hours until one of them suggests that they return home. Picture that scene; that is exactly what was going on in my Shack.

Matt and I were biting our lips trying to control our giggles. It was a horrendous atmosphere, I felt like a naughty school girl that had been summoned by the headmaster and because I was nervous I started to laugh. I couldn't hold it in any longer, it was my house for God's sake. I just laughed and laughed.

Matt gave me a nervous 'I'm not sure that is appropriate' look but I couldn't help myself.

I peeped through my tears of laughter and noticed that Penelope was not amused and Rupert had gone green. He was actually looking very ill. It suddenly hit me and I stopped laughing almost immediately – maybe he'd had an allergic reaction to a chilli in the curry, or maybe he was just allergic to Penelope.

Rupert spoke slowly, 'I don't feel well,' and before he could say any more, he threw up.

This wasn't just a tiny bit of vomit, it was vomit that bounced off the table, up the walls, all over the food and, unluckily for Rupert, all over Penelope's new sheepskin slippers that had cost her seventy quid. She had been ripped off in my opinion, she could buy her own sheep for that sort of money.

There was no sympathy for Rupert being unwell, she just shouted, 'Rupert, how could you make such a show of me? My slippers are ruined. Get up, we are going home.'

I glanced around the room and was convinced I hadn't seen vomit like it since I was nineteen years old and had sneaked some of my dad's whisky from the cellar.

Outside, the rain was pouring down. Penelope stepped over her husband's vomit and pushed him out of the door. She didn't even let him put on his shoes or his coat. They walked down the path, both wearing their slippers and looking like they had just escaped from the funny farm. You could still hear Penelope shouting at Rupert as they disappeared out of view down the lane.

I turned to Matt and said, 'Oh no, I need to go after them.'
'Why?'
'They've forgotten their bloody kids!'

It was mid-afternoon the next day before Penelope remembered she had kids. I had watered and fed them and given them beds for the night. Rupert knocked on the door to pick up his shoes and children – in that order! He looked terrible.

He thanked us for taking care of the kids and said, 'See you next Saturday, no doubt.'

Surely not, I would be too embarrassed to show my face, especially as neither of them had offered to clean up his vomit.

The next morning I was woken by the sound of my phone beeping. I grabbed my phone and there on the display it read, 'Penelope Kensington has tagged you in a post'. I was obviously off her Facebook 'restricted' list this week as I counted at least twenty notifications from Facebook with various people sending me 'Good luck' messages.

I didn't have a clue what they were referring to until Penelope commented on the post numerous times. Not only did it seem she was lapping up all the attention, she was loving it!

'Yes we will do our best,' she posted.

'It's going to be hard work but training starts this morning,' read another response.

What training? Had she entered us into the world championships of one-sided talk-walking? This is an event where two 'friends' walk for miles but only one of them is allowed to speak and the topic of conversation must be themselves – or their firstborn. I didn't think we'd be seeing the event at the Olympics any time soon.

Penelope seemed to know what everyone was talking about but I certainly didn't until I read the post. It was official; Penelope had put it out there in cyberspace for everyone to see.

She and I were going to climb a mountain.

There was no way out of this now. Did I want to climb a mountain? No! Did I want to climb a mountain with Penelope? NO!

The sheer magnitude of the task ahead suddenly hit me. Not only did this mean I had to climb a mountain, it also meant spending a whole weekend away with Penelope. A weekend spent with Penelope would feel like a lifetime.

What on earth would Penelope and I talk about for forty-eight hours? This was already beginning to worry me but I was certain she would take care of the situation; no doubt she would talk about herself for the whole time. I could suggest a ban on talking, since we would need to conserve all our energy for the last stretch to the peak. Or better still I could take a gag. What more could she possibly tell me about herself, there was nothing I didn't already know.

On venturing downstairs, there, posted through the letterbox, was an A4 piece of paper. I bent down to pick it up and saw the words TRAINING PLAN written in capital letters. Penelope had actually drawn up our training plan. There was an entry on the plan for every day of the week except Saturday. I was relieved that there would be at least one day of respite from Penelope, until I discovered that she had kept Saturday free so we could continue our family get-togethers.

Fay once said to me, 'Friends are the family we choose for ourselves.'

I wouldn't pick Penelope or her family to be my family. They were on my bus; they were over that cliff.

I concluded that Penelope must be having a mid-life crisis. Why couldn't she just buy a sports car, have a tattoo or take Rupert's lead and have an affair?

People start to do daft things when they worry where their path is leading them in life – good job she didn't know she was soon to be driven over a cliff in a make believe bus! I wasn't panicking, I was quite happy minding my own business, pottering around my Shack with the odd bit of work in the afternoon.

Initially, the training plan consisted of an hour's exercise each day. This increased to nearly three hours by week four. The mountain climb was pencilled in for the first weekend in October. I contemplated saving her seat on my bus for someone else as I could simply push her off the bloody mountain. It wasn't the climbing of the mountain that would be the problem. The greatest challenge was going to be putting up with her for the whole weekend.

Penelope had not even considered that I may not want to participate in this adventure; I was unwillingly roped in – end of. Maybe I needed to purchase some rope in case I did decide to put her on the bus after all – I could use it to ensure Penelope was tied tightly to the seat of the bus so she couldn't escape. Fay said I was lacking a very important word in my vocabulary. That word was the word 'No'. Fay made me say it over and over again on the phone and told me to phone her again the following day for more practice.

Luckily for me, training started tomorrow. Today was the day we bought the kit. I wasn't sure what kit I would need – I had two legs, two feet and walking boots – all I needed was earplugs so I couldn't hear her drone on up the mountain and it would all be sorted.

The local climbing shop was miles away as there wasn't much call for that type of gear in the village. For most people the only time they needed to climb was a Friday night – climbing out of the local drinking hole after a particularly heavy session!

As usual it was left to me to navigate and drive to the shops in the city. She grabbed a trolley at the entrance of the store and before we had even reached the end of the first aisle her trolley was half-full. There were whistles, water bottles, thermal socks, thermal vests, thermal blankets, a sleeping bag and a flag. A flag – what the bloody hell was the flag for? Which mountain did she think we were going to climb, Mount Everest? I decided to have the conversation to confirm the intended mountain sooner rather than later, before I found myself at base camp in the Himalayas.

I thought I had better show willing so I purchased a water bottle and a thermal vest. Penelope had already moved on to the next aisle and was looking at tents. Why did we need a bloody tent? Had she contemplated being stranded up the mountain or was she simply covering all bases in case we suddenly became ill? There was no way on this earth she would lug a tent up the side of the mountain, heaven forbid she broke a finger nail. If push came to shove, I would probably prefer to die of hypothermia than spend a night stuck up a mountain with Penelope.

I reminded her that these days there were inventions called mobile phones. I would just make sure my phone was fully charged before we set off and in the event of an emergency, I would simply telephone the mountain rescue services – I didn't worry about trivial things like mobile reception! Penelope seemed a little more relaxed once I had mentioned this fact and after I refused to go halves on a tent, she didn't have much choice anyway. My 'No' training from Fay was starting to pay dividends. She'd be proud.

My shopping expedition resulted in one carrier bag containing only two items. Penelope summoned the shop manager to assist her to carry all of her gear to the car. Rupert was going to flip. She had bought another two new coats from the shop – one for minus temperatures and another for the wind and rain. She had seven carrier bags full to the brim, one of which was topped off with two boxes of Kendal Mint Cake. Allegedly these seventy-two bars were for energy up the mountain. I sarcastically asked Penelope whether she would prefer a donkey or a Sherpa to cart all her stuff up the mountain. There was no way on this earth I was helping her to carry any of it.

The next morning, Penelope turned up for training wearing … well if I'm truly honest I hadn't got a clue. It was August, the weather was reasonably hot and on her head was some sort of road-kill. I couldn't make up my mind whether it was a fox or a badger that had been run over. Who did she think she was, Davey Crockett? She looked ridiculous.

'Nice … erm hat?' I murmured.

I wasn't sure what to call it. She informed me it was a present from Camilla. It wasn't a hat as such, more half a hat so the heat could escape out of the top of Penelope's head when she got too hot walking up the mountain. How thoughtful of Camilla! She wasn't that bloody thoughtful when she was having it away with Penelope's husband.

Failing that, I thought to myself, if we got hungry and by some miracle managed to eat all the Kendal Mint Cake, then we could throw the road-kill onto a fire and eat that too.

Strapped to her back was a rucksack and in her rucksack were some of the items she intended hauling up the mountain. She had a torch, a blanket, thermals, socks, four bottles of water and a coat. Flippin' 'eck Penelope, where was she going to store her food for the day – and her cigarettes as she was still smoking at least forty a day? Penelope hadn't given food a second thought. We hadn't even set off for the first training session yet and she had already packed and unpacked her bag umpteen times.

I was dressed in my walking trousers, boots and a shirt with no rucksack – one step at a time. We hadn't even reached the top of the hill on the way out of the village when I thought I had gone deaf. I was relieved when I realised I wasn't deaf, it was just that Penelope was extremely quiet. Maybe she was conserving her energy because we had planned to walk approximately twelve miles that day.

The next thing I heard was a thud, which was the sound of Penelope hitting the pavement when she collapsed. Then she threw up everywhere. Twice in less than a week I had observed the contents of her and her husband's stomachs and there was no way I was cleaning this lot up, I'd gone 'above and beyond' cleaning up after Rupert. The so-called hat had slipped right off the top of Penelope's head as she hit the ground and landed slap bang in the middle of the vomit. It now looked more like an unfortunate freak of nature than road-kill.

If this was a ploy for me to carry the rucksack she had no chance. Unusually, I wasn't immediately overcome by the noxious aroma of sick, which would normally have me gagging immediately. All my nostrils detected was the very strong scent of mint.

Penelope was starting to murmur faintly.

'It's the cake, it's the cake.'

Penelope had only decided to stuff five bars of Kendal Mint Cake into her system before setting off this morning. Apparently this was to provide her with more energy to walk the miles. There was no way we were walking anywhere today with all that stuffed inside her. Luckily for her, Rupert was driving down the main road in his bubble car – you could spot him a mile off but I decided it was probably best not to mention this to Penelope as she had made him buy a car that she thought was inconspicuous.

He spotted Penelope on the floor – let's face it you couldn't miss her – dressed in her minus temperatures coat, with her rucksack strapped to her back. He stopped the car and bundled her into the passenger seat and drove her home. I politely refused a lift, plugged in my headphones and went on my merry way, being careful to avoid stepping in her vomit. I had a lovely walk all by myself, just the way I like it.

After a couple of hours I returned home to discover a bunch of flowers on my doorstep. The flowers looked a little more alive than the weeds I had previously received from Penelope. I glanced at the card and found that they were sent by Rupert. I plonked myself down on the step, untied my boots and wondered why the heck he was sending me flowers. I read the card.

I'm so sorry for the mess on Saturday night and for everything else. Rupert x

Two things immediately crossed my mind. Did Penelope know he had sent me flowers and what would Matt think? I wasn't even sure what I thought. Maybe they had both sent the flowers but then the words 'I'm' and 'Rupert' did suggest he was working alone.

The flowers were pretty enough to deserve a vase and water so I placed them on the kitchen table. Matt arrived home from work and didn't even notice them, moving the vase to one side while he ate his tea – which immediately took care of the conversation about where the flowers had come from. I decided not to mention them to Penelope unless she did first and I would just thank Rupert discreetly next time I saw him, more than likely on Saturday night!

For the past week Matilda and Daisy had been booked into the local nursery whilst the training sessions became a little more intense. They were enjoying their time integrating with other little people who hopefully they would become friends with.

The next morning's training session was free of Kendal Mint Cake and road-kill hats. It amused me that we didn't go for walks any more, we went on training sessions! We were walking the same routes and everything else was the same except for the bright pink fluorescent rucksack that she carried on her back. In the shop, Penelope had chosen the bright pink one so she would be easy to spot by helicopter on the side of the mountain if she needed to be rescued. If it made her feel more important thinking she was on a training session rather than on a walk who was I to argue?

Penelope seemed a little giddy. She had news. Penelope was delighted to finally be giving up her afternoon child-minding duties to be employed by Camilla Noland. 'Can you believe it? I've got a new job, who'd of thought? I'm going to be Camilla's internal domestic environmental status executive,' Penelope gushed with excitement.

Staring up at Penelope in disbelief, no, in fact I couldn't believe it one little bit.

In simple terms, Penelope was going to be Camilla Noland's cleaner.

I thought this was unbelievable, not because Penelope wasn't capable of cleaning Camilla's house but because Camilla had had an affair with Penelope's husband. Maybe she felt guilty about the whole affair but then I didn't believe that for a moment – you need a conscience to feel guilt and it appeared she had no conscience at all.

It was incredible; Penelope had agreed to be employed by the woman who had spread the gossip about Rupert's affair with Annie around the village. This was also the woman whom Penelope had spent a great deal of time slagging off during our walks and the woman who took advantage of her child-minding time while she entertained Penelope's husband in the back of her horsebox. Maybe it was a match made in heaven.

Her employment was due to commence on the first Monday in September when the long summer holidays were over and the children returned to school. At this time the only advice I could offer to Penelope would be to stock up on nit lotion as I was sure her hair would be crawling by the end of her first week. My other advice would have been to keep her husband away from Camilla but it was way too late for that. I wonder what Rupert thought of it all? He'd had a lucky escape from making up the foursome with Elvis and Camilla but now his wife was off to work for his ex-mistress. What happens when it all goes pear-shaped or comes out in the wash?

It was now just over a month until we climbed the mountain and Penelope kept bursting into song, singing 'Ain't no mountain high enough,' every two minutes.

I wished she would burst a blood vessel otherwise she would be doing a forward roll down that mountain in a few weeks if she didn't shut up. I left the booking of the hotel in Penelope's capable hands – she took care of all the arrangements and all I had to do was drive us there.

Initially, I thought I had the better deal, before it dawned on me that she only had to click on a few websites and make a couple of phone calls. I, on the other hand, had to drive for hours while she sat back for the entire journey and talked about Little Jonny or herself for a change. Actually that would be a bit of a change as lately it had all been about her new position of Internal Domestic Environmental Status Executive and Camilla Noland.

CHAPTER 9

September

Penelope began working for Camilla as planned at the beginning of September. It seemed the pair of them became inseparable overnight and it felt like my friendship with Penelope was disposed of instantly; I was replaced by what Penelope thought was a more upper class model. Penelope was Camilla Noland's lackey on the minimum wage. I wasn't upset by her sudden change in loyalties; I still had a seat reserved for her on the bus. It was unlikely she would now pass the seven-year rule of friendship and we would be lucky to make it to one year at this rate.

Camilla's seven-seater Land Rover had always taken up two car parking spaces outside the school gates but now she edged up further, sharing the prime position outside the school with Penelope. I was a little confused and upset by Penelope's actions; had she forgotten we were climbing a mountain together in a few weeks? I spoke to Fay about my concerns but she reiterated that trying to understand what went on in someone else's brain would be a challenge on its own but trying to avoid getting lost in the vast empty space that occupied Penelope's head would be damn near impossible.

In the playground, I carried on standing where I had always stood, saying 'Hello' to whoever passed me by. The next morning the spectacle in the playground cheered me up no end. Penelope arrived dressed in exactly the same horsey gear as Camilla. To my knowledge Penelope didn't even like horses. It looked like she was dressed in extremely tight jodhpurs. I had to look twice. Yep, Penelope was definitely wearing jodhpurs.

As she set off walking down the playground my eyes were transfixed on her backside – I couldn't help staring. As she walked it looked as though there were two small puppies having a fight in a sack as her backside jiggled up and down.

There was a silver lining to this cloud; Matt and I had been completely dropped from Saturday nights because Penelope and Rupert were now spending all their time at Camilla's house. I pictured the three of them sitting cosily in the garden sharing a bottle of wine until I remembered there was no garden, she had no land. It seemed Penelope was incapable of having more than one friend, Imogen had been right all along. When she thought someone better had come along she put all her energy into that new person. Unfortunately for her, this new person had already entertained her husband on numerous occasions. Rupert had spent plenty of time in the garden she did own.

At this point we were still walking every morning even though I had to venture over to the 'dark side' of the playground to catch up with Penelope. Botox Bernie was a neighbour of theirs on that side of the playground and had teamed up with Imogen of late to become the best of buddies. I could imagine the two of them shoplifting together and when they got caught they could share a cell with Botox Bernie's husband. BB – Botox Bernie – had been getting thinner and thinner over the past few months and had also become less vocal. It was hardly surprising; the local newspaper had recently reported that her husband had been sent down for a short stay at the big house for fraud. She was a fraud herself with all her hooky designer gear and her fake boobs. I liked my usual quiet spot on the playground and didn't want any of these mothers as neighbours.

The hotel for the climbing weekend away had already been booked and paid for, so I gritted my teeth and carried on with the training, which was really hard work. The training itself wasn't hard work; the hard part was listening to Penelope singing Camilla's praises every two minutes. It was amazing how she could spend months slating her but now Camilla was paying her the minimum wage to clean her house she was suddenly her new best mate. Jealous? No chance, I just needed this climb to be over. I just wanted out of this friendship. Where was the genie in the lamp when you needed him? My wish was about to be granted.

Every morning Penelope walked off the playground with Camilla but waited for me by the front gate. Penelope always left her car parked outside the school and drove home after the training session. I was fed up now, this morning walking lark was becoming a chore. The conversation was tiresome; the whole situation was tiresome. One morning, I had just set off with Penelope when we heard a voice shouting my name. I glanced behind to find Wendy Barthorpe waving her hands frantically in my direction, clearly trying to flag me down. I looked at Penelope and she looked at me. I wasn't quite sure what to do but I waited in anticipation for Wendy to approach us and speak. Penelope just glared at me. I knew exactly what Wendy was going to say but had no idea how Penelope would react. As Wendy sauntered up to us her eyes fell upon Penelope's new horsey clobber. I have to admit I was with Wendy on this one, as she coughed to disguise her laughter at the sight of the puppies fighting in the sack in Penelope's tight jodhpurs.

Wendy's own weight loss was incredible, she had shed pounds recently without the effort of walking; she too had been on the divorce diet. I'm not sure if I'd suggested this diet to Penelope before or whether I'd just thought it. I could feel Penelope's eyes burning in the side of my face.

Wendy only wanted to confirm that I had received a party invitation for one of my children from one of hers. This was something I hadn't intended to mention to Penelope but there was no getting out of it now. After I confirmed in front of them both that Eva could make the party, Wendy smiled and thanked me politely then went on her way. Turning around towards Penelope I waited for the backlash, but she was no longer at my side. I spotted her stomping off in the distance, no doubt in a rage.

Powering my legs I put on a spurt and sprinted in her direction. I caught Penelope up quite quickly and I think it was safe to say that she was fuming, so livid in fact you could almost see the steam coming out of her ears. She looked more amusing than any cartoon character I had ever seen.

'Whatever is the matter?' I enquired.

I wasn't exactly sure what the problem was but had concluded she was maybe a little annoyed that one of my children was visiting Wendy's house for a party.

'How could you send your child round there?' she demanded. 'I thought you were my friend?' she continued.

You'd have thought I was sending my child off to the childcatcher rather than a child's birthday party at Wendy's house. I had been on the receiving end of Penelope's jealous streak before. The million text messages flashed back through my mind – the ones I'd received when I landed my new job. Thank God I was standing next to her otherwise there was a possibility she may have crashed the whole mobile network system by now. As far as I was concerned I hadn't done anything wrong but I was willing to listen to Penelope's side of the story, not that I was quite sure what the whole story was. We started walking and Penelope starting talking; actually more like blubbering and whining than talking.

'How could you? How could you? You know what Wendy has done to my family.'

As far as I was aware, Wendy and I were about the only people in the village who had not played any sort of poker games with Rupert. If I was Penelope, I would have probably tried to hold on to both our friendships.

'She is still friends with Annie, how could you send your child to her house? You're unbelievable.'

I'm unbelievable!

What did it have to do with me if Wendy was still friends with Annie? I didn't see the logic but I let her carry on.

Over the course of the next hour I received a full character assassination from Penelope. She began by telling me that Wendy Barthorpe detested the ground I walked on. Apparently, she really hated me.

'Wendy can't stand the way you talk with your funny accent. She can't stand the way you put your hair in a side pony tail, she thinks you are way too old for that. She can't stand you full stop.'

I had often wondered myself whether I was getting too old for a side pony but sod it, now I was going to wear one much more often.

This was just what I needed – an hour's walk listening to a so-called friend describing in great detail why someone detests you. Penelope seemed to take some delight from passing all this information on to me. I wasn't exactly sure why I needed to hear it – or even know it. I wasn't impressed with Penelope. I thought she was calculating and cruel and there was no need for any of it. She kept going on and on and on.

By the end of the walk I was completely drained and deflated. I know our walks were never what I would describe as 'jolly' but usually it was only the monotone soundtrack of self-indulgent waffle that left me wanting to slit my wrists. On this occasion, if our walk would have taken us anywhere near the coast, I could have easily carried on walking straight off the top of a cliff.

Surely Wendy couldn't hate me that much? After all she had invited my child to a party. I left Penelope at her car that was parked outside the school gates and strolled off without saying goodbye. As I wandered towards home I tried to figure out how something as innocuous as a pony tail could have caused someone to have such a negative opinion of me. I put the key in my front door, closed it behind me, sat at the bottom of my stairs and cried.

Penelope was merciless. I couldn't believe how deliberately vindictive she had been, causing me this pain and distress. By my reckoning we are only on this planet for an average of seventy years so what's the point wasting time on people you don't really want or need in your lives? If Penelope couldn't see what I had done for her in the last nine months, what more was there to say? I had been discreet about Rupert's affairs while her new best friend was the one who had spread it around the village in the first place – after taking advantage herself of what Rupert had to offer. I had been walking in sub-zero temperatures to help her lose weight, I had put up with her constant drivel about Little Jonny – and lack of drivel regarding Annabel. I had also listened to her constantly slating Imogen, Wendy, Annie and Camilla, but the thing that riled me most was that I had given up Saturday nights with my family to support her, as she was incapable of spending any time with her own family. What exactly was I gaining from this relationship? Absolutely nothing. I made a decision there and then, this was to be the last day I walked with Penelope.

The next morning in the playground was really difficult for me. I stood by myself trying to hold my head high and gave my side pony tail the occasional swing from side to side as a metaphorical two-fingered salute to anyone who thought I was too old to wear it. I spoke to no-one and I looked at no-one. I was there for one reason and one reason only – to drop my children at school. These mothers weren't my friends, these mothers were full of their own self-importance and they used their kids to score points in the popularity war of the playground. I asked myself a question.

'Would these people be my friends if I didn't have kids at the school?'

The answer was loud and clear. 'No!'

However, one problem lay ahead of me – the weekend away for the mountain climb. This was something I wasn't looking forward. Airing my concerns to Matt he was extremely sympathetic but he also knew I was a person who didn't like confrontation. He suggested I still go ahead with the climb, that way there would be no major falling-outs with Penelope. After thinking for several hours I decided Matt was right, I needed to remember that living in a small village and with children at the same school I was more than likely going to bump into Penelope on a daily basis and if we were still on speaking terms that would be more comfortable than the current situation with Imogen, who was in fact still ignoring me and I didn't want that. The best thing to do was to go ahead with the climb. The weekend could prove there was no hard feelings and afterwards I would leave Penelope to drift away to her new BFF, without any major fallout – assuming she didn't accidently drift off the summit of the mountain in the meantime!

That week in the playground was pretty uncomfortable to say the least. I could see Imogen smirking in my direction as if to say 'That didn't last long' now Penelope was standing with Camilla. BB had the audacity to invade my spot on the yard in a clear attempt to extract the gossip from me; she too was trying to discover why Penelope had suddenly switched to the other side of the playground. If there was any good to come out of this situation at all, it was the fact that Camilla Noland had been reminded that she had a daughter.

In their divorce settlement, Camilla and the farrier were fighting it out in court. He put up a good case to win sole custody of their daughter Rosie but unfortunately Camilla was driven by the financial gain of monthly child benefit. She won the battle and was now solely responsible for picking Rosie up from school each day.

The day of Wendy Barthorpe's kids' party was upon us. Her house was in the same village but I'd never visited before. On arrival it was a modest-looking detached house, overlooking fields and streams, very similar to Penelope's house but with country views. I knocked on the door and waited. Wendy answered the door with a beaming smile and made Eva and I feel very welcome when she invited us in.

Slipping off my shoes at the door we followed Wendy down the hallway. Glancing at the wallpaper it all looked familiar to me but I couldn't work out why. Wendy led us both into the kitchen and I had a very strange feeling that I had been here before. It all looked so familiar – the kitchen cupboards, the blinds, the ornaments. Eva ran off with the other children towards the front room to join in with the birthday celebrations whilst Wendy made me a cuppa. Scanning the room I had a quick look towards the back of the house into the conservatory. I must have been here before. I recognised the cushions, the rug and the lamps. It was all very bizarre unless this was the first sign of dementia – maybe I had been here before but just couldn't remember. I racked my brains, but nothing.

Asking Wendy if I could use the facilities she pointed me in the direction of the downstairs toilet. Once inside, I recognised that space too, even down to the colour of the toilet paper. I sat on the loo quite puzzled by it all. Then it suddenly hit me and I let out a small laugh before reaching for my phone. I sent a text to Matt.

You are not going to believe this, I am in Wendy Barthorpe's house and it is decorated exactly the same as Penelope's!

It was unbelievable. Their houses were identical, even down to the tea cups and coasters. Even though they were virtually identical, the decor seemed to work much better in Wendy's house. I'm not sure if it suited her house better or whether the extra detail, such as the vase of flowers in the hallway or the ornaments stood on the floor by the fireplace, just made it feel more homely. I was beginning to think I'd had a lucky escape from Penelope. There was no doubt Penelope had copied Wendy – with the effort Wendy had clearly gone to with the balloons and party bags for the kids, I could tell she was a very selfless thoughtful person. It was no wonder Rupert was confused when he copped off with Annie in Wendy's house, maybe he thought he was at home.

On the way home from Wendy's I made a mental note that she wouldn't need to be allocated a seat on my bus. I found her a lovely, down to earth, approachable lady. The effort she had put into organising such a fantastic party was to her credit and her interaction with the children was mesmerising. My guess was Penelope never wanted me to become friends with Wendy, which was probably more down to Penelope's insecurities.

This village was getting more bizarre by the minute; there were affairs, frisky pensioners, identical dwellings and let's not forget that Elvis and Marilyn Monroe were both alive and kicking in the village too! This village could have been used as the inspiration for a TV serial drama but no-one would watch it – everyone would think it was too far-fetched.

I wasn't quite sure how I fitted in around all these mad people, not that I particularly wanted to fit in. I had made two friends – sorry, acquaintances – and lost two acquaintances. I suppose technically I had only lost Imogen but I was about to distance myself from Penelope once the mountain escapade was over. I felt a little sad towards Rupert – I actually thought he was a good bloke who just made the wrong choices and found himself trapped, probably because he was unhappy.

I had two hours to kill before I picked up Eva from the party. Matt had taken Samuel, Matilda and Daisy for a walk up the forest with the dog so I used the time to clean the house for most of that time and finally sat down with a cuppa nearly an hour later. Resting my feet on the chair opposite I opened my laptop, balancing it on my knee and checked my emails. I couldn't believe what I was seeing – never mind what I was reading. There in front of me in my inbox was a rambling email from Penelope. I suppose sending this lot by text may have used up all her credit. The main gist of the email was about how I had let her down.

HOW I HAD LET HER DOWN!

How the heck did she come to that conclusion and what was wrong with knocking on the door and having a face-to-face conversation if she was so upset? Apart from the fact it was all a little pathetic, she was hiding behind an email which probably made her feel brave about what she was saying.

Penelope had decided I had let her down by sending Eva to Wendy's house for a party. The only thing this email had done for me so far was remind me to pick her up; I had completely forgotten she was there. Apparently, if I was any sort of friend I would delete Wendy from Facebook and ignore her in the school playground because of the pain she had caused Penelope.

I was confused, very confused. It might not take a lot for me to be confused but this was bordering on the verge of insane. I looked out of the window but I couldn't see any men in white coats ready to take me away – more's the pity. Penelope claimed she was deeply hurt that I had taken Wendy's side. I hadn't taken any sides – it wasn't my argument – and actually it wasn't even Wendy's argument. Any rational person could see the argument was between Penelope, Rupert and Annie. Wendy hadn't done anything wrong and neither had I.

That email had pushed me to my limit. It was ludicrous; it was ridiculous and it was all playground stuff. The bottom line was if Rupert hadn't played away so close to home, none of this would even be happening. Drama is a spark that will extinguish when it is ignored and I did the sensible thing and ignored the email. I decided to stay clear of the lot of them. If I responded it would just add fuel to the fire, it would give Penelope something to gossip about with Camilla and quite frankly I was past caring what any of them thought of me. New Year's Eve would be here before I knew it when my make believe bus would take them all over the cliff, never to darken my days again.

For one whole week Penelope ignored me, which didn't upset me in the slightest. Penelope was acting like a toddler. She hadn't got her own way and was stamping her feet. She could stamp them all she liked, I didn't care. It gave me the opportunity to get on with my life without listening to her woes. It was always about her.

After a very quiet week and a Penelope-free Saturday night I was relaxed and enjoying myself, pottering around the Shack without the tedious schedule of meeting up with her every day.

This very morning I was enjoying myself playing with Matilda and Daisy, something I felt I hadn't been able to do with the training schedule that occupied my time. Hearing a knock on the door I made my way up the hallway to open it. There standing on other side was a tearful Penelope.

'Can I come in?' she sniffled.

Opening the door wide I gestured and welcomed her in.

Making our way up the hallway I put the kettle on and handed her the box of tissues. I secretly hoped that the tears were down to the fact that she had changed her mind about climbing the mountain the following week and had come to let me down gently. That would mean there would be no confrontation and an amicable friendship would continue. The best of both worlds.

Penelope spilt the beans that the tears were because of a niggling gut feeling that Rupert was still having an affair and she wanted me to help her find out with whom. My jaw dropped; why did she need my help and where was Camilla, her new best friend, to help her discover Rupert's latest misdemeanours?

Why couldn't Camilla take a turn at playing Dempsey and Makepeace with Penelope? I'll tell you why, because she would gain nothing from finding out what Rupert was up to now, and if she started following him it may soon come to light that she herself had once been sneaking around with lover boy.

I wanted to inform Penelope that it seemed I was no longer good enough to be her friend but, in reality, she wasn't good enough to be my friend. It was all take, take, take on her part and not once in the last few months had she ever asked how I was. Not that I would tell her if she did ever ask but I would have liked to have been given the choice. I still had her email – in a fashion. It was just about readable after being pinned to the dartboard along with her mountain training plans, with numerous holes punched all over it.

Sighing to myself I took pity on Penelope and agreed to help her one last time.

Apparently Rupert claimed that he had landed a new job. I was surprised he hadn't landed a sexually transmitted disease the way he seemed to put it about the village. He was now a supervisor, working shifts and the occasional weekend. He was still with the same company but had moved to a different department. He had taken to wearing a new set of blue overalls with the word 'Supervisor' stitched onto the back of them in neon yellow thread. I didn't hold back and suggested to Penelope that she had absolutely nothing to worry about when Rupert wore the new uniform. Under no circumstances would any woman fancy him wearing those overalls, as he looked like an outcast from the Village People.

Penelope had a plan. Unfortunately I remembered her last plan, which resulted in a full-on cat fight in Home Bargains. Such class. Her plan involved me taking a copy of Rupert's shift timetable and following him when he set off for work, to confirm that he was actually going where he said he was going. I suppose it wasn't as though I had anything better to do with my time except look after my children, animals, Matt and fit in my part-time job.

'Mission Infidelity' was due to begin that night. I was so excited … not. It was Saturday night and yet again Penelope was impinging on my time. Matt was beginning to think he was single father always in charge of the children and I could see his point. Rupert's shift was due to start at 7pm and I was to sit up the road and wait for him to pass me, then follow him to his destination. I took my satnav just in case I fell too far back and missed him make a turn – what I really wanted to do was go straight back home and crack open a beer. I had been sitting in the car since 5.30pm, which was Penelope's idea to guarantee I didn't miss him. There was no way I was going to miss a bloke with neon lettering across his back driving a black bubble car, was there?

As I set off on Mission Infidelity Matt was abandoned yet again with his arm around the dog, the children to put to bed and then a night of watching re-runs of *Fawlty Towers* until I returned. I did suggest maybe Penelope could keep him company but, after the death stare he gave me, I left the house immediately. I was dressed in dark clothing and wore a baseball cap, sunglasses and trainers – not at all conspicuous. I've no idea why I agreed to Penelope's request to wear this stupid attire because Rupert would recognise the car anyway, regardless of what I was wearing.

I had received strict instructions to return with evidence – any evidence. While I was sitting in the car waiting for Rupert, I saw Annie drive through the estate. At least I had evidence that it wasn't her that Rupert was meeting. Penelope would be pleased. I sent her a text to put her mind at ease. She went off on one with her reply, she was back to being the texter possessed!

How dare she drive through the estate, why can't she go all the way around on the main roads, she had written.

Annie had every right to drive through the estate. The roads were public and I'm sure she paid her tax and insurance. I didn't have time to respond to this outburst because at that very moment I'd spotted Rupert driving up the road in his bubble car. I'm not sure how he clambered into that car; it looked like his head was cranked to one side as he contorted himself to see out of the windscreen.

I set off after him in hot pursuit, well actually chugging along at twenty-five miles an hour. He drove for approximately fifteen minutes before pulling his car into the drive of a lovely, old thatched cottage. The cottage was surrounded by established trees, shrubs and beautiful brick archways with flowers clambering and entwined all around them. There was even a stream running through the front garden, complete with a little wooden bridge. Camilla would be miffed if she could see this now – there was loads of land attached to the property, something she could only dream of. This was my ideal home.

I imagined myself on the television programme *Through the Keyhole*.

'Well who lives in a house like this?' I muttered, complete with the silly accent.

That's the question Penelope would soon be asking Rupert. Actually I wanted to live in a house like this, it was magnificent.

Rupert uncurled himself from the car, stretched out his legs and arms and went to retrieve a beautiful bouquet of flowers from the boot. The front door of the cottage opened and Rupert disappeared inside. I couldn't quite make out who had opened the door, as I was currently hiding in one of the hedgerows with a thorny rose sticking in my backside and unable to move without letting out a squeal. I think it was safe to say there was only one type of 'shift work' Rupert would be participating in tonight.

I headed back to Penelope's, being careful not to get the house mixed up with Wendy's, convinced I had one of the thorns from the bush still stuck in my rear. When I arrived, I found Penelope pacing up and down her kitchen and shouting at Little Jonny for not completing his workbook quicker. In her agitated state she was clutching her mobile phone and showed me the messages she had sent to Rupert. He was lucky, she had only sent twenty-three messages so far! Goodness knows how many it would be by the morning. Rupert hadn't replied to any of them. I therefore had two choices; I could comfort Penelope by telling her that Rupert would be unable to reply because he was at work in a factory and probably didn't get a signal, or I could shatter her world further and tell her he was in the most gorgeous cottage you could ever imagine, about to start some overtime on his latest mistress who no doubt lived there. I did wonder what the heck he was doing turning up at the cottage in those shocking overalls. If that had been me I would have stopped off to change before I arrived to see the other woman. Not that I had any expertise in this area at all I should add.

I dived straight into the 'shattering her world further' option. This was selfish of me and I only took this option to avoid being sent out night after night to follow Rupert, while wearing this stupid disguise. Before I knew it Little Jonny had been bundled in the back of the car and we were driving towards the Shack. Her idea was to drop Little Jonny with Matt while I drove her to where Rupert was located. I sent Matt a quick text to warn him of the situation. I received a text back.

I would quite like my wife back, the Shack is going up for sale and when we move house make no friends and talk to no-one. He joked but there was a serious undertone.

Penelope was becoming a pain in the backside – a bit like the rose thorn which continued to stab me every time I sat down.

Matt opened the door of the Shack and Little Jonny clambered out of the car. The poor kid didn't even have his shoes on.

Matt looked into the back seat of the car.

'No Annabel?' he enquired.

Oh gosh, I had forgotten all about Annabel, which just went to prove I had been hanging around with her mother way too long. Penelope had also forgotten all about her daughter – not for the first time I might add. She was fast asleep, tucked up in bed at home. Matt shot me a stern look, took Penelope's house key from her and headed back there with all the children in tow. I had déjà vu when I glanced down at Little Jonny who was heading back home in his slippers. Like father, like son.

Mission Infidelity was now in its second hour and I'm sure Rupert would be looking forward to the second hour of his shift, no doubt hoping it was as rewarding as his first. I'm not sure what union he was with but I hoped he didn't plan on going more than four hours without a break. I drove back to the thatched cottage and pulled up outside. Penelope just stared open-mouthed.

'It's b-b-b-beautiful,' she stuttered.

I had the feeling that whoever owned this property would be beautiful too…

Penelope stomped up the gravel drive. She walked over the little bridge across the stream and rapped the lion's head knocker onto the door. The time was now 9.30pm and I was more than a little peeved that yet again it was a Saturday night and not a drop of alcohol had crossed my lips. This was starting to become the norm. I commented on the pretty clematis climbing up the front of the house and the roses tangled amongst them. Penelope shot me the death stare – which was a bit of a cheek, as I was the one giving up my evening tracking down her husband for her yet again.

The door of the cottage opened and both Penelope and I looked at each other in a state of shock – our jaws simultaneously hit the herringbone block doorstep. This was the first time in a long time that I genuinely didn't know what to do or say, which is most unusual for me. The woman stood before us was dressed in exactly the same cardigan, top, trousers and shoes as

Penelope. She was the spitting image of Penelope too. Her hair was the same, her complexion was the same, they were even the same height – they were like twins. She even had Penelope's mannerisms. Penelope and the other woman just stared at each other before the other woman broke the uncomfortable silence. Penelope and I digested her words, one at a time.

'He has done it again, hasn't he?'

I was a little confused and I was supposed to be the intelligent one, so Penelope didn't have a cat in hell's chance of figuring out what was going on. Every person has an unstable friend in their lives, yet here was I, stood with what looked like two unstable Penelopes. Why was I so unlucky?

The woman introduced herself as Charlotte and invited us into a magnificent period-style kitchen that looked like it was straight out of a *Country Living* magazine. I wanted to make an offer on this house there and then but surely the only thing on offer at this moment in time was Rupert's head – or maybe his whole body – on a silver platter.

Charlotte offered us a cup of tea and watched us curiously while we scanned the area looking for Rupert. I didn't see him in person but noticed a photograph on the wall of a young Rupert with his arms around Charlotte.

'Where the hell is Rupert?' Penelope enquired.

'He left about half an hour ago to start his shift. He has just started a new job,' Charlotte replied.

My phone beeped and I glanced down to see a text from Matt.

What's going on? Rupert's turned up back here and is asking why I am looking after the kids in his house and wants to know where Penelope is. He's got his shifts mixed up and he's not supposed to be working this weekend.

Jesus, how the hell was I going to explain what we had discovered in only a hundred and sixty characters?

Play dumb again, just say we are out for drink and we will be back soon.

I didn't have a clue if we would be back soon. I didn't have a clue what was going on, full stop.

It was strange being in the same room as two Penelopes dressed in the same clothes. I did think of suggesting that Charlotte could buy Wendy's house and then they could have matching houses and matching clothes but share the same Rupert. At least then he would feel right at home in either house and save a few quid on petrol too – Wendy only lived down the road.

Penelope, who had been staring into her tea cup, finally spoke again, directing her question at Charlotte.

'What do you mean he has done it again?'

'Rupert has had an affair again,' replied Charlotte, coolly.

'Well obviously – with you,' snapped Penelope. 'He can't have an affair with me, I'm his wife,' she continued.

OH MY GOSH…

It hit me before it hit Penelope – further evidence that I was the intelligent one. Was Rupert actually married to both of these women?

Penelope was slow on the uptake and hadn't quite grasped that she was in a room with Rupert's other wife. This was the most interesting Saturday night without alcohol I had had in a long while. I immediately renamed this assignment to 'Mission Bigamy'.

I couldn't keep the fact that they were wearing the same clothes to myself a moment longer. If I was in the same room as someone wearing an identical top I would be mortified, never mind the fact they also had matching cardigans, trousers and shoes. I tried to catch a glimpse of their socks but this was probably the least of their worries. So before I could stop it, the obvious question popped out of my mouth.

'Do you both realise you are wearing the same clothes?'

They should have been grateful that I didn't say, 'Do you both realise, you're dressed identical, look exactly the same and are sleeping with the same man.'

Penelope was definitely getting the worse deal out of the two of them as this house was beautiful and hers, apart from being an analogue of Wendy Barthorpe's house, was just another house on the estate.

Charlotte began her story. She wasn't angry; in fact she was very pleasant coming face to face with herself. I wasn't sure if I should leave because technically this was nothing to do with me but I was Makepeace – I had found Penelope mark two and I wanted the bloody gossip.

Charlotte stated that Rupert had had numerous affairs over the years and this wasn't the first time the 'other woman' had knocked on the door. I wasn't sure yet which one of them was the 'other woman' and didn't like to ask for clarification at this moment, so I thought it best to keep quiet.

Charlotte continued by telling us that every time Rupert had bought his mistress a present he would buy her the same, whether it was clothes, shoes, handbags or perfumes. There was a method to his madness – if he bought them both the same things he could never trip himself up by forgetting what he had got each of them. At this point, both Penelope and Charlotte confirmed that Rupert had bought them the same outfits and presents for Christmas.

I was amazed how calculating Rupert was. I would have never thought of that but I suppose I'm not married to two people. Christmas must cost Rupert a fortune, unless he sought out the 'buy one get one free' offers for gifts. I wondered how he would get away with having two families on Christmas Day but that's where his shift work could always be used as a cover story.

It transpired that Rupert had lived with Charlotte for over fifteen years but they were never married or able to have children. Charlotte wasn't shocked that Penelope had two children with Rupert. I was shocked that Penelope actually remembered she had TWO children as she was always forgetting about Annabel. This was a psychologist's dream, what went on in Rupert's head? He was living a double life with two different women who looked the same – living only fifteen minutes apart – and then continued to be unfaithful to both of them.

What amused me most about this situation was Rupert wearing the neon lettered boilersuit out of choice rather than necessity. He didn't really have a shift job, goodness knows where he was earning his money to support and sustain two separate families and lifestyles. The boilersuit was his cover; why in God's name did he not pretend he was a business man so he could swagger around in a fashionable suit impressing the ladies? He could then invent the odd business trip so he had legitimate cover for nights away from either – or both – of them!

Although I suppose he didn't need to reel in any more women, he had more than his fair share in the same postcode area. I felt sorry for Penelope, she looked physically battered. It was one thing forgiving your husband for having an affair with your best friend but how on earth do you get over him leading a double life for fifteen years and living with another woman who looks exactly like you?

It was getting late when I began to drive Penelope back to her normal house in the village. Penelope could probably picture herself as the lady of the manor but that was Charlotte's house

– left to her by her late mother – so there was no way Penelope would get her hands on it, even if she chose to divorce Rupert.

What do you say in a situation like this? There was absolutely nothing I could say. The Verve's 'Lucky Man' was playing out on the car radio so I switched it off quickly. Rupert had been a lucky man up to this point but I assumed his luck had just run out. I drove Penelope home in silence. She had trumped all my dramas with Imogen and Frisky Pensioner. It was all about her and she was welcome to it. Little Jonny no longer wanting to become a palaeontologist and deciding he wanted to work in McDonald's was the least of her worries.

I dropped Penelope at home. It was a bit of come-down compared to the cottage we had just left behind. Rupert opened the door and greeted us.

'Where have you pair been?'

I thought I'd leave Penelope to explain that one. I picked up Matt and our kids and drove home to the Shack. At least Matt didn't wear a boilersuit – he'd look like an inmate from the local funny-farm if he did.

CHAPTER 10

October

October was the month Rupert disappeared from the village for two whole weeks – not by choice but on Penelope's insistence. If it was down to me Rupert would have disappeared on a permanent basis – under the bloody patio. Luckily for him he wasn't married to me, thank God. Penelope sent him off to rehab to help him understand and control his addiction. I wasn't sure if it was the addiction to the boilersuit fashion disaster, sex or lying – I didn't like to ask. Penelope swore me to secrecy. That wasn't difficult; who was I going to tell? I couldn't believe she even wanted to save the marriage. Had it really been a marriage when Rupert had been sharing her with another woman for the past fifteen years? Penelope couldn't even spend a weekend with Rupert at the best of times but she decided they should stay together for the sake of the kids. She thought the children deserved a father figure that they could look up to but since they didn't have one of those, Rupert would have to do.

While Rupert was out of the picture for two weeks, I was stuck with Penelope. It was as though she had suddenly become an incapable human being and had regressed back to a child. She might as well have moved into the Shack as she was there more than Matt was. He was at the end of his tether and fed up with the sight of her and became a part-time alcoholic, venturing to the pub with the dog and a newspaper most evenings for company. I suggested he could join Rupert in rehab if he was going to carry on in that manner.

He thought he was having it tough but being stuck with Penelope twenty-four hours a day was more than torture – that would turn anyone to drink. She was driving herself insane trying to imagine what Rupert was up to every minute of the day. Paddy Power's odds suggested Rupert would have copped off with his counsellor by now and was probably living it up while away from his wives – but I didn't like to comment.

The weekend of the mountain climb was fast approaching. I could hardly contain my excitement; a weekend away with Penelope, just the two of us. Yippee! It was times like these when I pondered how bad I must have been in a past life. Matt was landed with the school run for the very first time ever as Penelope and I were due to head off on the Friday afternoon, before school finished.

The morning of the expedition, the scene in the playground was unbelievable – there were flags, good luck banners and lots of cheers. One of the teachers had even made us a 'Good Luck' cake – thankfully there was no Kendal Mint in sight! I thought it was a little over the top – wishing me luck for spending a weekend away with Penelope – but soon realised it was actually to do with the climb. She lapped up the attention while I, on the other hand, was a little bit embarrassed. We weren't climbing Everest, just some overgrown hill in Cumbria.

Camilla handed Penelope a good luck gift – a new ridiculous fur hat for her head. That woman certainly liked making Penelope look stupid. On the plus side, Penelope appeared to have lost the 'puppy fighting' jodhpurs for the weekend. Imogen looked over at all the kerfuffle in the playground, wandered over to me and handed me a small gift bag.

She gave me a wink and whispered, 'you may need this' before walking off.

I glanced into the bag to find a pill bottle with 'Valium' written in hand on the label, a small bottle of whisky and a card. I opened the card and read the message.

'To dull the pain,' it said, followed by a smiley-face symbol.

I quickly caught Imogen's eye as she left the playground and winked back in her direction. It had been a while since we'd spoken and I really appreciated the gesture.

Penelope and I drove back to her house to load up the car before we set off on our long journey. I waited patiently in the car for her to reappear with her overnight bag. I had to do a double-take in my mirror when she appeared with numerous bags; it looked more like she was moving house.

'What's in this bag?' I enquired.

She reeled off a list.

'My denim jacket, a lightweight rain coat, a fleece, a mountain coat, a heavyweight raincoat and my puffa jacket.'

I was no Carol Vorderman but that added up to six coats. We were due to be away for less than forty-eight hours and the weather forecast for once in Cumbria was actually quite sunny. I would look forward to her swapping her coat every eight hours.

'What's in this bag then?' I continued.

'My shoes.'

'How many bloody shoes do you need?'

This bag contained flip-flops, Converse, walking boots, a normal pair of shoes, slippers and Wellington boots. All in all she was taking six pairs of footwear. When was she going to have time to wear all these? Did she intend taking them all up the mountain?

'Why in God's name do you have flip-flops?' I quizzed.

Penelope enlightened me; apparently her feet swelled up at night and became really sweaty so the only footwear she would be comfortable in was the flip-flops. So why take the slippers, what was the point in that? The next bag was full to the brim of makeup. Then there was another bag of food, snacks and the boxes of Kendal Mint Cake. Finally there was the rucksack, which contained her climbing clothes and night stuff.

'Have you got your toothbrush?' I added sarcastically.

The panic-stricken look on her face suggested the answer to that was 'No' as she rushed back into her bathroom to retrieve it. I placed my one small bag that mainly consisted of the Valium and whisky that Imogen had given me into the boot of the car.

After taking thirty minutes to load Penelope's bags, we were finally on our way. You would think we were royalty as the streets were lined with her neighbours waving us off. I'm sure they were waving Penelope off hoping for her non-return.

We had only travelled three miles up the road when Penelope needed to stop for the toilet, have a fag break and to touch up her lipstick. I consulted my parent handbook and suggested she should have gone to the toilet before we set off. I gave her a sarcastic 'tut' and shook my head in disbelief. After waiting ten minutes for her to finish her fag she finally got back into the car reeking of smoke. I just knew this was going to be the longest forty-eight hours of my life filled with fag breaks, footwear alterations and numerous coat changes. Penelope took a CD from one of her many bags and she slipped it into the player.

I knew her fashion sense was a throwback to the eighties, in fact it was actually a very brave look, but I hadn't realised her music taste was no better than mine. Out of the car speakers blurted The Weather Girls. I was only aware of one of their songs. Come to think of it, it was probably their only song. The temperature was definitely rising in the car and I was beginning to feel agitated and we were only five miles from home.

I pride myself on being able to multi-task but there was no way I could listen to this and the details of Little Jonny's latest career choice while I was trying to concentrate on driving. Without saying a word, I pressed the eject button and took control.

I turned to Penelope and in the words of the song I sang 'Have I got news for you.'

I started how I meant to go on this weekend.

'My car, I'm driving, we are listening to the radio.'

It was going to be torture enough without any added pain. It was a long journey – a bloody long journey.

Penelope waffled on about how great Camilla was.

I wanted to add, 'Yes Penelope, such a good friend that she knows your husband much better than you think,' but I didn't.

Penelope carried on talking about their new celebrity clients and how much money Camilla was raking in at her saddlery business. She couldn't be raking it in that much as she still had no land.

'Pay rise for you then Penelope, managing director next!' I suggested. 'Just think of all those new coats you can buy.'

I could see the cogs turning over in Penelope's mind as she clearly hadn't been offered a pay rise and no doubt Camilla would keep all the profits for herself. Well I suppose she would try – if the farrier managed to secure half her business in the divorce settlement, Penelope may be out of a job. I guess Camilla would then become an ex-mate and Penelope would get back to slating her. She had given up a job working for herself, with time off during school holidays, to be Camilla's cleaner for the minimum wage. I know which one I would have chosen.

The evening was closing in and the sky was beginning to darken and after numerous toilet stops and fag breaks we made a visit to the nearest McDonald's. Penelope managed to shovel two burgers down in less than four minutes. I needed to consult the *Guinness Book of Records* for burger shovelling because I was gobsmacked how quickly she made them disappear. As we finally approached the village where our hotel was located, I was tired, fed up and couldn't believe I was wishing it was Monday morning already and I was back in the playground.

The satnav took us to the road where the hotel was supposed to be. We passed some magnificent houses situated along the riverbank, quaint little shops and ice-cream parlours. Luxurious hotels complete with swimming pools, spas and cinema rooms. I couldn't wait to arrive and head off for a quick relaxing swim and a small tipple, before climbing into bed in preparation for our long day ahead.

I drove up and down the road umpteen times but couldn't locate the hotel. Penelope double-checked the address on her confirmation and declared that we were definitely on the right road. I handed her my mobile phone and suggested she rang the hotel to get the exact location. The telephone was on loud-speaker as Penelope dialled the number. The phone clicked and a very unpleasant bloke answered.

'Yes? What do you want?'

I raised my eyebrows and stared hard at Penelope. Surely she had dialled the wrong number. Penelope spoke and asked if she had called 'The Yates Hotel'.

I was hoping the irritable man would confirm it was the wrong number and I could sigh with relief. No such luck – he verified we had called the right number and we needed to head another mile up the road. He told us to be quick too, as he wanted to close up for the night.

When we arrived I couldn't prevent the words, 'You seriously have to be joking,' from leaving my lips.

'We have passed some fabulous-looking hotels and you have booked us into a dive. How much has this dump cost?'

The look of horror on Penelope's face said it all.

'It cost a thirty pounds a night,' she replied.

'No shit, Sherlock … no bloody wonder. They need to pay me to stay here.'

I was a little angry to say the least, after driving for hours and ending up at what looked like a rundown youth hostel or 'halfway house' for those recently released from prison. Even the hotel sign was lopsided and numerous light bulbs were out. There was no swimming pool, telly, bar or Wi-Fi. Even ten quid a night for this place was steep. I reluctantly parked the car, climbed out and headed to the door of the hotel. It creaked and jammed against the floor so I gave it a shove with my shoulder, dislodging a massive spider which fell down and landed on Penelope's shoulder. Thank God I had Imogen's Valium and whisky tucked away. I had a feeling I was going to need a lot of help to survive this weekend.

We looked around and couldn't see anyone. There were lots of chairs covered in cobwebs and antique tables draped in lace tablecloths. In front of us there was a hatch with a bell and a rope. Stuck to the wall adjacent to the bell was a scribbled note, telling us to ring the proprietor again when we arrived. I was willing to lose my thirty pounds a night and leave this dump there and then. I was willing to find a vacancy at one of those lovely hotels down the road, crack open a bottle of champagne and pay a hundred pounds per night if I had to. Penelope was anything but willing. In her words she couldn't afford to lose her money.

I felt like saying, 'OK, your choice, I'll meet you tomorrow' and leaving her to enjoy her couple of nights in the hotel from hell.

Before I could decide whether to pay Penelope not to stay, she rang the bell. No sooner had her hand left the rope when the hatch opened and a miserable-looking bald man stood in front of us.

'What do you want?' he demanded, in a very unwelcoming tone.

He was a funny-looking thing – he reminded me of the farrier, small and stumpy – and he was staring at us in a funny way which I eventually deduced was because he had a glass eye. Penelope gave our names and he checked his guest list, which didn't take him long as ours were the only names on it.

'I'll show you to your room,' he muttered.

'Will someone help with our bags?' Penelope enquired.

He looked at her as though she had said something in another language.

'No, you will have to take your own,' he barked.

Watching Penelope struggle with her numerous bags up three winding flights of stairs to a room situated right at the top of the hotel was the only time I'd smiled to myself in the last few hours. The man stopped outside our room, handed us a key and left us standing there without saying a word.

We opened the door and peered in, not knowing what to expect. The swirly carpet was more dated than the carpet back at the Shack and the walls were covered in horrible beige patterned wallpaper that made the room look completely dull. There were no tea-making facilities or telephone in the room. In the corner was a free-standing wardrobe with only one door. There was no way that would fit any of my stuff in, let alone the contents of Penelope's multitude of bags. We decided to keep our belongings at the sides of the bed and leave them packed, just in case we needed to make a quick getaway.

Thankfully there were two beds in the room; both with grubby grey-coloured sheets and ghastly lemon floral-patterned duvet covers. On the back wall there was a small window but it was too high to look through. I had had high hopes for a room with a view but I couldn't even reach the window, never mind see through it. I was damn certain Rupert's room in rehab would be more comfortable than this. There was basic but I was certain that this was less opulent than the worst cell in the Bangkok Hilton. On reflection, Rupert's bill would be in excess of a hundred and fifty quid per night – I should have checked myself into rehab for my addiction to nutters.

The room was cold and the sheets were damp but I didn't dare ponder too much on why they were damp. There was a small hole in the door so I cracked a joke that if the bloke was spying on us, he wouldn't get to see much with his glass eye. Penelope was not amused.

Penelope blankly refused to sleep on the bed by the door just in case. In case of what? She had a bloody cheek, especially since she was the one who had selected such a luxurious hotel. I wedged one of Penelope's many shoes by the door and placed another one on the small table next to my bed.

'Why've you put that there?' queried Penelope.

'You never know. I might need to bludgeon someone to death in the middle of the night – and on this occasion I don't mean you, Penelope.'

This hotel was more risky than climbing the mountain, I would be lucky to make it home alive. I sent Fay a quick text which read, *Make room for those Five Star records, they may be yours by Monday. I've left them to you in my will, in case I die!*

Penelope took out a cigarette, lit it and took a drag that was so long you would have been forgiven for assuming it was her last ever. I don't smoke but I did consider that maybe this was a good time to start. Almost immediately a loud siren rang through the room. The voice of the one-eyed hotelier blared out over the Tannoy.

'Extinguish your cigarette immediately, no smoking is allowed in the deluxe rooms.'

Surely that couldn't mean us, could it? There was nothing deluxe about this room? I scanned the room quickly looking for a hidden camera but couldn't find one. There was only one thing for it – the whisky – but we didn't have any glasses. If I had to sleep closest to the door with one eye open, Penelope could go and locate some glasses. I needed a drink – fast.

She wouldn't go alone so we ventured down the winding stairs together. From the deadly silence that surrounded us we concluded we were the only residents. We didn't dare to speak. Each stair creaked and groaned as we descended. Reluctantly, we headed back to the hatch and rang the bell. It was like déjà vu when the hatch swung open again and the one-eyed man appeared.

'What do you want?'

'Can we have a couple of glasses please?' we asked politely.

He handed over two dusty beakers and demanded a fifty pence deposit for each of them. I wasn't going to argue as I actually did value my life and for the first time ever I was glad Penelope was by my side. We quickly hurried back to our room, piled all the bags up against the door and lay down on our damp beds. We started to relax after a few drinks and eventually climbed into bed. Our alarms were set – the plan was to venture out bright and early in the morning to climb the mountain, then we could hit the town the following night.

I must have seen every hour of the night, there was no need to even set an alarm clock. I lay in bed frightened and rigid as a shadow constantly appeared to be moving back and forth under the door. I kept hearing what sounded like a shuffling of feet and my mind ran into overdrive wondering if the bloke that owned this place was a distant relative of Frisky Pensioner. I slept holding Penelope's boot and that isn't a euphemism – I did actually clutch her boot all night.

I could still see darkness through the tiny window as I finally dozed off around 5.30am. Penelope, on the other hand, had slept soundly – very bloody soundly – snoring her way through the night. Each time she snored, her fringe blew up in the air and created a shadow on the ceiling which freaked me out.

When I finally woke around 7.30am, I glanced over at sleeping beauty and bolted upright. Where was Penelope and who was the bloke in the bed next to me? My heart was racing as I frantically tried to establish what had happened to her, surely I hadn't drunk that much whisky? The tremendous beard and moustache combination had definitely reached its peak as this bloke looked like a yeti. On a closer inspection I couldn't believe my eyes, it was actually Penelope. She had facial hair. She stirred then woke up and spotted me staring intently at her face.

She grabbed and stroked her beard like it was the norm and whimpered, 'It doesn't matter how regularly I wax my moustache, it still grows extremely fast.'

No shit, Sherlock, I could plait that facial hair!

After a shower – and shave for Penelope – we laced up our boots, packed our rucksacks and went in search of the big hill to climb.

We escaped out of the hotel without breakfast and managed to avoid being spotted. The car was still parked outside with all four tyres so that was another bonus. My car was the only one in the car park and on the pavement next to the car we stepped over a bra and a sock. It would just be my luck if a woman with a bare foot and her boobs hanging by her knees came hopping towards me. She would fit in well with such a classy joint.

Penelope had opted for an eighties look to climb the hill. She was wearing her hair in bunches (and she had the nerve to mention I was too old to wear my hair in a side pony!) and perched on top of her bunches she wore a baseball cap switched round the wrong way, like some Toni Basil wannabe. The bargain basement tight-top had made a reappearance along with the hot pants. This time the outfit was accessorised with bright pink legwarmers. There was no way she was dressed to climb a mountain, she looked more like she was about to attend a reunion of the Fame Appreciation Society.

The lack of donkeys and Sherpas for hire in the area meant Penelope had to make the heart-wrenching decision to leave all her coats at the hotel – there was no way I was lugging any of them around with me all day. The weather was sunny and even though the temperature would be cooler at the summit there was no need to take a coat. I had one rucksack packed with lunch, water, tissues and wet wipes. Penelope had the same, plus some Kendal Mint Cake and the flag.

That was it, we were off! We had between three and four hours of walking to the summit ahead of us, plus approximately the same time to venture back down. So all in all I could look forward to a minimum of six hours' riveting conversation. Matt had provided me with a game he had devised himself to help relieve the boredom. This was a list of words that he was certain Penelope would bring up in conversation over the next few hours. Every time she said one of these words I had to cross it off the list. There was no winner in the game, Matt was just curious how many he would get right.

As we were at the foot of the mountain looking up at the summit, Penelope said, 'Little Jonny would have loved to climb with us.'

Those were the first words in Matt's game – 'Little Jonny' – immediately ticked off. I smiled to myself. If nothing else, Matt's word game would be a source of amusement for me for the next few hours. We headed up a steep slope to start with. Penelope raced off but I held back and went a little slower, as I thought it was better to pace myself and not burn myself out right at the start of the journey. I was absorbing the breathtaking scenery all around me, it was absolutely stunning.

Penelope had attracted a hanger on – an old bloke with a walking stick and was chatting to him a little further on in front. I was praying he wouldn't go into cardiac arrest at the sight of her in those hot pants because I was certainly not giving an old bloke mouth to mouth. I think he thought he had already died and gone to heaven as Penelope took him under her wings – her bingo wings to be precise.

They shouted for me to hurry up but I was certainly in no hurry. I was enjoying lagging behind, ambling along at my own steady pace in the sun. My conversation with me was a lot more entertaining than that up front, I'm sure. For once Penelope must have been listening – no doubt to a conversation which revolved around hearing aids, piles, bed-pans and Murray Mints – because if she'd started with the usual monologue, the old codger would have chucked himself over the side by now.

I noticed they were quite a way in front but they had perched down on a rock. I tried to walk slower, assuming they had decided to wait for me but I didn't mind walking by myself, I preferred it. We were only twenty-five minutes into the ascent and Penelope was already tucking into her packed lunch. She offered a limp tuna sandwich to the old bloke – he must have thought he'd won the lottery. That would be a lovely combination for Penelope – fag breath mixed in with fish breath – I bet the old bloke couldn't believe his luck.

'How slow are you?' Penelope shouted back at me as I approached them both.

I hadn't realised it was a race. Penelope's t-shirt was sodden with sweat. Her face was so red and flustered, she looked like a walking beetroot. She announced that she was hot and the old bloke looked her up and down – he thought she was hot too. I suggested to Penelope she should remove her legwarmers to cool her down a little. Once the legwarmers came off the old bloke made his excuses and set off on his own again. I had never seen a bloke move so fast, especially after a woman revealed part of her body. He moved so quickly you would have thought they had just announced a free bar at the British Legion – he was up off the rock and gone. The rock can't have been doing his piles any good anyway! I suggested to Penelope that maybe she should put the legwarmers back on before she frightened any other fellow climbers away.

As a result of the old bloke's rapid departure, I was now stuck with Penelope for the remainder of the climb. Why hadn't I just kept my mouth shut about the legwarmers? He could have kept her company and I could have carried on alone, enjoying the scenery.

After Penelope's initial energetic spurt she was beginning to slow down – any slower and she would be rolling backwards down the hillside and starting again from the bottom. Then she informed me that the lovely fishy sandwich – which she swilled down with too much water – had made her feel a little sick. I had already encountered Penelope's and Rupert's vomit first-hand and there was no way I was holding her pigtails back while she threw that lot up. I suggested a twenty-minute rest so she could get some colour back in her cheeks.

We encountered numerous people on the mountainside, all different backgrounds and walks of life brought together with the common goal of reaching the summit. Penelope was the only one dressed like a one-woman tribute to the eighties, so we stuck out like a sore thumb. Even on the side of a mountain it was always about her. Penelope's conversation turned to Imogen. I glanced down at Matt's list – that was another word ticked off. Matt knew Penelope too well, which was a little bit of a worry.

As it was approaching November, Penelope decided she was going to hold a bonfire party at her house. She was going to invite Little Jonny's classmates – all except Miles that is, Imogen's son. I wasn't sure why you would invite the whole class and leave just one child out, it was cruel. How would that child feel when all his classmates were off to Little Jonny's and he realised he was the only one not invited? Penelope's logic was that she didn't get on with the mother but I didn't understand that logic – a child is a child – so I made a mental note that my children were not going to attend. I was not having any part in child mental cruelty. Penelope seemed to take great pleasure in annoying Imogen by leaving Miles off the guest list. She even seemed a little excited by her plan. If she carried on with this enthusiastic cruelty I would forget my bus theory and have her Fed-Ex'd off the mountainside and catapulted to another planet.

We were now at the halfway point and the climb was beginning to get steep. My legs were beginning to tire but not as much as my brain. Moan, moan, moan – that was all Penelope had done up to this point and that's all that she did after this point. Fortunately for me I didn't hear anything else. I couldn't take any more so I powered my legs and took off at speed on the second part of the climb, leaving her lagging behind wiping her brow with her lurid legwarmers. I glanced back on a couple of occasions to make sure she hadn't fallen over the mountainside. Alas no, she was still with me, more's the pity.

I could see the summit and the air was beginning to cool down a little. Other climbers were on their way down, chattering excitedly, thrilled that they had reached the top. They looked like they were having a ball. I wanted to join their gang – I didn't have an adrenalin rush like these climbers, I had an allergy, an allergy to Penelope.

One last step on my weary legs and I had finally done it. I stood at the summit, looking at the misty haze all around me. I felt delighted, I felt ecstatic. By some miracle I managed to get a phone signal so I phoned home to tell them my news. I could hear squeals of delight from my children as Matt relayed the news of my achievement. All the words in Matt's game had been ticked off – all except one final phrase.

I sat down not far from the summit, where I could observe Penelope approaching.

'Why didn't you wait for me,' she panted.

That was it, the list was complete. She had muttered the final words right on cue. I took Matt's list out of my pocket and proudly put the final tick on the sheet, quietly cheering to myself.

We took photographs of each other on the summit and I scooped up a couple of stones from the mountain as souvenirs for the kids. There were no sewing kits or shampoo to pinch from the hotel – only the bra and sock from the car park and they looked more like Penelope's size than mine – so I needed to take something back. After a short rest we started our descent.

The journey down was equally painful but somehow we managed it in half the time. I was looking forward to a nice cool beer and putting my feet up in a beer garden once we had reached the bottom. The pub was in sight and so was the old bloke that had latched on to Penelope at the start of the day. The free beer offer at the British Legion must have finished and he was now taking advantage of the Happy Hour at the pub. He was letching over some young floozy, without a legwarmer in sight. He was definitely high on life – or something stronger – especially if he had managed to beat us two athletes to the bottom.

My legs ached, my arms ached and muscles I didn't even know I had ached. Even though we were still booked in at the hotel from hell I couldn't face another night in that place, especially with Penelope. I had done what I had agreed to do and reached the summit with Penelope but her verbal attack and assassination of my character on one of our last walks had hurt me deeply. I wasn't gaining any joy from this unhealthy relationship. It was time to move on. We rescued our stuff from the hotel and packed up the car.

Penelope turned to me and said, 'Shall we run a marathon next?'

That mountain air must have affected my hearing, I'm sure I heard Penelope suggest we run a marathon! It appeared she was still in the middle of her mid-life crisis. Fay's words of wisdom flashed through my mind.

'Learn to say no. Just learn to say no!'

'I'll have to think about that one, Penelope,' I replied as I started up the car engine for the long journey home.

CHAPTER 11

November

Rupert was out of rehab and had ditched his horrendous blue overalls for a more sophisticated suit. He had landed himself a training management position at the store where Penelope had previously had a scrap in the cat litter aisles with his ex-mistress. Penelope had let Rupert back into the family home to save face. She couldn't possibly have any of the Playground Mafia finding out he had been leading a double life for the last fifteen years. Imagine the humiliation that would cause her.

Rupert reckoned he had turned over a new leaf and had seen the error of his ways. Only time would tell, I suppose. I bet Penelope had 'Lucky Man' on repeat play on the stereo in their house. He had more lives than a bloody cat – in fact he had more lives than every cat put together.

Around the same time, Penelope seemed to disappear from my life and I wasn't upset by this at all – in fact I was slightly relieved. It occurred to me that in the last eight months Penelope had learnt nothing about me except that my kids attended the same school as hers.

I stood by myself in the playground and observed the latest fallings-out and playground politics that blighted the lives of us playground mothers every day. Matt and I finally had Saturday nights back to ourselves and he had removed the Kensingtons' coat pegs from our cloakroom.

November was now upon us and I smiled to myself as I flipped the kitchen calendar over to reveal the month ahead.

One date on the calendar had me smiling no more. On the first Saturday night, written in bright red, was the word 'Penelope's'. She had invited us round for a meal. She was in the habit of booking the next get-together before the previous one had even ended. I think she liked to have something to look forward to.

I wasn't sure if she still expected us to go as I had barely seen her since the mountain climb. I decided to try Matt's favourite pastime and play dumb, I wasn't going to mention it or contact her. If the invitation was still open I'm sure she would be in touch at some point in the week.

Matt and I were still in the dark on Saturday morning because Penelope hadn't yet been in touch. As he badgered me to find out what was happening – probably so he knew whether he could watch *Match of the Day* or not – my phone beeped and the dreaded text arrived.

Are you still OK for tonight, about 7 o'clock?

Damn, there was no getting out of it now. Matt agreed to go one last time – at least we would get a free feed, if nothing else.

We all walked over to the Kensington house in the early evening, swigging a couple of cans of beer as we went for Dutch courage. The children weren't thrilled about coming with us but we promised them this would be the last time. I thought about taking my slippers but decided we wouldn't be staying that long, much to Matt's delight. Once we arrived the children ran off to play except Daisy who was fast asleep in the pram; placing a blanket over her we left her in the hallway to sleep. Penelope took our coats and directed us into the living area. The room resembled a florist shop with bouquets of flowers scattered all around the room. Penelope needn't have bothered with the fresh flower look on our account. It was way over the top. On the coffee table there were various cards.

Even though the heating was blasting out at tropical temperatures the atmosphere seemed a little frosty. While Penelope went into the kitchen to fix us some drinks, I picked up one of the cards.

It read 'Happy Anniversary Rupert and Penelope'.

I showed the card to Matt.

'Please tell me they haven't invited us around for a meal on their wedding anniversary?'

Matt shrugged his shoulders as Penelope walked back into the room and Rupert appeared from the conservatory. It was the first time we had seen Rupert since he had been released from rehab and he looked subdued, as well as a little thinner. The conversation was a bit awkward to say the least. I mean what were you supposed to say to him?

'Hi Rupert, what happened to the woman that lived in the beautiful cottage?'

No, that wouldn't go down too well.

I could try, 'You are one lucky man to still have a home and your children.'

I wasn't sure if he was still lucky to have Penelope or not. Rupert saved us the embarrassment and thanked us for coming and for supporting Penelope over the last eight months. To be honest we hadn't had much choice in the matter, she had just dumped herself on my family and our Saturday nights.

He continued his impromptu speech.

'Today is the first day of the rest of my life.'

Then he raised his glass for a toast.

'Here's to my family and Happy Anniversary to my beautiful wife.'

Matt and I exchanged glances.

'It *is* their bloody anniversary,' he mouthed at me.

So there we were stuck with a couple on their anniversary who, by the looks of it, didn't want to be stuck with each other. I thought it was very strange to invite another couple round to share a meal on your anniversary. I thought it was even stranger that Penelope hadn't thought to mention it was their anniversary. But I suppose if she had we might not have gone and then she would have had to spend time with Rupert all by herself.

Penelope had confiscated all devices from Rupert until he could be trusted. He had no mobile phone, iPod, iPad or Xbox – nothing at all. He had even deleted his profile from the dating website. He wasn't allowed to leave the house without Penelope and she had taken it upon herself to drop him off and pick him up from work every day. There was no way Rupert would be given an opportunity to stray in the near future.

'Happy Anniversary,' I offered, as we sat down at the table to start our meal.

I wasn't entirely sure what was happy about it as they both looked as miserable as sin.

Penelope had cooked a chilli. It was bland to say the least and the only flavour came from the lumpy, burnt bits. The garlic bread wasn't much better. It could only really be described as bread as it seemed to be lacking a certain key ingredient – garlic – and it was stale. There was only thing for it – sink a few more beers to wash the taste away.

While we were away up the mountain, Penelope had been delighted to inform me that Little Jonny was doing rather well at school. He had been chosen to attend another school for one day a week. Apparently, he was now deemed to be gifted and talented – I hoped for his sake that he didn't share his father's more dubious 'talents'. Penelope was gushing with pride when she told me he was the obvious choice from the class, no other child came close to his intelligence level.

I decided to warm up the frosty atmosphere by asking Penelope how Little Jonny was getting on with these 'gifted and talented' days. I wasn't remotely interested but I knew Penelope would relish this conversation and hopefully she and Rupert would be reminded of what beautiful children they had made together. I had consumed enough alcohol to numb the pain of the impending 'Little Jonny' conversation.

Almost immediately her face turned crimson. Rupert coughed and then spoke.

'They made a mistake.'

'Made a mistake about what?' I replied.

'There are two Jonnys in the class and the letter was meant for the other one, they gave it to us by mistake.'

I bet Penelope was livid. Never mind coughing, I nearly choked with laughter.

I turned to Penelope and said sarcastically, 'Surely not? You were so adamant that no-one even came close to Little Jonny's intelligence levels the other week. There's only one thing for it then, Penelope, you need a tutor. You can't possibly have another child beating Little Jonny in class.'

Recently Little Jonny had started to become unbearable at school, making the other children's lives hell. It was understandable given that his home life was far from stable. He had started to throw his weight around at school. At this present time he was the talk of the Playground Mafia.

He was always starting fights and calling names, before putting on his 'It's not me, Miss' sweet face and of course Penelope couldn't see any wrong in him.

He was her golden boy. There were two boys in particular that Little Jonny made fun of – one was our Samuel and the other was a boy called Jacob. Both boys struggled at school and were dyslexic. Little Jonny knew they were different and singled both of them out, preying on who he thought were the weaker boys in order to make himself feel more important. Little Jonny was losing friends fast. Even Josie, whose son was in the same class, was having difficulties with Little Jonny and everyone was encouraging their children to stay away from him.

Penelope wanted to make her children popular. Little Jonny had different friends back to his house almost every night of the week for tea. Of course, when I say friends I mean that in the loosest sense of the word. These were children whose parents welcomed the opportunity to offload their offspring for a few hours after school and save a few quid while they were fed elsewhere.

The constant flow of children through the Kensington house wasn't for the sake of the children. It was to ensure they had someone to play with and didn't bother Penelope. She was probably rifling through their book bags to find their reading levels while checking the labels on their coats to see if they were worth listing on eBay. The thing that amused me the most was that even though she had all these children playing around her house it was very rare anyone ever returned the favour.

Matt decided to change the subject quickly with a corker of a question.

'Have you done anything nice for your anniversary?'

I rolled my eyes at him.

'Obviously not as we are here for dinner.'

I didn't think it was good time to go over how happy Rupert and Penelope had been for the last fifteen years, as he had been living his double life for the majority of that time. I also thought it was best not to remind Rupert he could be curled up with Charlotte now in a beautiful cottage instead of being with us on his anniversary, eating burnt chilli and un-garlicky garlic bread.

Rupert changed the subject to holidays.

'Are you going anywhere nice next year on holiday?'

'Yes, we are off to our other house in the sun,' I replied.

As soon as the words left my mouth I wanted to rewind thirty seconds. There was deadly silence as our hosts swapped puzzled glances.

'What other house in the sun?' Rupert enquired.

'We have owned another property in southern Spain for the last ten years,' I answered. 'So we will be off there again for our holidays as usual.'

'You own another property and you've never thought to mention it?' exclaimed a very jealous but curious Penelope.

You could see she wasn't happy about the fact I had never mentioned it but to be perfectly honest, why would I? What business was it of anyone else? All our close friends knew we owned a second home. It wasn't as though I was trying to hide the fact; it was just nobody else's business.

This conversation usually goes two ways. The first way being that we rapidly lose friends as they become jealous and fall out with us, claiming we've got too big for our boots. The second is the antithesis of the first – we immediately acquire new best friends who won't leave us alone until they obtain a free holiday out of us. My money was on the Kensingtons blagging a free holiday then falling out with us immediately afterwards when their holiday euphoria ended and the jealousy kicked in.

The questions were then fired at us relentlessly.

'How many bedrooms does it have?'

'Has it got a pool?'

'What's the address?'

There's only one reason why she wanted the address and that was so she could have a good nosey on Google Earth before deciding if she should blag a free holiday.

'When are you going?' Penelope enquired.

'At the end of May, in the school break,' I reluctantly replied.

'That would be great wouldn't it, Rupert? That would fit in brilliantly with our plans. How many bedrooms did you say the villa had?'

'I didn't,' I answered.

And I certainly didn't give a monkey's about their plans.

Had I just heard right, had Penelope just invited the whole of the Kensington clan on our next family holiday? I began choking on burnt chilli bits while Matt stared straight at me and kicked my ankles under the table.

'No…No…NO!' he muttered under his breath. He was damn right it was a 'No!' There was absolutely no way we were sharing our house or our holiday with them.

'What do you think?' enquired Penelope. 'I think it's a fantastic idea,' she continued.

Which bit was fantastic? I would rather spend two weeks locked in a pit full of snakes with only the PTA for company. Spending two weeks with the whole Kensington clan was NOT on my 'To Do' list this year – or any other year for that matter.

Before Rupert could slip his feet into his flip-flops and shake his cocktails in Penelope's direction she had fired up her laptop and was checking out our holiday home on the Internet. Matt passed me a glass of water in the hope that it would stop me choking on my burnt chilli.

'You own this house?' Penelope asked in disbelief.

I glanced at the computer screen.

'We do indeed,' I answered, rather smugly.

'But it's beautiful, look at that pool and hot tub, look at the rooms and the view. We are definitely going there, Rupert.'

I know it was their anniversary but I couldn't work out why either of them would want to celebrate the pantomime of the past fifteen years. Even so, there was no chance they were coming on holiday with us.

After the mountain climb I had hoped to shake Penelope off and it had been working until now. She had hardly spoken to me since we arrived back and she'd paired up with her new best friend, Camilla. So why couldn't she go on holiday with her? I got the impression I was about to become flavour of the month again, just because we owned a house in Spain.

'Have you booked your flights?' Penelope enquired.

I thought Matt was about to spontaneously combust, he was holding his breath and making a small whining noise while muttering, 'Please no, please no.'

I couldn't be rude and not answer her, after all we were sitting in their house on their wedding anniversary, eating their burnt chilli and drinking their wine.

'Yes, we are all booked, thank you,' I replied, hoping that would draw a line under the conversation.

No such luck. Before Matt and I knew it Penelope was screaming at Rupert.

'Quick, get the credit card now, we could even be on the same flights, hurry quick.'

Matt and I sat there open-mouthed when Penelope shrieked, 'I've booked it, it's booked,' as she hit the 'confirm' button.

I felt like I had been hit by a truck. In fact being hit by a truck would probably be less painful than spending a fortnight with Penelope, Rupert and their bloody kids.

For a minute I thought it would all be OK as my bus was scheduled to pick them up on New Year's Eve and drive them out of my life forever. Then I remembered my bus theory wasn't reality – it was just a dream, a fantasy that was never going to happen. Surely I knew enough dodgy characters from my 'dole days' with Fay to make it a reality? I was prepared to pay good money – well any money in fact – not to have to go on holiday with these people.

Matt and I were still sitting at Penelope's table with our mouths wide open and chilli dribbling down our chins. We were numb, there was no other way to describe it.

'This is the best anniversary we have ever had,' squealed Penelope.

The tactless retort would have been, 'Bloody hell, you must have had some really crap ones,' but clearly they had.

The past fifteen years had not been great for both of them. OK, maybe a little fun for Rupert but for Penelope there can't have been much joy. There was a loud bang as Rupert suddenly popped open a bottle of champagne and quickly filled our glasses.

'A toast,' he declared, 'to a great holiday.'

The holiday was booked for May, which meant I would have to endure another six months of Penelope in my life. I only had myself to blame. I nipped to the bathroom and fell to the floor. As I slumped against the bathroom door, I sent Fay a text. If there was anyone who would know what to do, it would be her.

I need a solution and I need it fast. Penelope and Rupert have booked to come on holiday with us.

I only had to wait a few seconds for her reply.

LMAO. Stop sending me prank texts, it's not 1st April. Do you seriously expect me to believe you are going on holiday with Penelope and Rupert?

I would do anything – and I mean anything – to reverse the clock. I was that desperate I would even become the next chairperson of the PTA and run the Summer Fair single-handed if it would mean I didn't have to spend a fortnight with them – and believe me, those were desperate measures. I didn't want a bus any more – I wanted a time machine to transport me back to yesterday.

It's no laughing matter, I'm being serious! Help! I sent back.

Well I suggest you climb another mountain and push her over the edge. Or get your calendar out and plan the bikini shopping trip!

The flights were booked. There was nothing I could do. From the bathroom I could hear the happy chatter around the dinner table – well everyone except Matt – maybe he had choked on the burnt bits in the chilli. If he hadn't, he was probably wishing he had.

When I returned to the table, Little Jonny and Annabel were jumping around the room with joy. My children were staring at me in disbelief.

Samuel shrugged his shoulders at me and mouthed, 'Why?'

He was not happy and after Little Jonny's torment towards Samuel recently at school he probably couldn't think of anything worse than spending his two-week holiday with the budding palaeontologist – or was Little Jonny the professional footballer this week?

Penelope announced at the table that she wanted to start her exercise routine again in order to get fit for 'our' holiday. She decided she needed to up the ante and seriously lose weight, ready for May. I had technically been dumped of all joint weight loss activities since the mountain climb and I wasn't sure I could cope with being chucked out of her house again when I started losing more weight than her. I couldn't face walking with Penelope so I came up with a genius proposal, we would go bike-riding instead. This way it would be difficult to talk – or listen in my case – and the torture would be over more quickly. Penelope agreed that it sounded like a plan and the first ride was scheduled for Monday morning.

After booking Matilda and Daisy back into the nursery for the odd few mornings, our exercise regime began again.

Monday morning arrived and after Penelope wrestled her bike from the garden shed – dragging it from behind the plant pots, bits of wood and old paint tins – we set off on our first bike ride. I did think that I should suggest she sold the shed's contents on eBay to make some money, instead of fleecing everyone else in the village.

As we rode past the school a toddler pointed at Penelope and shouted 'Bike … Bike.'

This was the funniest thing I had heard in ages. At that age kids don't know how to lie so I started to wonder if the toddler knew something about Penelope that I didn't. Maybe she had been taking a leaf out of Rupert's book and riding a few local blokes. My cycling companion went bright red and remarked that she found the toddler's comments deeply embarrassing and insulting, until I reminded her he was just a toddler, pointing at her mode of transport.

The start of the ride went pretty slowly and we didn't really have a route mapped out. We rode side by side which gave Penelope the chance to remind me that she was still going ahead with her bonfire party on the Saturday after Bonfire Night for the children in Little Jonny's class. Well when I say all the children, that isn't quite correct – she had invited all the children in the class except two. The first was Miles – Imogen's son – and the other was Jacob – the dyslexic lad. Miles wasn't invited because Penelope thought it would rile Imogen. Jacob wasn't invited because Penelope had decided he wasn't intelligent enough to mix with Little Jonny – her words, not mine. For everyone who thought the playground bully was a thing of the past, think again. They are now older and pushier than ever, breeding the next generation of bully in every town and village.

I kept quiet during the whole conversation. I thought it was absolutely diabolical that anyone would consider leaving two children out. How would those kids feel when everyone else was talking about the bonfire party? Penelope needed a firework up her backside to make her see sense. Jacob was no different to my Samuel. The only difference was that I had never told Penelope that Samuel was dyslexic too, so his invitation still stood.

My blood was starting to boil. I've said it before and I will say it again – the only thing that is wrong with primary schools is the mothers. If it wasn't for the Playground Mafia the children would all get on together. It's the mothers that create the cliques, it's the mothers that segregate the children and choose the people that they think are good enough to play and become friends with their child and it's the mothers who place pressure on the children to be the best in class.

There was only one thing for it. I made the decision that Samuel would not be going to the bonfire party. Instead, he would be having his own small firework party at home and Miles and Jacob would be invited.

That decision was bound to go with a bang when I finally got round to telling Penelope. It would also give Matt and me a legitimate reason to avoid yet another night at the Kensingtons'. Penelope was lapping up all the attention in the playground as the other mothers thanked her for their child's invitation, one by one.

I watched from afar and for three days running saw Imogen handing tissues to Miles as he came out of school. I could only assume he was upset by the lack of a party invitation. Unfortunately for me I was involved by proxy just for being Penelope's friend. It was at that moment that I decided to invite the excluded boys to our house on Saturday night. What's the worst that could happen? The Kensingtons cancelling their holiday? Now that would be a result. They hadn't even offered to pay towards the villa; they had just taken it for granted that it would be a free holiday.

As Imogen and Miles walked past me I grabbed Imogen's arm.

'Have you got a minute?' I asked.

I could see Penelope watching from the other side of the playground, probably wondering why I was speaking to them both. Hopefully she would blast off in a rocket on Saturday night and never come back. Imogen was a little weary and Miles was heartbroken.

'Is everything OK?' I asked.

'What do you think?' she curtly answered.

'How about Miles comes over to the Shack on Saturday night and has a small firework party with Samuel and Jacob, how would he feel about that?'

Imogen appeared astounded.

'That's extremely kind of you.'

Miles wrapped his arms around my stomach and gave me a massive hug.

Penelope looked like she was about to give herself a hernia as she struggled to stay rooted to the spot, desperately trying to look like she wasn't interested.

'What about Penelope's party?' she responded.

'I'm sure Penelope will have enough kids at her house to even notice we are missing and this way no-one has to miss out. See you Saturday about 6.30pm.'

Once Imogen had left the playground, Penelope was over quicker than a lit firework blasting up into the sky.

'What was all that about?' she demanded.

'I was just inviting Miles over for tea. He's had a very upsetting week at school,' I replied.

There was no doubt that I was in for an interesting week. Penelope had spent an absolute fortune on fireworks, food and drinks for her party. She had gone over the top baking cakes and organising party bags. It wasn't even anyone's birthday, it was all about making Little Jonny popular and securing future invites to these so-called friends' future parties. Samuel was entitled to choose his own friends – whoever he felt comfortable with – that was good enough for me.

Penelope had spent in the region of three hundred pounds to impress these kids. I, on the other hand, had baked some cakes with eggs from my own hens, bought a twenty quid box of fireworks and had some hot dogs and chips at the ready. For me it wasn't about putting on a show, it was all about making the children feel happy and confident about themselves.

Penelope banged on all week about her party preparations. I, on the other hand, was glad I was going to be a mile up the road in the comfort of my own Shack.

Saturday night was upon us and Jacob and Miles arrived with big beaming smiles on their faces. We huddled around together in the garden. My children and the boys squealed with delight as they watched the fireworks whizz, crackle and bang in vibrant colours that flashed across the dark night sky. They stuffed their faces with hot dogs, chips and cake and we made toffee apples, which were delicious. The boys then retreated into the Shack and settled down to watch a film, all happy and all having the best time.

Then the text arrived from Penelope.

Are you thinking of arriving anytime soon x?

Sorry Penelope I forgot to mention we can't make it tonight.

What do you mean you can't make it?

No kiss at the end of the text. I smiled to myself. It would be the shouty capitals next.

I was disappointed in myself for behaving this way but I felt I needed to make a stand.

We are having our own firework party and Samuel has Miles and Jacob around for tea. Hope your party goes with a bang! Have fun, see you on Monday.

I would be able to hear the hissing and whizzing of Penelope's temper over the noise of our Catherine Wheels and Roman Candles once she read that text. What Penelope thought of me was not important and I couldn't care less. Penelope was bitter, insecure and it could be worse – I could be with her at this moment in time with almost thirty kids in the house. No doubt she would make Rupert clean up!

CHAPTER 12

December

The festive season was upon us – again. The weather in recent days had changed drastically and there was a proper wintery chill in the air. The snow was fresh and crisp on the ground. Temperatures had dropped to a whopping minus ten degrees.

I love this month, Christmas time is my favourite time of year. I love the hustle and bustle of the shops, the decorations, the Christmas trees, the twinkling of the fairy lights, the log fires burning and the dark, cosy nights. We had lived in the village of Tattersfield for almost a year now and it certainly hadn't been dull.

Since I'd hosted the substitute bonfire party for the lads that had been snubbed by Penelope, she had not spoken to me. I had been relegated in her friend list, no doubt replaced by Camilla. That suited me just fine, especially as it meant I didn't have to put up with her relentless self-important dialogue or follow her wayward husband at stupid o'clock in the morning to ascertain his whereabouts. Rupert would be flush this Christmas, not having to buy numerous instances of the same presents for various women. Matt and I and our beautiful family were chugging along nicely in the Shack, enjoying the time to ourselves and looking forward to a lovely, chilled family Christmas.

The latest Playground Mafia rumour suggested that Penelope and Rupert were spending Christmas Day at Camilla Noland's house, which was still up for sale. This hardly came as a surprise to me and confirmed that Penelope was still unable to spend any time alone with Rupert. I cringed as I imagined the likely topics of conversation that would dominate the lazy evenings on our holiday that they had gate-crashed; obviously women, shift work, boilersuits, sports cars, Christmas presents, etc., would be totally out of bounds.

School had now been closed for a couple of days due to the freezing snow conditions. The children loved the time off school, building igloos, sledging and generally having fun in the snow. I too was overjoyed that school was closed – probably more so than the kids – as it meant I didn't have to make the school run, which gave me a break from the Playground Mafia.

It was the morning of Christmas Eve and Matt was finishing work at lunchtime. In the meantime, the children and I headed to the local hill for some general snow-based fun, pulling our sledges behind us. There were three other figures standing on the hill, glancing over in our direction. I noticed the familiar figure of Penelope sporting yet another new coat.

Penelope looked straight at me and ignored me which I really couldn't believe after all the effort I had put in with her over the last nine months. My monster slippers had been laid to rest because of her. My poodle was no longer a virgin after she took his doggy-cherry at our summer BBQ and I had provided beds for her children – both of them – on numerous occasions.

Even from a distance I could see that Penelope looked sad. Maybe Rupert had decided he couldn't afford to buy her – and therefore Charlotte – an iPad for Christmas. Or maybe he had finally come to his senses and left her.

I wanted to tell her not to worry, that she would meet some fabulous characters next week at the New Year's Eve bash I had arranged for some 'special' friends. There would be Mrs HSM, Mr ISG, FP, BB and of course the opportunity to meet up again with the White Witch of Narnia. The bus would be picking her up at midnight and would drive her to her destination to party to her heart's content.

However, I quickly decided it was her prerogative to ignore me and that suited me just fine. I carried on walking to the other side of the hill with the children, where we sledged for nearly two hours. When we finally decided to head home, Penelope was gone.

Christmas Day was a quiet, family affair for us. The children had a wonderful time and Matt cooked the dinner – like he does every year – while I put my feet up. This time next week in the Shack I knew would be complete mayhem. New Year's Eve was approaching and we had come a long way in the last twelve months. There was no threat of spending New Year's Eve with the likes of Mr ISG and Lois.

This year our good friends from back home were coming to stay for the weekend, after all it was my birthday too. We would be a little squashed in the Shack but Eva and Samuel would bed down on the inflatable air beds at the side of our bed, leaving some space for our guests. I was glad I didn't have to inflict the pain of Penelope and Rupert on these quality friends. We had known Mark and Jane for over twenty years and they were the salt of the earth, a couple you could always rely on for anything. They had one young child so a night of games, drinking and general fun – once the children were tucked up safely in bed of course – was on the cards for all.

We decided to have a kitty for our evening and I offered to go and buy all the food and alcohol the day before. I purchased balloons, party poppers and enough food and drink to sink the *Titanic*; the party celebrations were waiting to begin.

When New Year's Eve arrived the snow was falling lightly around the Shack. The log fire was burning and I sipped a small sherry while reflecting on the last twelve months. It had been eventful to say the least. I quickly concluded that I had made no new 'real' friends. A lot of people who had crossed my path were no longer speaking to me. Paddy Power was spot on with the odds of who wouldn't go the distance. I had simply met people who wanted to use me in one way or another. I was probably a novelty being the new blood in the village. It was definitely a local village for local people. The playground scene was no different to the place I had left behind. All the same characters were in attendance; they just had different appearances and names and drove different cars. Considering we lived in the country, there were nowhere near as many 4x4s at this school as there were at the last school.

I symbolically raised my glass to wish the likes of Mr ISG, Lois, Mrs HSM, FP, BB, the White Witch of Narnia, Camilla Noland, Penelope and Rupert a 'Happy New Year' which I thought was very kind of me considering what they had all put me through in the previous twelve months. I chuckled to myself as I pictured them climbing onto the bus to be driven out of my life forever.

I was interrupted by a knock at the door. I was excited thinking that it would be our good friends arriving and shouted to Matt to hurry and open it for our guests. I waited for the inevitable chatter as people spilt down the hallway but none came, it was deadly quiet.

Matt popped his head around the living room door and said quietly, 'It's for you.'

Standing up I headed towards the front door. There standing in front of me was one of the people I was least expecting to see – Mr Fletcher Parker – Frisky Pensioner himself. He needed to get himself back home and wait for my bus to pick him up.

His hands were clasped behind his back.

'Thank God for that,' I thought. At least he wouldn't be able to grope me again.

'Can I help you?' I asked.

This was the most polite I had been towards him in a while. Suddenly he swung his arms forward from behind his back and thrust a bottle of red wine straight into my chest. Well, at least it wasn't his face.

'I believe it is your birthday tomorrow, have a drink on me,' he said, merrily.

I didn't want a drink on him and I didn't want to take the bottle from his sweaty hands but as his hands were still pressed against my chest, I needed to remove him and the bottle from my doorstep quickly. Before I knew it, he had me in a head-lock and had thrust his lips onto mine, again. His geriatric ninja qualities didn't end at silently creeping into houses, he could contort himself and his unwilling victim into a compromising pose faster than you could say 'Bruce Lee'.

'Happy Birthday,' he mumbled as he un-puckered.

Why me? Why did it have to be my birthday? And more to the point, how did he even know it was my birthday? I stepped backwards, just as Mark and Jane's car pulled onto the drive. Frisky Pensioner was startled and shuffled away quickly, still holding the bottle of wine.

Mark, slamming the car door, had witnessed Frisky Pensioner's antics and reached out to grab the bottle from him as he passed.

'She'll need that to get rid of the vile taste in her mouth,' he declared.

If FP was the geriatric ninja, Mark was definitely the wine ninja!

'That's the last time you will ever kiss me. Your bus leaves at midnight, make sure you are ready,' I shouted up the road after him.

Mark and Jane looked at me with a puzzled stare.

I ushered Mark and Jane and their daughter Poppy inside and shut the door behind them. I then left them rolling around laughing in the hallway whilst I marched quickly to the bathroom to scrub my teeth. That wasn't a great start to what I hoped would be a great night but I suppose it could be worse; I could be spending the evening with Penelope.

After my unexpected birthday kiss the party celebrations were properly underway. The buffet was prepared, the wine and beer were flowing and the children were all having a great time. They played games and sang songs, dressed in their pyjamas – it was better for them to be dressed in comfy stuff instead of being trussed up like chickens, and we knew that we would be in no fit state to help any of the children get changed for bed later on.

With only a few hours until midnight the children snuggled down in one of the bedrooms with a pile of snacks to watch a film. That left the adults to drink more and become even merrier, if that was at all possible.

Then Mark asked, 'What's that banging noise?'

Matt, Jane and I stopped to listen but we couldn't hear anything. We concluded that Mark was probably imagining things. After all, he'd already drank way too much alcohol.

'There it is again!' he exclaimed.

This time I thought I had heard something but was distracted by Jane handing me a birthday present to open. Technically it wasn't my birthday for another few hours but I ripped open the paper anyway. I couldn't believe my eyes; there inside the package was a brand new pair of monster slippers. And even better – they matched perfectly with the monster onesie I was wearing. I put them on and jigged around the living room showing them off to everyone.

The next song that blurted out from the stereo made me laugh.

It was 'It's Raining Men', the song that was playing in the car on the way to the mountain climb with Penelope. I was more than merry by now, continuing to dance around in my comedy footwear.

'Hey,' I shouted over The Weather Girls. 'At least these monster slippers will survive the antics of Rupert Kensington. I bet they are stuck with Camilla listening to Elvis records all night.'

Samuel entered the room, turned down the music and made an announcement.

'Unfortunately for you they are not. They are standing in our hallway listening to you. That banging was them knocking on the front door.'

I wanted to die on the spot. Right there and then I hoped the floor would open and swallow me up. Why couldn't I have a birthday without any gate-crashers knocking on my door for once? What on earth did they want? I wasn't going to find out stood where I was so I went to face the music – they would have heard every word of my drunken outburst. I smoothed down my onesie, and poked my head around the door. The Kensingtons were definitely standing there in my hallway and they were looking straight at me.

'Happy New Year,' I offered with a hiccup and a drunken smile.

There was no getting out of this one. I remembered my manners and asked, 'What can I do for you?'

I could hear Matt, Mark and Jane whispering behind the door, clearly trying to figure out what had brought them to our party – uninvited I might add. Of course not one of them had the bottle to come out from behind the door to help me out of this tricky situation.

'We had nowhere to go,' replied Penelope.

I know I was a little worse for wear but had Penelope just told me they had nowhere to go? She had a nerve, she hadn't spoken to me for the past month and now she wanted to gate-crash my New Year's Eve party with my good friends. The others had gone quiet behind the door, except for Jane who was trying to whisper, but in her tipsy state, was trying too hard.

'We believe Camilla Noland is having a garden party, get yourselves over there,' she boomed, immediately followed by even louder 'shushing' from the boys.

Then they all shouted, 'She can't be having a garden party, she hasn't got a garden!'

The dog wandered up the hallway from the kitchen, obviously curious about all the commotion. When he noticed it was Penelope he retreated back to his bed with his tail between his legs; he was definitely embarrassed after his one-night stand and couldn't face her again.

I threw open the living room door, smashing it into the three drunken adults who subsequently fell backwards into a heap on the floor. I looked down at them and threw my arms into the air.

'Well you'd better come in and join the party,' I reluctantly announced.

Little Jonny and Annabel disappeared upstairs to find the others. Little Jonny and Samuel were friends again at the moment but with children that could all change next week.

Matt quickly disappeared and Mark hurried into the kitchen to get everyone a drink. If they were going to reach parity with our alcohol consumption levels they had better start on the hard stuff. Rupert started drinking before he had even taken his slippers out of his carrier bag and removed his coat. It was like he had never been away. Jane took Rupert's coat from him and asked where she should hang it. Before I had chance to answer, Penelope piped up.

'We have our own pegs with our names on in the cloakroom.'

Not any more they didn't – we had removed them once we thought we were rid of the Kensingtons. I looked around for Matt and caught him sneaking back into the garage with a screwdriver and a hammer.

'What are you up to?' I quizzed. 'Don't leave me with this lot on my own.'

He winked in my direction and pointed towards the cloakroom. The Kensingtons' coat pegs were back in place. Matt returned from the garage with a bucket, which he promptly handed to Rupert.

'This is for you,' he said. 'I may not be opposed to the odd bit of DIY on New Year's Eve but I am certainly not cleaning up any of your vomit.'

Rupert knew the score, they were lucky to be back in the Shack – bloody lucky!

Jane and I were drunk, absolutely stinking drunk. We danced to every cheesy song that was played, jumped off the furniture playing air guitar and sang 'Agadoo' completely out of tune. Penelope, however, did not join in with any of our fun and games. She was sitting on a chair in the corner of the room wearing an expensive black cocktail dress – and even more expensive slippers – slowly sipping her drink. She definitely didn't look in the party mood. Rupert, on the other hand, was getting into the swing and had joined us jumping around like lunatics playing air guitar. I handed out a deadly cocktail that I had concocted earlier and Rupert looked like he was having the best New Year's Eve ever.

Jane was the first to notice that Penelope had disappeared from the chair. I mimed to Jane the actions of smoking a fag and pointed outside to where Penelope was standing. I glanced through the window and saw her dragging on a cigarette. Rupert was now beyond tipsy and was doing a great job of catching up with the rest of us. I decided as much as Rupert had his faults he was actually all right, I quite liked him.

It was thirty minutes before midnight and Matt had put the champagne on ice and retrieved the posh glasses – that only seem to come out on New Year's Eve – ready for the chimes of Big Ben. Penelope still hadn't returned to the room when Jane decided we had time to play one last party game. Everyone sat down in a circle on the floor for a game of 'Shag, Marry, Avoid'.

Jane went first…

'I would shag Gerard Butler.'

'Why?' I enquired.

'Because he looks dirty,' she replied.

'Fair play,' I thought.

'I would marry Colin Firth – in his Mr Darcy days of course – and I would avoid Roy Cropper.'

We all fell about laughing.

I followed Jane's lead… My answer was not going to be a surprise to anyone. I love this man, the only man I would ever leave Matt for.

'I would shag Gary Barlow, I would marry Gary Barlow and I would avoid his wife!'

The jovial mood continued.

Then Mark took his turn.

'I would shag anyone, I'm a bloke, aren't I,' he grinned. 'I would marry no-one and I would avoid "the clap"!'

We were all howling with laughter.

The only contestants left to declare their intentions were Penelope and Rupert – Matt had disappeared to fill up his glass, no doubt desperate to avoid revealing his drunken desires. Penelope had also disappeared off to the toilet – after finally returning from her fag break – and had still not returned. Rupert was beyond drunk at this point and sat in the circle making funny faces pondering his choices.

Rupert hushed the room for quiet.

We looked at him expectantly but we did not expect the words that came out of his mouth. 'I would shag Camilla Noland, I would marry Annie and I would avoid Penelope.'

Our jaws hit the floor.

Awkward silence.

The whole room remained quiet whilst we all gazed up at Rupert with astonishment; he of course was completely serious. If there was any moment to sober up it would be now. Not only was he being completely serious, he had chosen to make his declaration right at the moment Penelope returned to the room. She had heard every word from where she was standing in the doorway. We all cringed, waiting for the leftover bonfire party fireworks to go off. We didn't have to wait very long. This was definitely going to be a night to remember.

Penelope walked straight over to him and we all flinched, waiting for the inevitable slap across his face. Instead she picked up the champagne bottle and poured the finest Lanson Black Label all over his head. The rest of us gasped – what a bloody waste of good champagne!

Just at that moment the clocks chimed. We quickly joined hands and sang 'Auld Lang Syne' at the top of our voices. Penelope and Rupert were standing silently, right in the middle of our celebrations. Party poppers were flying and champagne glasses clinked together. Everyone was kissing each other's cheeks and wishing one another a 'Happy New Year' – and of course wishing me 'Happy Birthday'. Jane winked at me and went over to Rupert. Putting her arms around his neck, she pretended to give him the biggest snog ever. Then before any of us knew what to do, we heard a loud intermittent beeping noise coming from outside.

We all raced to the window to look out. Jane put Rupert down so she could see what was happening too. I couldn't believe what I was seeing. At first I thought it was a vehicle that broken down in the snow but it was actually a shiny red bus – and it was being reversed onto my drive.

I strained my neck for a better look out of the window and spotted Fay giving me a cheeky wave from the driver's seat!

Not only was it a bus, it was THE bus and there were already passengers occupying some of the seats, people who I sincerely hoped I would never set eyes upon again. Sitting on the bus was Mr International Sex God and Lois, Mrs High School Musical, Botox Bernie, Camilla, the White Witch of Narnia and Frisky Pensioner!

Fay gave me a wink and shouted, 'Bus for Penelope and Rupert Kensington.'

I knew Fay was my best mate in the world ever… I always knew she wouldn't let me down. A true friend that had passed the seven-year rule of friendship. There was no way on this Earth that she would ever let me go on holiday with those two lunatics!

This was turning out to be the best birthday ever.

Happy New Year!

To be continued…

LETTER FROM CHRISTIE

Dear readers

I would just like to say a HUGE heartfelt thank you for choosing to read *A Year in the Life of a Playground Mother*.

The idea for the book was launched one rainy afternoon. Once hitting my mid-life crisis (but dodging the tattoo and the fast car) after wholly dedicating my life to the care of my children, they asked me what I wanted to do with my life. 'I've always wanted to write a book,' I found myself answering.

After muttering to myself for nearly a fortnight and wondering what could I possibly write a story about, it hit me one afternoon whilst I was on the school run. With all my children at various stages in their education it was then I decided to write a book based on purely comedic scenarios that occur in a mother's life on a daily basis.

I love writing about Rachel Young's adventures but sometimes wish she'd learn to say NO! Penelope and Rupert Kensington are characters that I simply love. I'd often find myself giggling away whilst writing the story. They are both entertaining yet annoying. It is important that I am able to relate to my characters and love who they are – faults as well.

Thank you so much to everyone that has been involved in this project, my family, friends and readers for all your lovely messages, tweets and emails along the way. I love reading all your messages! Writing fiction is certainly a lonely job and most of the time it is spent on my own tapping at the computer with only my mad cocker spaniel Woody for company.

If you enjoyed my book and have time to post a review that would be amazing. It can really make all the difference in persuading a new reader to try my book.

I am delighted to tell you there is a sequel coming very very soon…Watch this space!

To keep right up-to-date with the latest news on my new releases just sign up using the link below:

www.bookouture.com/christie-barlow

Warmest wishes
Christie x

 @ChristieJBarlow

 ChristieJBarlow

www.christiebarlow.com

Printed in Great Britain
by Amazon